W9-CCI-998

"HOLD ON TO YOUR CHAIR!"*

PRAISE FOR DOUGLAS CLEGG
Winner of the Bram Stoker Award
Winner of the International Horror Guild Award

"Clegg establishes himself firmly as one of the leading authors of the horror genre . . . a powerhouse of a read."
—*Cemetery Dance*

"This is pure imagination, and it is wearing speed skates."
—Peter Straub

"Clegg approaches horror with a stark and vital simplicity that is utterly convincing. Fans of Stephen King and Dean Koontz will appreciate." —*Library Journal*

"Clegg is one of the best!"
—Richard Layman, author of *To Wake the Dead*

"Clegg pulls out the stops of terror. Psychologically astute and genuinely shivery. Suspenseful and relentlessly spooky . . . one of horror's brightest lights."
—*Publishers Weekly* (starred review)

"Clegg gets high marks on the terror scale."
—*New York Daily News*

"I was compelled to keep turning the pages as fear . . . raised my pulse to racing level from cover to cover." —DarkEcho

"One of the best." —*Fangoria*

"Complex, suspenseful, and exciting horror."
—*Midwest Book Review*

"Every bit as good as the best works of Stephen King, Peter Straub, or Dan Simmons." —Hellnotes

"Douglas Clegg is one of horror's most captivating voices."
—BookLovers

AFTERLIFE

Douglas Clegg

AN ONYX BOOK

ONYX
Published by New American Library, a division of
Penguin Group (USA) Inc., 375 Hudson Street, New York, New York 10014, USA
Penguin Group (Canada), 10 Alcorn Avenue, Toronto,
Ontario M4V 3B2, Canada (a division of Pearson Penguin Canada Inc.)
Penguin Books Ltd., 80 Strand, London WC2R 0RL, England
Penguin Ireland, 25 St. Stephen's Green,
Dublin 2, Ireland (a division of Penguin Books Ltd.)
Penguin Group (Australia), 250 Camberwell Road,
Camberwell, Victoria 3124, Australia (a division of Pearson Australia Group Pty. Ltd.)
Penguin Books India Pvt. Ltd., 11 Community Centre, Panchsheel Park,
New Delhi - 110 017, India
Penguin Group (NZ), Cnr Airborne and Rosedale Roads,
Albany, Auckland 1310, New Zealand (a division of Pearson New Zealand Ltd.)
Penguin Books (South Africa) (Pty.) Ltd., 24 Sturdee Avenue,
Rosebank, Johannesburg 2196, South Africa

Penguin Books Ltd., Registered Offices: 80 Strand, London WC2R 0RL, England

First published by Onyx, an imprint of New American Library,
a division of Penguin Group (USA) Inc.

First Printing, December 2004
10 9 8 7 6 5 4 3 2 1

Copyright © Douglas Clegg, 2004
All rights reserved

REGISTERED TRADEMARK—MARCA REGISTRADA

Printed in the United States of America

Without limiting the rights under copyright reserved above, no part of this
publication may be reproduced, stored in or introduced into a retrieval system, or
transmitted, in any form, or by any means (electronic, mechanical, photocopying,
recording, or otherwise), without the prior written permission of both the copyright
owner and the above publisher of this book.

PUBLISHER'S NOTE
This is a work of fiction. Names, characters, places, and incidents either are the
product of the author's imagination or are used fictitiously, and any resemblance to
actual persons, living or dead, business establishments, events, or locales is entirely
coincidental.

If you purchased this book without a cover you should be aware that this book is stolen
property. It was reported as "unsold and destroyed" to the publisher and neither the
author nor the publisher has received any payment for this "stripped book."

The scanning, uploading, and distribution of this book via the Internet or via any
other means without the permission of the publisher is illegal and punishable by law.
Please purchase only authorized electronic editions, and do not participate in or
encourage electronic piracy of copyrighted materials. Your support of the author's
rights is appreciated.

For Dean Koontz—mentor, friend, colleague, who continues to write and inspire.

Thanks to Laura Anne Gilman, Dan Slater, Sharon Gamboa, and Leslie Gelbman for bringing me into the Penguin Group (USA) fold. Thanks also to Raul Silva, Jane Osnovich, Matt Schwartz, Pam Sayer, and M. J. Rose for the right words at the right time.

The author invites you to write to him at ebook@ DouglasClegg.com, to find out about getting a free ebook and screensaver.

"We sometimes congratulate ourselves at the moment of waking from a troubled dream; it may be so at the moment after death."

—Nathaniel Hawthorne

"There are monsters in the world. They're called human beings."

—Michael Diamond, from *The Life Beyond*

Prologue

1

In the testing room, the boy stared at the others from behind the glass. He raised his fists and began hitting the thick pane. His cries for help went unheard. Flames shot up in the booth around him, moving rapidly up the boy's back as he pounded harder, his mouth open impossibly wide. He shut his eyes as if trying to block it all out or to send his mind to another, safer place.

The others watched from behind triple thick glass and waited as the fire burned away the boy's shirt. They all held hands, and one of the girls said, "Look at how scared he is."

"We need to get out," a teenager said. "Now."

And then, the heat of the fire shattered the glass, moving beyond the booth, beyond the testing room, as if the air itself burned out of control.

2

The rumor went that in the 1970s, a small, privately funded school in Manhattan existed where young children with special talents were being observed and tested for what were then labeled "PSI" abilities. Little is known about the school, other than it remained enshrouded as yet another urban legend of the city. The conspiracy theory was that the government—or several governments—funded the school and used it to learn more about the human mind and child development of extrasensory ability, and perhaps in some covert way. Another story was that it was simply formed by a group who believed that these so-called special children should have a safe place to develop their talents. Still another suggestion had been that this was one of the city's many small private schools that didn't contain a trace of the psychic or the occult, but that some of the former students themselves spread that rumor as a joke to discredit the school.

Another of the rumors had to do with a little boy who had precipitated the closing of the secret school when he somehow was responsible for the death of another child.

Other than hints in *Rolling Stone*, in the *Village Voice*, in *New York Underground News*, and even now, an occasional mention of the school on the Internet, nothing substantiated this tale, which some thought had grown out of the drug culture and the increasing interest in the paranormal during the sixties and seventies.

The school was supposed to have existed somewhere near the Chelsea district of New York City, although its exact location was anyone's guess.

The school was called Daylight.

PART ONE

chapter one

1

She opened her eyes to darkness. Her breathing slow, warm, but too shallow. Something was wrong. Blindfolded? Not sure. She pressed her eyes closed and then open again. Nothing but claustrophobic night. Her breath came back at her, along with a feeling of dizziness, an enclosed space and pins and needles in her toes and fingers. Paralyzed?

Buried. Buried alive.

Throat dry. A thudding—her heartbeat? No light at all. Not even cracks through the box. Coffin? A large trunk? She was squeezed in, and her limbs felt numb.

Dear God. Dear God.

Slow, deep breath. Hammering in her head. Wetness along her neck.

You won't get anywhere if you panic.

This crawlspace. This . . . casket.

Blurred images came to her: the white room, the feeling of being laid gently down on some bed, twine wrapped around his hands as he reached for her . . .

Your hands. Move. Reach.

Her hands were bound in front of her. Thick twine connected her wrists, and as she tugged as hard as she could—

barely able to move—she remembered how he'd spoken gently to her. She had been drugged, after all. He had incapacitated her in some way she didn't understand.

Blocked. No matter how hard she tried to roam with her mind, something blocked her.

Her lips were parched. She opened them, but only a ragged whisper of a sigh came out. *Help me. Please*, she wanted to say. *No, there must be a way out. Must be. This may be another test. It may not be what it seems. It's just a test. Surely. Please, dear God.*

Please, she tried to say. *Someone.*

Then she heard the voice, barely a whisper. He must be pressing his face near the sealed lid of the box. "Don't be afraid, Gina. Don't be afraid. Just let it happen."

His words had the opposite effect on her. She felt as if she were hyperventilating. She fought back tears.

And then she felt the heaviness of her breathing—it hurt her lungs. She tried to take in too much air, and there wasn't enough.

Please, somebody, help me.

A sound above her. Just above her face.

On the other side of the box.

And then, she gasped, because the air was running out too fast.

2

Miles from the city, in the wilds of northern New Jersey, out along the lakes beneath the great and small houses rising up among dense woods, spring has only just awakened. The ice melted only just weeks before, the new grass exploding with bright green, with the lavender and yellow of crocuses and wildflowers.

Someone's hunting.

3

A man stood on an empty plateau in a brief but undisturbed wilderness overlooking a placid silver lake.

It was a day of winds, a good sign as far as he was concerned. He carried his burden through the tall grass that twisted as the breeze whiffled through it. His boots sank into the deep mud, and he pressed slowly through the swampy land until he'd reached the slight rise of the bank.

He set the man down, relieved to be free of the heaviness.

The man looked up at him drowsily.

He felt the push of wind at his back; he knelt down beside the man, reached into his breast pocket for the blade, and set about his grim task.

The man beneath him. Eyes open. Watching.

He matched his victim, breath for breath.

The killer caught his breath as he brought the small blade down with the precision of a surgeon.

He closed his eyes and delved inside the mind of his victim, just as surely as his knife pierced the man's sternum:

The sweetness of the air. Electrical impulses sparking. The smell of ozone—a whiff of ecstasy, and then, gone, thrown into another.

Penetrating.

He broke through the barrier.

The blade cut into his chest. He looked down at it; his vision went to pinpricks of darkness, and his victim could barely see the face of the one who had stabbed him.

He experienced what his victim felt.

Burning pain. Along his neck and the back of his head. But not in his chest area. Instead, that was a dull throbbing ache. Then, stabbing close to his heart. He lost his vision entirely. Weakness flooded him. The pain was located in his head—a screaming. But he had already begun to discon-

nect from it, as if a cord had been snapped from its power source, and he had pulled back into the source itself. But still, he had a lingering connection to his body. He felt, but the feelings did not concern him.

A feeling of numbness was followed by the dead stop of the heart. Yet he had the curious sensation of still being aware.

Not precisely lucid, but aware.

He felt as if his breath contained his essence, and it coughed into a darkness—he moved, propelled, through some dark void. All the while, he was aware of the others there, around his body, as if his memory still held them, and the place, the last moments of his life—held them in perfect balance with this new feeling.

It wasn't a sense of being a physical body but of being a solid form, undefined by material barriers but kept in place, an entity.

He moved through the darkness, half expecting to open his eyes. Any anger or resentment he'd felt had run its course just as his blood had trickled from his body. He was on a new voyage now and knew that the thread holding him between his last breaths and the doorway through Death was slender.

Then, he felt a shift—as if something weren't working right. He kept waiting to be brought back into life, but instead, he felt a general weakness, as if his mind were growing tired.

A steep descent. Falling. Smells came up, almonds and peaches, wonderful odors that he hadn't experienced in years—since childhood—of jasmine and fresh, running river water, orange blossom, and even a sharp vinegar bite. His senses felt as if they were releasing memories, of tastes and scents, all exploding as he fell.

Fear came, as well.

Fear that leaked into madness, and he tried to cling to his memory, and tried to shout himself back to consciousness.

The killer kept the knife in his victim's chest and his eyes closed, experiencing everything with his victim, feeling the descent into death, trying to stay with his victim so that there was no fear of what was to come.

chapter two

1

In the early afternoon, off the trails of the Jenny Jump Mountain of northern New Jersey, deep in the woods bursting with new green growth, beyond the slight hills above a placid brown lake, a woman and her young daughter hunted for fossils alongside a creek. The outcroppings of rock between patches of forest had fascinated the little girl as they'd wandered, and her mother had pointed out what she remembered from her college years about the area. "Some of these rocks are one point six billion years old."

"That's old," her daughter said, making her mother chuckle at how mature Livy could sound, even at six and a half.

"That's why you can sometimes find fossils."

"Like you used to with Gramma. When you were little."

"Yep. Right along here."

"I love days like this," Livy said.

"Why's that?"

Livy hesitated, then sighed a little. "Well, it's just you and me, Mommy. After school. And you don't have to go to work today. And Matty doesn't come home till later. I just . . . I just sorta like it."

"Me, too, sweetie."

The view beyond them, over the ridge, was of the Kittatinny Mountains and Great Meadows. The sky was damp with the recently passed rain, and the fresh, pungent smell of the wild permeated the countryside.

They'd found a possum skull, two arrowheads, and what they thought might be a small cracked trilobite print on a rock fragment. "This was once part of a glacier," Julie told her daughter. "That's why we have all these lakes."

"Like Ghost Lake. And Forest Lake. And . . . Lake Pe-something."

"Lake Pequest."

"Where'd it go?" Livy asked.

"What?"

"Where'd the glacier go?"

"Well, the earth changes. The earth shifts, the ground warms, the glaciers melt, and then they recede. Over millions of years a lot of stuff can happen."

"That's scary," Livy said. "What if the ocean comes back?"

"Well, if it ever does, we'll have beachfront property. See this?" Julie Hutchinson held the bit of trilobite fossil up for her daughter's inspection. "Once, these lived all over the place here. Swimming underwater." Julie tried to remember if that was precisely correct—she had come up to these woods with her grandmother, who knew a lot more about the trilobites than she ever would. She and her grandmother had never gotten along all that well, except for their mutual love of nature and exploration.

Livy took the fossil into her cupped hands and looked at it. Then up at her mother. "Is it a dinosaur?"

Julie considered how she'd respond. She was screwed when it came to the precise classification of a trilobite. "Sort of."

"Wow."

After a minute of turning the fossil over in her hands,

Livy passed it back to her mother, who dropped it into the small green knapsack they'd brought that contained their bottles of water, smooth pebbles, bits of shell, and arrowheads they'd collected during the late afternoon. Then Livy went back down to the creek, crouching down to look around the rocks and fallen logs for more fossils.

Julie felt a gentle tingling in her hand, and for some reason, it made her think of Hut, the way he grabbed her hand sometimes. The way he did when she thought he was in love with her. Back in the courtship days. Back before the storm clouds had come into their marriage.

An animal scent nearby—dead raccoon? Possum? She hoped it wasn't too close. Immediately, she glanced over at her daughter, who was teetering back and forth on a log at the edge of the creek, her small feet curving around the wood as if trying to clutch it. Livy had an enthusiastic smile on her face, and she leaped from the log into the sandy edge of the creek, causing a splattering that nearly reached Julie.

"Liv," she scolded. The hem of her daughter's dress was already soaked. "Olivia Hutchinson, get out of the water."

Her daughter looked down at the water around her ankles. "I'm only a little in it, Mommy. It's freezing. I like it."

Julie let it go. She glanced across to the other bank. That warm odor of a rotting wild creature wasn't unusual in the woodlands and the several creeks just beyond their town. Sometimes she saw deer pausing between thickets, and recently, she and Livy got to see a beaver swimming down toward its dam.

"We should get back to the car. We need to pick up Matty next," Julie said.

Julie crouched down to pick up some small, nearly round pebbles her daughter had dropped. She glanced over at Livy, who stared across at the view beyond the ridge, to the slope that led down to the lake.

Her daughter's face had a curious slant to it—Livy

squinted, and her nose wrinkled slightly, her head gently turning a bit, not quite looking up at the trees, but nearly.

"Mommy?" Livy asked, detecting something was wrong. "Daddy says it's all right."

Julie pushed herself up from the muddy grass. "He always says that."

"He said it just now."

"On your brain radio," Julie said, grinning. It was a joke between Livy and her father that they could communicate on a higher frequency that Hut had made up.

The wind came up again; it got a bit chilly. Julie was about to lift Livy up out from the muddy water, afraid she might get a cold from being out when the weather was about to make such a sharp change.

"Daddy's in the city. He won't be home till suppertime."

"Silly you," Livy said, teasing. "He's here. He just said it." She glanced around through the ferns and trees, as if her father were playing hide-and-go-seek with her. "Daddy?" She turned her head side to side and then scrunched her eyebrows up, confused.

After Julie wiped her daughter's soles off with her own shirttails and slipped her small feet into the small white and pink socks, what Livy called her "sockets," and then into her shoes, they walked back down the path that led to where Julie had parked the car at the shoulder of the road below. As the wind picked up, her daughter clutched her hand as if she were afraid of being blown off the path. They watched some Canadian geese that had gathered on a large patch of grass near a creek, and Livy told a joke that her father had told her: "Do you know how I know those are Canadian geese?"

"No."

"They say 'Quack, eh,'" Livy said, and giggled as if it were the funniest joke in the world.

"You need a new joke," Julie said, smiling.

The cell phone began vibrating in the pocket of Julie's overstretched wool sweater.

"Is it your job?"

"Maybe," Julie said, trying to ignore the slight downward turn to her daughter's voice whenever Julie's work at the hospital came up. In some respects, Livy seemed like an old soul and could see right through her mother. "Liv, weren't we having fun?"

"I guess I just miss you when you're gone."

"But you see Daddy."

Her daughter didn't answer. The awful and stupid guilt that Julie had worked so hard to overcome—about going back to work in the hospital again after having stayed home with Livy for her first four years—warmed her face.

"But you want to work in a hospital, too, you told me," Julie said. "When you grow up? And you like all the stories I get to tell you from the ER. Aw, honey, I get five days with you each week. Two days away isn't so bad."

"I know," Livy said, sighing. "It's okay, Mommy. I know they need you."

When Julie looked at the number on her cell phone, she saw that it was not the hospital at all.

2

Julie dropped Livy off with Laura Reynen, a young mother who ran daycare out of her house and babysat for Livy far too often. Laura was in her mid-twenties, with two young children, and had arranged her life such that she could stay at home and run the business from her small cottage-like house. Laura could take one of the kids on a moment's notice, and Livy adored being at her home, complete with wisteria creeping up the trellis at the side of the house and an enormous fenced-in backyard full of swing sets and sand-boxes and a double-slide. Laura was the mother that Julie knew she never would be—happy with the clutter, happy with kids all over the place, happy in a way that Julie barely understood, since Julie felt like a screw-up of a mom. Laura always had the aura of joy around her, as if young children were somehow meant to be attached to her arms and legs and running in and out the backdoor all the time.

At the front door, Laura, with a baby in her arms, said, "So I can expect you back when?"

"Two hours, tops," Julie said. Then, looking down at Livy, "We'll eat junk food tonight, okay?"

"Mommy, you look sad," Livy said.

Julie leaned down and gave her daughter the tightest hug she could, kissing her on the forehead. "You go play, all right?"

"Only if you promise to read to me tonight."

"Promise," Julie said. She hoped she wouldn't have to break that promise.

3

The Rellingford Learning Academy was a small private school for children with certain behavioral issues. The academy occupied a circle of buildings on three well-manicured acres. Although there was a blacktop and a baseball diamond, there was little else to suggest a school other than the name at the front driveway. The school had on-staff medical personnel as well as a psychologist and a psychiatrist on-call who conducted therapy sessions among the student body of sixty-four, from grades six through twelve. Although it was expensive and at times administratively pigheaded, Julie had convinced Hut that it was the best place for Matt, despite the added expense, at a time when Matt had been getting increasingly violent and uncontrollable at the public school—and at home.

Julie tried to put that episode out of her mind: that mo-

ment when Matt had pulled a kitchen knife on his father.
Matt's face full of rage, his eyes wild as if he wasn't even
seeing who stood in front of him, spit flying from his lips as
some of the worst language that Julie could imagine came
out of that boy's mouth.

*It wasn't Matt. It was something else. A mental disorder
that hasn't yet been diagnosed. When he's older, they'll find
something. They'll get the right meds to fix his problem. I
know they will.*

At the front desk, near the secretary's office, Julie flipped
through a *Psychology Today*. Finally the headmaster came
in.

She glanced up from the magazine. "He's all right?"

"He's resting. He's fine now. I'd like you to speak with
Dr. Maitland first."

"Maybe I should drive him over to his own doctor, Dr.
Swanson."

"We already put a call in. Our nurse, Miss Jackson, thinks
that's not necessary at this time. He's fine, really."

Julie refrained from commenting, *Cut the condescending
attitude. I'm a nurse, too. I'll decide what's fine for Matt.*

Instead, she said, "I'd like to see him now."

4

The school psychologist was named Renny Maitland, and
he looked like a ski bum to Julie, and far too young. He was
on-hand every day for the students. A psychiatrist was in
once per week for special consultations, but Maitland handled the day-to-day issues.

"It's not as big a concern as we're making it," Maitland
said. "It's just not the first time it's happened, and we
wanted you and Mr. Hutchinson to be aware of it. It may be

the added pressure of the exams right now. We've been going through standardized tests these past few weeks. Nothing the students have to prepare for—but they're timed, and there's some pressure, so there's some . . . well, some students act out a bit when doing them."

"What exactly are we talking about here?"

"He's been carving things. Into his skin."

"He got hold of a *knife?*"

Maitland shrugged. "Just a pen. A good old ballpoint pen."

"He's done this before?"

"Well, just with drawings. Sometimes on his hands. He seems to have an issue about his hands."

"You need to call either me or my husband when Matt does this. We can't be kept in the dark."

"Mrs. Hutchinson, I did call your husband the last time it happened," Maitland said.

She felt a brief flush of embarrassment in her face.

"He said he'd talk it over with Matt. When a child draws with a pen on his hands, we simply have him wash the ink off. It's not abnormal for kids to draw on themselves. But today, well . . . he cut."

"Is he all right?"

"I think so. This isn't the first time a child has done this. It doesn't always indicate anything more than a preoccupation on the child's part. But based on Matthew's history . . ."

Julie nodded. "Of course. I can't . . . I just can't think of anything that might be bothering him. I thought with the camera, he was doing better."

"Most definitely. That was a stroke of brilliance. He videotapes everything. He's communicating much better because of it."

Julie smiled slightly, but still felt worried. "Where is he?"

5

It was a long walk from the front offices down to the nurse's office. Julie glanced at the green walls as she went down the corridor: pictures that the kids had painted, essays pinned to bulletin boards, the odor of sawdust and a strong odor of paint. She glanced down a hallway as she passed by, seeing two men working on ladders painting the walls. She passed a girl of thirteen or so and smiled at her. The girl stopped. Her arms crossed over her chest in anger, a pout on her lips. The girl watched her as she passed by.

She tapped at the open door of the nurse's office.

The room was white and large, with an empty cot pushed into a corner, the blinds drawn on the windows, and an examination table.

"Yes?" The nurse turned from an open folder on her desk and smiled. "Mrs. Hutchinson?"

"I'm here for Matt."

"He's resting," the nurse said, nodding toward a closed door. "Sometimes a good nap does the trick."

Without realizing it, Julie let out a brief sigh. "How's he doing?"

"It was rough. It started on the blacktop—one of the kids had found a hornets' nest and they were kicking it around."

"Wait, he got bitten?" Julie lingered in the doorway, glancing at the door beyond the office.

"Along his arm. It swelled up, no more than normal, but it just made him furious. He got completely out of control. He started kicking when anyone tried to keep him from drawing the pictures on his arms."

"Why wasn't I called right then?"

"Mrs. Hutchinson," the nurse said, a slight but undeniable condescension in her voice. "Our job here is not to pick up the phone every time a student gets a bee sting, unless we're aware of any allergies. Within twenty minutes of the bite, he was drawing all over where the swelling was."

"I was told they were carvings."

She nodded. "When he calmed a bit, he told me that they were pictures in his head he was trying not to forget. That's why he put them on his skin." The nurse suddenly had a look of puzzlement on her face. "It was odd. I don't mean because of how he hurt himself doing it. Or even his acting out. It was odd because he said something about his hand. How his hand couldn't work without all the fingers. Or something like that. But his hands are fine." As if dismissing something from her mind, the nurse added, "Has he been getting enough sleep?"

6

"Matt?" Julie said, stepping into the darkness of the small room. It was little more than a walk-in closet—just enough room for a cot and a bit of crawlspace around that.

At first, Matt didn't stir. Then, after a minute or so, his eyes opened. "Julie?"

She noticed that his Sony camcorder was pressed against his back, almost as if it were a comforting stuffed toy. "Right here, Matty."

"I had a bad dream."

"Oh. Well, it was just a dream. Everything's fine."

"No," Matt said, turning over to face the wall. "No. It was real."

"Do you want me to call Dr. Swanson?"

Matt glared at her. "Eleanor? No. I don't like her."

"How about . . . well, Dr. Maitland?"

He lip-farted at this.

"Did you mean to cut yourself?"

He didn't respond. She bit her lower lip. *Shouldn't have asked that. He doesn't need to be grilled right now.* She wanted to go lift him up and hug him, but she resisted what Hut would've called her "smother mother instinct."

"Matt?" she asked. "We can go home now. It's all right."

Still facing the wall, he said, "She's in a box. I heard her." Then his voice seemed to change. It sounded . . . girlish. Like he was imitating someone. *"Dear God. Dear God. Somebody help me.* That's what she said. She said it until she couldn't breathe anymore."

7

When they got out to the Camry, it had begun raining again. Julie drew Matt closer so that he could keep under her raincoat a bit. His body felt too warm.

"I'm sorry," he whispered, shivering as she unlocked the door to let him into the front seat. He was a funny kid in too many ways—violent at times, in a rage; sweet at other times. And somewhere in between he reminded her of a little kid who was smart beyond his years. Yet he had learning disabilities that she couldn't figure out. *Maybe it was his mother. Maybe it was whatever had driven her to alcohol and then drugs and then . . . the accident. Maybe whatever brain chemistry was there had gotten a little into Matt.*

Julie leaned forward and hugged him, kissing him on the top of the head. "Nothing to be sorry about, honey. Want to go grab a bite at McDonald's?"

"What about Livy?"

"She's at Laura's. We'll bring something back for her. Okay?"

He brightened slightly. "Okay."

8

After making sure his camera case was secure between his feet on the floor of the car, Matt poked around the bun of his Quarter Pounder. He lifted it up and picked out the pickle. He dropped it back in the bag.

They were at the McDonald's off the main road through town. She'd parked in front. Her cup of coffee was on the dashboard. She leaned the driver's seat back and took a bite of a Chicken McNugget.

"I know it's crazy," Matt said, chewing.

"What?" she asked, trying to hide her interest.

He swallowed the bit of burger. And then reached for his soda, took a sip, slurping. "It was like I was in a movie."

"Movie?" She glanced through the windshield. Cars went too fast on the road. Across the street at the strip mall, a little red car was nearly backing up into an SUV that wanted to quickly take a parking space.

"It's okay," he said. "I just was somewhere else. In my head."

She tried not to glance at his arms, to give him that privacy. The nurse from school had done a messy job bandaging and gauzing his elbow and forearm. She saw what looked like the drawing of a spider, a little too deep in his skin—a faint image, the ink of his ballpoint pen washed away, a lightly raised line of skin.

"Does it hurt?"

He gave a brief peripheral glance at his arm and shook his head. "Not much."

"You were stung by a hornet."

"Bitten," he corrected her. "And I think it was a yellow jacket."

"Oh. I didn't know there was a difference." She smiled. "I'm not too smart about insects."

"Maybe not," he said, closing his eyes briefly as if a headache had suddenly come on. When he opened them seconds later, he got a wicked grin on his face. "It hurt like hell when it bit me."

She reached forward for her coffee and lifted the plastic

lid. Mixed in two small cups of creamer and then a packet of sugar, but couldn't find the plastic stirrer. She took a sip. Better than she had expected.

"What about what you saw? In your mind? Did it frighten you?"

He nodded. She offered him a McNugget, and he glanced at it, then at her, then reached his thumb and forefinger into the little box and plucked it out.

"Not anymore," he said.

She touched the edge of his arm. Next to the raised skin.

He looked away, jerking his arm. Glanced out the side window. Sparrows and starlings were over by the round tables outside, and an old man tossed French fries to them.

"Is there anyone else you want to talk to? It's all right."

"No."

"I just want to help."

"I'm not mad at you," he said, gently.

"I know."

"I just got scared."

"I know you did. But it's over."

"No, it's not," Matt said. "It's just starting."

She tried to crack a grin, hoping that somewhere behind his eyes he was teasing her a little. "What is?"

"Julie," he said, sounding wise beyond his years with a voice that was utterly serious. "It's a test. She told me. In my dream. Her name is Gina. They gave the test to her. That's all there is to it. But you only get three days to pass."

chapter three

1

After picking Livy up from Laura Reynen's, Julie drove Matt and Livy home, listening to Livy describe her afternoon with the babysitter and her family. Now and then Julie glanced over at Matt, but he'd already gotten his camcorder out and was taping the blur of woods and strip malls and suburban houses.

As she turned onto their street, which would take them first up and then down a hill to the house, Livy began singing a funny song about "After you gone, and left me cryin'. After you gone there's no denyin'."

Matt howled with laughter and told his little sister she was certifiable. "You made that stupid song up."

"That's an old song," Julie said. "Gramma might even be too old for it. Was Laura playing it on the piano?"

Livy shook her head. "I heard it in my brain radio," she said. Then she continued singing, "You feel blue, you feel sad, you miss the bestest pal you ever had."

"It's called 'After You're Gone,'" Julie said. "I bet your father taught it to you."

2

By eleven that night, he still hadn't called, and she didn't want to call him because sometimes he went into a tirade when she did it. And she didn't need that—*not tonight.*

Sometimes he had to stay in the city late. It wasn't that unusual, but she expected at least a call or a message.

Julie tried paging him, but got no response. She thought she heard him come in, and went down to the front door and opened it. Just a car turning around in the driveway. It seemed misty outside—not quite rain. She stood on the front porch, feeling the chill and enjoying it a bit.

She heard some noises from downstairs and went to the finished basement.

Matt was watching television.

"Matt? It's a school night. Let's hit the sack."

He ignored her.

"What are you watching?"

"Some guy," Matt finally said.

On the TV, it was Jerry Springer. A man with a ponytail who looked a little too old for a ponytail shouted at another man, who was fat, had his shirt off, and was covered with tattoos of naked women. A middle-aged woman with short blond-red hair wiped tears from her eyes. The audience screamed.

"Let's turn it off, okay?"

"I can't sleep," Matt said.

She watched the back of his head. "All right. But get to bed soon. Okay?"

No response.

"Matt?"

"Okay," he said.

"Don't forget. You promised you'd walk Livy to the bus stop tomorrow."

"I do it every Thursday, don't I?" Then he turned around

to look at her. In his hand, his camcorder. "Smile for the camera, Julie."

"Aw, you're catching me at my best," she laughed. "Are you videoing the Springer show?"

"Nope. Just documenting my life," he said.

"To bed," she said. "Another half hour, okay?"

"Watch the birdie," he said, following her movements with the camera as she left the room and went back upstairs.

3

She lugged her laptop to bed, plugged it in, and then went online to check her email. One email from Hut, sent early in the day. She tried to open it but it was marked as "unavailable." It bugged her that her email service did that sometimes—or Hut might've even done it if he had recalled the email. She wondered what it had said. Maybe he had sent a note about what time he'd get home and then had to change it. Or maybe one of the assistants had sent it. She could've called the clinic, but decided against it. No need to be paranoid. No more Clinging Julie, as Hut had sharply called her when she'd shown up a little too much, too often, unannounced at the clinic. She'd heard enough stories about his first wife and how she'd never given him any space for his work.

That won't be me. I wouldn't want him hanging around the ER, either.

She saw her sister's name come up on her computer screen—an instant message.

"Want to Scrabble?" her sister asked, the words appearing in a text box on the screen.

"Sure. What a day."

"Let's phone."

Julie picked up the phone and speed dialed her sister's

number. "Mel. Melly. Melanie. How'd you know I'd be up?"

"Telepathy," Mel said, her voice upbeat, as usual. "Naw, just a guess. Julie, I've got to tell you. There's a new hot guy at work. I know I'm too old to chase teenagers, but he's in his twenties, and I just want to do him."

"Mel."

"Oh. Sorry. I forgot. You're married. You're not allowed to look at the menu anymore."

"He isn't home yet. It pisses me off. And drives me nuts."

"You marry a doc, you marry a god. And God does what God wants."

"Enough."

"I'm sorry. You married him, not me. You could've had my life. The revolving door of men."

The Scrabble board appeared on the computer monitor's screen. Mel had already begun putting letters on it. The word "round" came up.

"What if he's had an accident?" Then Julie added, "I can't believe you got all five letters for 'round.' You must be cheating."

"Luck of the draw," Mel said.

Julie figured out her word for the online Scrabble board: she just added a "g" to "round" to make it "ground." A genuine coup in Scrabble, as far as she was concerned.

"He hasn't had an accident," Mel said. "It's not like this is the first time. Shall I remind you of the other nights he's been late?"

A slight pause on the line. Something left unsaid. Better left that way, Julie thought. *Don't think about the phone number you found in his jacket. Don't think about it.*

"He's fine," Mel said. "You work long hours, too. You know the life. Maybe it's completely innocent." Mel had that edge to her voice, and Julie hated hearing it. It meant

that her sister was just saying what she thought Julie wanted
to hear.

"You think everybody cheats on everybody," Julie said.

"Maybe Hut's different." Mel said it with her liar voice
that was a little too cutesy.

On the online Scrabble board, Met added the word
"under" to "ground."

"You are too lucky to have drawn those five letters. Now
I know you're cheating," Julie said.

"The luck of the draw."

"Okay, I'll trust you. Cheater," Julie chuckled, glancing at
the letters she had to see how she could score triple points.

"Look, Julie, if you and Hut are still having problems . . ."

"You know," Julie said. "When we met, I thought I'd be
working beside him. The way Mom and Dad did."

"And that would lead to a fast divorce. Just like Mom and
Dad. Hey, is Matty over his fever?" Mel quickly changed the
subject.

Julie put out the word "nod," adding an "od" to the first
"n" of "underground."

"Over one obstacle and on to another. He's not doing
great. A bad episode today."

"You sound like a wicked stepmother."

"I am. I am. I love that kid. I just feel at a loss sometimes.
I don't understand so much about him. What he goes
through. In class, he was drawing things on his arms with his
pen."

"Kids do that, I guess," Mel said, putting in the letter "s"
under the "u" of "underground." Her voice had shifted
slightly as if she were hiding her alarm.

Then Julie closed her browser so that the Scrabble board
disappeared.

"Hey, did you just destroy our game?" Mel asked.

"Let's not play anymore. Too many things going on.

Look, here's the thing, Mel. He carved it into his skin. I mean gouged. These weird little drawings."

"Jesus. Is he okay?"

"They cleaned him up, and he seems okay. I guess."

"What'd the shrink say?"

"Not much. The usual."

"More meds?"

"I hate that stuff. But yes."

"What were they of?"

"What do you mean?"

"The drawings? On his arms?"

"I'm not sure. He wouldn't tell me. Looked like a sun maybe with sunbeams coming out of it, and then one of them looked like a bunch of circles. He talked about someone named Jeannie or Gina, and something about his hand not working. I guess it was just one of his moments."

"Aw. Poor kid. He's been through a lot. You got to give him credit. And you, too. Hang in there, wicked stepmommy. How's my darling niece?"

"Fine. Wonderful. She sat up with Matt and read him a bedtime story. He loved it. He was like a different kid from the one who cut into himself today. I wish the psychiatrist could . . . Well, wishing won't get me anywhere."

"Aw, you're quite a mommy. You give those kids extra butterfly kisses from Aunt Melanie."

"Oh, I almost forgot. Livy told me to tell you that she expects to see more of you in the next few days."

"She threatening me?" Mel laughed. "You know, she's a lot like her gramma. Did I tell you about Mom's new hobby?" Mel always knew how to pull Julie off her worries and into funny anecdotes about their mother's life. Mel regaled her with a long, involved tale with a funny punch line about her mother wanting to open a used bookshop that only sold self-help books. "She said it's because everyone needs to help themselves. She thinks that's what changed her life.

All those books on codependency and her diet books and that Dr. Phil book. And now she's getting into ESP. I think she'll end up being a witch." They both laughed.

As they finished up their call, it was nearly midnight, and Mel signed off with her usual, "When you were born, you know what I told Mom? I told her that you were going to be my favorite sister in the whole world. And you still are, thirty-four years later."

"And it's still easy, because I'm your only sister," Julie chuckled. "Say good night, Gracie."

"Good night, Gracie."

After she'd hung up the phone, Julie drew out the previous Sunday's *New York Times* magazine section and opened the page to the crossword puzzle. Puzzles helped her relax a bit, and although she nearly forgot the name of the state bird of Hawaii—"Nene," a crossword puzzle staple—it seemed to turn off some awful buzzing in the back of her head. She took a half dose of Ambien to help get her to the sleep point.

When sleep came not long after, she thought she heard the phone ring, but it seemed to be in the wonderful dream she was having, so she didn't try to answer it.

4

A feeling of intense physical excitement overcame her body, and he touched her hand lightly and held her wrist as if to restrain her. Then she felt a tender shiver go through her, a distinct sexual charge. Hut was there, rubbing her, licking her nipples, but she couldn't move at all—somehow she was tied to the mattress. She felt wave after wave of delicious sensation, and his hand moved down her stomach and crept between her legs.

She gasped. Something about his face had changed. It seemed to fade in and out of focus.

5

She woke to sweat-soaked sheets, in the dark of her bedroom.

Livy had crawled into bed beside her in the night. Julie felt embarrassed to have had such an erotic dream with her daughter sleeping beside her.

She watched Livy's face as she slept, and waited for the sun to come up.

6

The next morning, Julie checked the machine for messages, but there were none. Hut had not come home at all. She called his cell phone, but got the recording. She called the clinic, but got his voice mail.

I hate you, Hut Hutchinson. I hate you for doing this to me. For making me suspicious. For making me call hospitals in case you had an accident and then finding out you had just worked too late and hadn't thought it important enough to call me. Or your kids. I hate you for being this cold to me.

Another voice cut in to her head. *Julie, you are nuts. He loves you. He loves the kids. He is working on important things. He probably just pulled an all-nighter working on some emergency or other and is still asleep on that little cot in the filing cabinet room at the clinic.*

7

Matt had been up by six. He had his Sony camcorder out and was filming birds pecking at the backyard birdfeeder. When he saw Julie at the kitchen window, he turned the camcorder on her and waved. She waved back, opening the window to tell him that she had some oatmeal and toast with raspberry jam for him for breakfast. He lowered the camcorder from his face and scowled a bit. "Oatmeal? What about Pop Tarts?"

"I'll pick some up tomorrow at Shop Rite," she said. "In fact, if you want anything else special, let me know."

"Maybe some Dr Pepper?"

There was an everydayness about the two of them talking through the open window that made her smile and forget the bad day that Matt had, and nearly forget the little scratches and scars on his arms.

She had to rouse Livy from what must've been a fantastic dream, because even as she hustled her into the shower, Livy kept talking about the wondrous things she saw the previous night, including flying horses.

"And in my dream, Daddy kept asking me if I could get up, and I said, 'Of course I can, Daddy; I just want to keep sleeping.' But you know what? I did get up. I thought I heard him say something."

"Daddy had to work all night," Julie said, kissing her on the forehead, smelling Livy's hair—Johnson's Baby Shampoo, the last little vestige of babyness left in her six-year-old daughter.

"You never work all night," Livy said. "Daddy works all the time, but you don't."

"I know. I have a perfect job."

"Like on *ER*."

"Just like that," Julie grinned. "Plus, I get to be a mommy."

"Poor Daddy," Livy said. "He never gets to be a daddy anymore."

"Poor Daddy is right," Julie said, and tried not to think of the phone number on a slip of paper that smelled of perfume that she'd found in Hut's overcoat, a number she had never called, a woman whose name she didn't know, a woman who might not even exist except in a jealous, insecure wife's imagination.

8

She did her telephone punch-in when she got to Rellingford Hospital, and then proceeded down the long rose-colored hallway to the ER. She passed some medics and other nurses, said the obligatory morning hellos and listened to the lukewarm jokes, but her mind was elsewhere and she was craving coffee. The staff in the ER was small, like everything else in Rellingford. There was simply the doc—Dr. Davison—a unit clerk, and a few nurses on the day shift. The night shift was even more bare bones. Not a lot happened out in Rellingford that required the ER, and some days, no one came in except a patient with a twisted ankle or a kid who needed a few stitches and a hug. There were always lab techs around, the respiratory therapists, and an on-call staff in case anything major came down.

She picked up the report from Nancy Maier, the outgoing staff nurse, and then grabbed a cup of coffee from the vending machine room—and *Thank God it is Starbucks* or she would've been in a bad mood over the usual mud-in-a-cup—and then she went off to triage to get the long shift going.

By the late afternoon, two new patients had come in, one of them from a car wreck out on the main highway. It made her think about Hut and hope that he was okay. Surely, he'd page her or call, and, she had to remember, that if something had happened to him, she'd have been contacted.

The patient who arrived had been lucky—a broken leg, perhaps, and a dislocated shoulder. With her coworkers and the doc on his way, Julie got to work in triage.

Just before five, her shift supervisor called her over to an empty office and said, "Julie. Something's happened."

The supervisor had that tone of voice that meant something bad. Something tragic. She'd heard the tone when the news came about any tragedy—from the World Trade Center horror of a few years' previous to the sudden death of one of the visiting physicians. Immediately, Julie thought of the children. Of Matt and his troubles. Of the time she'd seen him with a knife, and even though he hadn't done anything to himself with it, she had known—he had communicated with his eyes—that he was thinking about his real mother, about where she was, the institution outside Philadelphia, about all the things that Matt had whirling in his mind at all times . . .

"Not Matty," Julie said, tears already forming in her eyes. Images of Matt, memories of him, his violent outbursts, his tantrums, his moods.

"No," her supervisor said softly.

chapter four

1

The morgue wasn't located in the hospital but at the sheriff's station one township over. It was an area of what New Jerseyans called the Lake District that was less wooded and natural than paved over and set up right off the major highway. The sheriff's station looked like an industrial park, and the morgue was toward the back. Julie had insisted that she could drive, that it was a mistake, that none of this made sense, and she was fine until she saw the staircase down to the morgue.

It looked like she had to walk down into limbo. It grew colder with each step, and she had to steady herself on the railing. She felt as if, at any moment, she might trip on the stairs.

A policewoman accompanied her, and Julie could tell that the woman watched her to make sure she wouldn't collapse or stumble.

She sat down on the seventh step down and covered her face with her hands.

"We can sit here for as long as you want," the cop said.

Julie wasn't sure how much time had passed. "I've seen dead people before," she said, steeling herself, wiping her eyes. "It's all right. It really is. I'm a nurse." She wasn't sure if she said any of this aloud or not as she got up and went down into the chilly floor below, where the lights were a flickering blue, smelling of talcum, alcohol, and something that reminded her too much of the emergency room.

And then the room itself: shiny and silver and garish. The overhead lighting was flat and made the coroner and the sheriff look as if they, too, were dead, as they stood there over the body. In the far corner of the room, three large blue plastic barrels seemed out of place. It wasn't as big a room as she had expected, and she felt crowded by the others there, and self-conscious because she was sure they were just waiting for her to do something irrational.

She didn't look at the face of the dead man until then.

2

"Mrs. Hutchinson?"

"It's not him," she said. "Thank God. Oh my God. It's not him."

The sheriff was a man named Cottrell, whom she knew only from the time he'd brought Matt in when Matt had stolen a car at the age of twelve. The sheriff had told her that the car was undamaged and the owners were willing to drop charges, and Matt had been bawling like a baby. Rellingford was that kind of town. Cottrell had told her then that he understood Matt's situation from "Dr. Hutchinson," and so he hoped it would just be an isolated incident. Dr. Hutchinson was known in Rellingford. They knew of his first wife and her "troubles." They knew of Matt and his "situation."

Julie had thought back then that she probably would never see the sheriff again on official business. How many times in life do you have to see the local authorities?

She took the tissue he offered and wiped her eyes. Her vision came back into focus. She felt a boundless happiness

and a distant sorrow for this murder victim. She looked at
the face. She didn't recognize him at all, but she could see
why the mistake had been made. Hut had floppy auburn
hair, too, and he had that kind of squarish jaw that reminded
her of the Midwest and cornfields for some reason. But that
was really it. This corpse in front of her was pale, and the
lips and nose were all wrong. "It's a mistake," she said. "It's
not him."

"This is Homicide Detective McGuane, from Manhattan," the sheriff said too formally.

Julie didn't glance up at any of them. *People make mis-
takes all the time. Errors in judgment. This is why they need
someone to identify bodies. Human error is the norm in life.
Of course that's true. Of course.*

"Mrs. Hutchinson, I'd like to talk to you for a few minutes. Perhaps not right now. Not today. But soon. The sooner
the better," the stranger said.

She couldn't look up at his face.

She kept watching the dead man. She was aware of the
wounds and knew that whoever had killed the man on the
table had a knowledge of where to strike—there were knife
entry wounds at the arm, the lungs, the neck, and the heart.
Lacerations on the shoulders and hands, possibly from a
struggle. She had worked in the city years ago and had seen
murder victims before when she had been a newly minted
RN and had often worked the graveyard shift in the ER.
She'd seen the victims of gang killings then, of domestic
homicide, of any number of ways that a human being could
be killed.

She had been able, quickly, to separate herself from the
dead, even in her mid-twenties, by viewing them as having
gone on—as being empty shells. It was as she'd been taught
in church, and although she only believed sporadically, it
helped to think of death that way, particularly a violent
death: *Their suffering is over. They're in heaven, now.*

They're in some afterlife that is somehow better than the raw deal they'd gotten in this world.

"It can't be him."

"He's your husband," McGuane said. "We have his personal effects. Wallet, keys, and so on. Mrs. Hutchinson. This is Dr. Jeffrey 'Hut' Hutchinson. I know this is a tremendous shock."

She had thought of him so much as "Hut" that she had nearly forgotten his real first name: Jeff. *It's not him. Why do they keep insisting it's Hut? It's not Hut.*

She looked at the wounds, at the arms, at the belly, and it wasn't until she saw the small circular tattoo on the dead man's left shoulder that it hit her, too hard. She felt nausea in her stomach, and heard a distant, shrill ringing in her ears.

Someone wrapped his arms around her, holding her up. Had she been falling? She tugged away from the arms and stumbled toward the wall, pressing her forehead into the coolness of the wall itself, as if she could press herself through it.

And then she knew that she was going to fall. It seemed in slow motion as she hit the edge of a small metal cabinet on her way down, and then her head hit the floor.

3

She awoke in a darkened room, the only light coming from beneath a door. The smell of fresh coffee somewhere, beyond the darkness. Gradually, as her eyes focused, she saw more: It was simply an office, probably at the sheriff's station. She felt achy and nauseated, but gradually, perhaps a half hour after opening her eyes, she pushed herself up from the cot. Her head ached, and she reached back to touch the back of her skull. Someone had already taped some gauze just under her hairline at the nape of her neck. She remembered the fall and winced with pain when she moved her jaw a little. She heard voices beyond the small room.

She stepped out into a too-bright light and went to sit in a large chair in a corner of the sheriff's office. He glanced up from his desk and laid the phone back in its cradle.

"We had you checked out," the sheriff said. "Your head. Are you sure you're okay?"

"I don't think it's a problem," she said, but the headache was pretty strong.

"How are . . . how are you doing?"

"I'm a little thirsty. If I could . . ."

"Certainly," the sheriff said, and then went out into the bustling main office to get a cup of water for her. Before the door shut behind him, she saw the man named McGuane again. He was gaunt and had lightly graying dark hair that seemed too long for a detective. He looked to be about fifty, and something in his demeanor and his wrinkled jacket made her think of a scarecrow. He stared at her as the door closed behind the sheriff.

Then she was alone again in the office, blinds drawn around the windows.

When the sheriff returned with a large plastic cup of water, McGuane followed.

She watched as he took a chair opposite her, pulling it in closer.

She couldn't look at him again. Not for a while.

"I wish I could be gentler about this," McGuane said.

4

Mel came to take her home and hugged her when she saw her. "What's that?" Mel asked, pointing to the padded yellow envelope in Julie's hands.

"Personal effects, they said. Wallet, keys, watch," Julie said, feeling dead on the inside.

"Did you hurt yourself?" Mel gasped when Julie turned away from her.

Julie felt the bandaging on her neck. "Oh. That. It's nothing, really."

"I don't even know what to say, sweetie," Mel said. "I just don't. We'll go home. Somehow, we'll sort this out."

You hated him, Julie wanted to say. *You told me on my wedding day that he was a poor bet for a husband. You told me he had too much baggage. Don't sit here and pretend everything will ever be all right again.*

Julie said, "Hut bought a gun two years ago. He said he didn't like the way there was too much crime, even in the suburbs. He bought it and I hated it and I tried to throw it away twice. He had it locked up at the top of the linen closet. I made him take the bullets out of it and put those elsewhere. I wish I hadn't insisted on it. I wish he had his gun with him. I wish he had it. He might still be alive."

She felt her sister's touch on her scalp, combing through her hair, just as her older sister had done when they'd been kids, when Julie had come home from a bad day in kindergarten or first grade, a day of fears and a day of friendships lost. Mel would comb her fingers through Julie's then-blond hair and whisper, "I'm going to brush all the bad things from your head, Jules. Don't worry."

5

At home, she lay down on top of her bedspread and stared up at the ceiling until her eyes lost their focus and she had to shut them.

In her dream, she saw the face again.

His face. Not dead, but alive.

Not on a shiny metal table, with pasty-white skin covered with blotches of brown-red and bright blue bruises.

But as he had been the last moment she had seen him. Alive.

It was morning, and she had just made coffee.

She turned to him, feeling the sorrow that came with the knowledge of the loss.

His warm brown eyes brightened when he finished telling a truly bad joke to her, and she chastised him for spilling coffee on the edge of his sleeve. He gave her that look that meant he was tired of the small, petty comments. In the dream, she tried to erase making a comment about the coffee stain. She looked at him and said, "Try to be home early at least one night this week."

"You know how demanding things are right now." His voice—had she even remembered it correctly in her dream? "It's not as if I'm making people get sick so I can work late and never be home with my wife and kids. You think I'm that kind of man?"

Even in the dream, the thought of another woman whom he might or might not be seeing came to her, a cloud that was both distant and close.

"Well, you don't even know your son at this point," she said—and something inside her said, *Don't keep doing this to him; he's going to want to leave you if you do. Don't become a bitch*—and yet she kept saying, "I got up in the middle of the night and he was cycling again." *Cycling* was their word for Matt's nearly manic phases when he would stay up all night, playing games of solitaire for too many hours, or doodling ridiculous images in his art notebook, or playing computer chess by himself.

"All you do is worry. I'd like to be home once and not have to be surrounded by this . . . this drama," Hut said.

And then the dream evaporated, and when she awoke in her bed, she thought for just a minute that nothing bad had happened to him, that he would be home later that night, that all of it had just been a dream.

But the yellow padded envelope lay next to her pillow.

6

She opened the yellow envelope and poured the watch and the keys out on her bedspread. The watch was from her, on their first anniversary. It had cost too much money—just under four hundred dollars at Saks—but she felt he needed a really good watch for his work. She wondered if she were still paying it off on her Visa. He had loved the watch and told her that it was the best gift he'd ever received next to Livy, who had arrived a scant six months after they married. His gargantuan key set—for the house, the clinic, his car, and even keys he'd told her he'd had since he was a kid. She'd joked with him sometimes, asking him if those were keys in his pocket or if he was just happy to see her. His wallet had the normal things she knew would be in there: his credit cards, his social security card, the pictures of the kids, the pictures of her, seventy dollars cash, and a few wadded-up receipts.

All I have left of you, Hut. This is it.

She switched on the little color TV above the dresser, clicking the remote to surf channels, and was afraid for a moment that the news would come on, detailing the murder. But no matter what channel she went to, no one mentioned Hut's murder. *We're not the news. We're not what people want to hear about.*

A gentle tapping at her bedroom door. The door slid open slightly. *Mel.* "You're awake." Her voice was smooth and soft.

Julie nodded, stretching. No headache. It would be back, but not just yet. She swung her feet over the edge of the bed, but was not ready to stand up.

"Can I get you some tea? Maybe some decaf chai?"

"I'm fine. Really," Julie said. She glanced over at the wide mirror that she and Hut had picked out at Pottery Barn two years before. Her face was all in brambles. Not her face at all, just as the dead man on the table had not had Hut's face. "I'm fine," she repeated.

7

She managed a shower, and while the steamy water cascaded over her, she didn't close her eyes. Didn't want to see inside her own head. Behind the opaque shower curtain, she could see the shadow coming into the bathroom.

Hut. It would be Hut. He would grin as he pulled back the curtain. Naked and happy as a puppy. Like in their first days. His grin infectious, his way of touching her so new and so right. Alive. Alive and fresh and younger than he should've been while in his mid-thirties. Not in a house with a mortgage too high for a debt-laden doctor to the poor and an ER nurse. But in her little apartment in the city, her crappy little place where they'd briefly made a nest before her pregnancy, where they'd made love too many times and for too many hours to count. Making love had been something more than pleasure. More than making a baby. It had been a bonding between them, a clasping of hands that reminded her not of sex but of absolute love. He had been everything to her. Everything.

The shower beating down on her face washed the tears from her.

When she emerged from the shower, and dressed, she wasn't sure why she even cared if she was clean. She wanted to go to Livy, and to Matt—she wanted her children. She wanted them in her arms and she wanted them now.

The detective showed up at six-thirty that evening.

chapter five

1

They sat in the living room. Although all the lamps were turned up, even the overly bright halogen one near the fireplace, Julie felt as if the room was cloaked in shadows.

She ate unbuttered whole-wheat toast and some tea with a little honey. It was all she had eaten that day, and all she had wanted to eat.

"I don't really understand," she said, after the first few questions.

"It's a pattern," McGuane said. He drank a Diet Coke and refused the cookies offered by Mel, who sat near the upright piano but said nothing. Julie noticed his wedding band and a ring that looked like a college signet ring. She didn't want to look back up at his face.

"Why haven't you got him yet?" she asked.

McGuane took a sip from his soda, and then glanced over at Mel. Then out the window. He nodded as if talking to himself. "I wish I had an answer for you. Can you think of anything that would connect your husband to this?"

"I don't know. I can't imagine . . ." Julie looked down at her teacup. *Keep your fingers from trembling. Just keep the teacup still.*

"We're hoping you might have records here. Not much to go over at the clinic."

She glanced up at his face. "He didn't bring his work home. That was important to him."

The detective passed her a beige folder with the photographs. She set her cup down on the red table beside her, and opened the folder.

"You know," McGuane said, more to Mel than to her, "I live across the Hudson all my life, and I had no idea Jersey is anything but an industrial tract and, you know, *The Sopranos.* Then I come out here and there are all these lakes and trees and it's like, I don't know, Pennsylvania."

"Except without the Amish," Mel said. She offered up a weak grin. Julie wished she'd had the presence of mind to thank her out loud for adding some humor to the somber atmosphere.

Death is everywhere. Death is all around, all the time, she thought. *At work, and now here. In my living room. In my house. Uninvited. I don't want it.*

Julie turned each photograph over.

More dead people. Just faces. Pale. Not really human anymore. Like white masks. Hollow.

"I'm sorry to do this to you," he said, his voice barely more than a mumble. "I'd rather catch this guy before he does it again."

"I've never seen these people before," she said. The sound of her own voice, weary and flat, made her feel heavier.

The pictures: two women and a man. Eyes closed. Empty shells of human beings. Gone.

Her half-Catholic, half-Episcopalian upbringing reared. *Their spirits have flown. They are in God's hands. They are in heaven. Or some other finer place. Beyond trouble. Beyond this world.*

Beyond the grasp of the one who killed them.

"There's another picture," McGuane said. "Inside."

She checked the folder. Under a thin piece of onionskin paper, one last photograph.

It was a man's back. Perhaps it was Hut's. Nothing reminded her of him, but she had barely recognized him in the morgue, so she didn't expect to identify him without seeing his face. That was why pictures like this were safe. They could be of anyone and no one at the same time.

All kinds of circles and drawings were carved into the man's back, from the shoulder blades down to the small of the back, just above the buttocks.

"Do you have any idea what this might be?"

Julie shook her head.

"He carves things into the bodies. He has a ritual. We know a little about what the symbols are. We just don't know where they lead us."

Julie remembered the carving on Matt's arm. *Don't be ridiculous. It's nothing like this. Matt's arm and this man's back have different things on them. Don't let your mind go with this, Julie. Don't.*

"No idea. What is it? They're like tattoos."

"Can I see?" Mel asked.

Julie glanced at McGuane, who gave a slight shrug. Mel got up and went over to retrieve the picture. After glancing at it, Mel said, "You're making her look at this kind of stuff *now*?"

McGuane kept his composure. "We want to do everything we can to stop this guy."

"It's all right, Mel. Really," Julie said. "We should help. I want to. I want to see who . . . what kind of monster . . ." She covered her face with her hands.

Just go away, she thought. *Everyone, go away. Let it be someone else who loses her husband. Not me. Let it be anyone else. Hut, where are you? Why did you leave? Why aren't you here with me?*

Mel and McGuane started talking, and Mel went to sit down on the two steps that led up to the dining area. Julie felt she could shut them all out. Just block them, like she was a child with her hands over her ears.

Then she brought her hands down from her face. Mel and McGuane were still there. They watched her as if she were something that was about to break.

"We've tried to locate the orphanage where your husband grew up," McGuane said.

She hesitated before speaking. She tried to grasp his meaning. "He had parents."

McGuane glanced at her sharply.

"Tell me," she said. "What is it?"

"Nothing," McGuane said. "Nothing at all."

"I know he was adopted," Julie said. "But he was little. Three or four. I think four."

"Mrs. Hutchinson, your husband wasn't adopted until he was sixteen. Before that he was a ward of the state of New York."

"What?"

"He was part of a special program, Mrs. Hutchinson. It was the 1970s, and there was some special aptitude your husband had to qualify for this program. As a boy."

"Are you sure you mean my husband? Jeff Hutchinson?"

McGuane nodded. "I'm sorry that you weren't aware. I assumed that your husband informed you about his past. About his childhood."

She sat there, stunned.

"Did you ever speak with his adoptive parents about his past?"

"No," she said, her face reddening. "What . . . what kind of program was he in?"

McGuane gave what looked to her like an ironic grin. "Not sure yet. I was hoping you could tell me, actually."

"I have no idea," she said, her voice taking on a faraway quality as if she were ransacking memories to try to remember one thing that he might've said about something from his childhood that seemed out of the ordinary. Her mother's annoying voice erupted in her head, the bad advice given when she got engaged to Hut: *Remember, wives never really know much about their husbands. It's just the way marriage is. That's why your father and I got divorced. They keep secrets. They hold back. To hell with it.* Then Julie remembered something. "Oh. He told me he was . . ." She glanced at Mel, trying to get her to confirm a memory of a conversation. "You were there. It was about some accident when he was little. He said he was in a hospital for a long time."

"All we know is that it was a school called Daylight. Or the Daylight Project. And it was not an ordinary program," McGuane said.

"Why is that important?"

"Your husband may have known one of the other victims. All of them were there. Your husband may have known the man who killed him. We're just trying to connect the dots," McGuane said. "A man, roughly your husband's age, was attacked by the killer. But not killed. His memory, after the attack, isn't so good. But he knew about your husband. He knew about two women who were also killed. We're having trouble with his story, simply because . . . well, he claims to have psychic knowledge."

"Psychic?" Mel said, shooting a glance at Julie. *What the hell?*

"Wait, are you saying that some psychic is claiming things, and the NYPD is listening?"

"We've had some help at times from the psychic community, Mrs. Hutchinson," McGuane said. "I personally don't really believe in that kind of thing. But sometimes, it helps."

"So you're going to use a psychic to find who killed Hut?" Julie could not repress a laugh.

McGuane glanced down at his soda. "There are all kinds of ways to find a killer, Mrs. Hutchinson. I'm sure you would want us to use every resource at our disposal."

Mel chimed in. "Mom told me that sometimes psychics feel they see a murder scene."

"Sure," Julie deadpanned. "Maybe we should ask Livy to tune in on her brain radio." Then, more seriously, to McGuane: "You think that my husband knew psychics?"

"No, nothing like that," McGuane said.

"Because he didn't. He didn't go for mumbo jumbo. That's one thing I can say for sure about him. He was a doctor. He was fascinated by scientific research. He didn't think life was mystical," Julie said.

"That's true," Mel said, and Julie was thankful she was there.

Mel got up to go get a glass of water, and McGuane made a joke about crazies who phoned in solutions to murders. "This guy may just be one of the crazies, that's true," he said. "Still, he knew some things."

"Where did the attack happen?" Julie asked, wanting to steer the conversation away from mumbo jumbo.

McGuane looked out beyond the living room window, as if thinking about how to delicately answer this question. "That doesn't really matter right now."

"It does to me."

"All right. Just outside town. Out in some hills beyond the highway."

"He died in the woods."

"We found his car on the side of the road," McGuane said. "In Newark."

"But you found him nearby."

"Yes."

"I want to go there."

2

Against his better judgment, McGuane agreed to drive her to the place where her husband had been murdered. The roads were slick from a previous rain, and he took the turns along the highway slowly, both for safety and because he felt as if he had a fragile item in his car.

They said nothing as he drove along the back road that led up to the hillside, beyond the suburbs, and Julie stared straight ahead the whole time, thinking of nothing whatsoever.

When they got there, to the edge of the road where the killer had left Hut's car, McGuane parked, got out, and went around to open her door.

"Thank you," she said.

He had positioned the headlights of the car to shine on the narrow gravel path that cut through the woods.

"He took your husband through there." McGuane pointed, and then made a circle with his finger in the air. "There's a clearing when you go higher."

"I suppose it's too dark to go up there."

"Mrs. Hutchinson, if you think this will help at all," he said, "I'll get a flashlight and we can go up there. But it's muddy, and frankly, any footprint we leave might obscure some vital piece of evidence. I hate taking that chance."

She nodded and glanced around the woods. "Do you know when he died?"

"We're not sure. Not yet. I'd guess it was early afternoon yesterday. Might've been last night. Some mountain bikers use that path. They were going up and down the hills around here this morning. One of them thought he saw a dead deer and went to get a closer look. Only, well, it wasn't . . . what he had thought. That was before nine this morning."

"It rained yesterday, off and on," she said.

"But it was fairly dry when the bicyclists came through here."

"Where did my husband's Audi end up?"

"Mrs. Hutchinson," McGuane said, "it's important to examine every little detail of this crime scene."

"So it's impounded." She nodded, understanding. "Livy and I were here yesterday. Well, not here. Miles away, really. To the west. But we were in the woods, up in the hills." She walked up to the edge of the path. She looked into the darkness between the trees as if half expecting someone to be there. Then, she turned, facing the headlights of McGuane's car, and said, "Please take me home now. I think I'm going to be sick."

3

Later that evening, Mel called to her from the top of the stairs. The kids were all ready for bed. It was nearly ten, and everybody was exhausted. Julie went to sit on the edge of Livy's bed.

Matt unrolled his sleeping bag on the floor near Livy's bed.

"It's okay for a night or two," Julie said. "It's wonderful in fact. But you need to move it back to your own bedroom soon. Okay?" Even as she said this, she wanted to bring both of them into her own bed and hold them for as long as possible.

Matt's reaction had surprised her. She had suspected he might have a violent outburst, or become agitated. But he had chosen silence instead. He had barely said a word since Julie had told him of his father's death, but stuck close to Livy, who had bawled for hours before she had just gone to her room and begun reading. Julie wasn't sure how Livy understood death, and even as she tucked her in, Livy looked at her as if she didn't quite believe that her father was not coming home again.

Mel sat next to Matt on his temporary bed, while Julie began singing "Lullaby and Goodnight" to Livy, who clung to her as she fell asleep.

"It's nice of you to do this," she whispered to Matt before

kissing him good night, which he shrugged away as if he were too old for kisses on the forehead.

"I want to keep her safe," Matt said.

Julie glanced around his sleeping bag. "You usually sleep with your camera."

"Not tonight, Julie. I don't feel like making a movie out of this," he said. He covered himself up to his neck in the sleeping bag and then rested his head on the pillow. "You won't let me go back to my mother, will you?"

Julie felt a lump in her throat. "Of course not. We're family," she said. "You and me and Livy. Don't even think it. Remember when all those papers got signed? You're stuck with me, bucko."

4

When the kids were asleep, she went to the linen closet and drew a footstool out so she could reach the very top shelf. She drew a metal box down. It clanked when she moved it. She took it into her room and set it on the dresser. She found the small key to the lock. She opened the box. The gun was wrapped in a thin cloth. She knew nothing about guns. She knew this was some special type of revolver that Hut had to get a license for. She hadn't wanted to know about it. She had pretended that the bad people never showed up at your door in the suburbs.

She went to find the clip to put in it. She didn't think she'd use it. She didn't think she'd ever need to. But she wanted to feel as if it was there for her if anything ever threatened her children.

5

Before Julie went to bed, she looked up the phone number in an old Day Runner that she'd kept since their wedding day. She punched in the number on her cell phone. California. The area code had changed. She had to tap the number in again, this time with another area code.

At first no one picked up. Then a man's voice: "Yes?"

"Mr. Hutchinson. This is Julie."

He said nothing in response.

"I'm sorry," she said. She could not help her tears.

"It's all right, it's all right," Hut's father said. His voice had a slightly Midwestern inflection. She visualized a husky man of seventy-one with salt-and-pepper hair. "We heard from the authorities. How are you doing?"

She didn't want to lie. She wiped at her eyes with her free hand. "I don't know."

"How's Matty and Livy?"

"Sad. Quiet. I can't imagine what they're thinking."

"The shock has just hit us both in the gut," he said. "I'm glad you called. We needed to get in touch at some point. Even if it would be against his wishes."

"I know."

"Joanne's sleeping. She's been sleeping since we heard."

"We can talk another time. Would that be all right?"

"Of course," he said. "And Julie, it's good to hear from you. Even under these circumstances. We want to try and keep up now, if possible. Would that be all right?"

Julie tried to erase the words her husband had used over the years about his parents, about how horrible they'd been to him, about how they could not come to the wedding, about how they had treated him like a piece of trash since the moment they'd adopted him, about horrible verbal and mental abuse at their hands, about how he had to use college scholarships to escape them, and get beyond their cold darkness.

It didn't seem to matter anymore. She wanted to know them. She wanted to know more about Hut.

"Of course," she said. "I want my daughter to know her grandparents. And Matt."

"Thank you," the man said. "He never thought of us as his parents. Not really. But we loved him, despite everything. We really loved our son."

It struck her as normal for him to say that, even though Hut had all but convinced her that his father was a monster and his mother was an overly passive contributor to his father's moods. Hut was dead now, after all. It was easy for his parents to remember their love for him. She had always assumed that Hut would deeply regret the rift he'd created with his folks when one of them died. She had never anticipated that Hut would die first and that she might finally get to know his adoptive mother and father, two people she had only briefly met during a trip when Hut had blown up with anger at them. He and Julie had had to retreat back to a hotel "rather than spend ten more seconds with those awful people!" Hut had yelled at the time.

6

She woke up late and couldn't pull herself out of bed until eleven. She had the vague memory of another dirty dream—something about a man pressing his fingers into her and licking her thighs. It made her feel a little guilty to have such a dream so soon after Hut's death.

She made some calls to the sheriff and learned that Detective McGuane had gotten some kind of ridiculous permission to transfer Hut's body to a morgue in Manhattan.

"It's necessary," the sheriff told her on the phone, and she immediately called Andrew Money, a lawyer she knew from work at the hospital to see what her legal rights were—she left an overly detailed message for the lawyer.

By noon, she had tried to reach McGuane by phone,

furious that she could not plan a funeral and have her husband's body safe from the dissectors of the autopsy room.

Finally, McGuane returned her call via cell phone. "Mrs. Hutchinson, we need to talk again. As soon as possible."

7

"I can drive you," Mel said.

"I can do it. I need the drive. I'll be fine."

"No, I'm going to drive you. Laura can stay with the kids. You should not be behind the wheel of a car right now. Not with all this," Mel said. "I can go shopping—he's right around the corner from Bed, Bath & Beyond. I need to get a few things. So you just call me when you're done. I can shop till midnight if I have to."

It took them nearly two hours to get to the city, so she was at McGuane's office just before three.

McGuane's office was full of maps and pictures of what might've been forensics snapshots. A gallery of the dead.

A young woman sat opposite McGuane. She glanced back at Julie, as if startled from a private conversation.

"Mrs. Hutchinson, this is Officer Donati. She's our point person in forensics."

Donati nodded in her direction, a warm but silent greeting.

"Coffee?" McGuane asked, pointing toward a filthy Mr. Coffee machine at the edge of his desk.

Julie shook her head slightly. "What is it you wouldn't tell me on the phone?"

"Please, sit down," McGuane said, overly politely, gesturing to an empty chair near the other officer.

Donati spoke up. "This happens from time to time with transfers between morgues and paperwork foul-ups, although in this case, it's somewhat unique. It's—"

McGuane cut her off. "Mrs. Hutchinson, your husband's body is missing."

chapter six

1

It was nearly four-thirty when she stepped out onto the street in Manhattan and just began wandering. She felt as if the woman named Julie Hutchinson had been hollowed out, and now she was someone else. She walked down to Sixth Avenue and cut east over to Washington Square. The great arch was fenced off, and the circle within the park had some acrobat passing a hat after a brief show. Dogs in the dog run were barking, and she almost wished she were an addict so she could buy something from the dealers at the edge of the park, some drug that would just put her further away from reality. Then along the streets again, past NYU, past the windows of shops full of shoes or books or pastries or trendy clothes. She stepped into Shakespeare & Company, a bookstore that had been a favorite of hers from her student days. She browsed the shelves, wondering what she should be looking for.

She remembered the conversation with her mother, after the news of Hut's murder had arrived: Her mother had recommended a specific book. What was it?

Something like *The Life Beyond.*

She touched each book on the shelf, as if it would speak to her. None of them did.

"Can I help you?" a young woman asked.

Julie smiled, shrugged a little. "I guess I'm looking for a book. I thought it would be in self-help. It's called *The Life Beyond*. At least, I think that's the title."

"Let me look it up," the clerk said, then retreated to the cash register counter. She emerged a few moments later. "I'm afraid we don't have that one in at the moment. Michael Diamond's books are a little hard to get these days. We could order it for you, if you like."

Julie felt normal for the two minutes or so it took to order the book, but when she was on the street again, it was as if she were afraid to run into her old self. The sky, seen between the overhang of buildings, was shadowy with clouds. She smelled rain in the air. Rain and the exhaust of taxis and buses.

2

She wandered neighborhoods, remembering how it had felt to be younger and living in the city. She glanced in shop windows along Greenwich Avenue, crossed over to Ninth and passed by Electric Lady Studios, thinking of Janis Joplin and Jim Morrison, the legends who had recorded there. She walked past the Barnes and Noble that had, when she'd lived there, been a B. Dalton's, past Gray's Papaya and other stops along her memory's lane, and there she was, outside her old apartment building. It was as rundown as it had been then, when she and Hut had their trysts, when she had just finished getting over a heartbreak of her twenties and decided that there was no such thing as romantic love. And then, suddenly, she had met Hut, and she believed again. She believed that love and romance and happiness were in the world for her.

She sat down on a stoop outside a junk shop on Breton Street, which conjured a scene from her twenties of buying funky lava lamps and scratched-up coffee tables, and she thought of her old friends—Alicia and Joe, whom she used to go with to hang out, see movies, explore the city, cry over relationships that didn't work, and laugh when life just became too absurd. Those were her old days. And then Hut had come along, and she'd left it all behind. She'd called Joe and Rick less and less, and then Alicia had grown cold (*Or had it been me?* Julie wondered). Alicia had an art studio somewhere now, and Joe was writing novels about the gay community. She had meant to read them, meant to follow up on Alicia's shows and installations, but Hut had brought her out to Rellingford, and they had quickly built a life that seemed at times beyond their means. She glanced up across the street at the window that had been her apartment. Then down the windows to the Chinese laundry and the overpriced Ethiopian restaurant next door to it. She had loved this neighborhood. She had loved her too-tiny place with its weird neighbors and its elevator that worked twice per year (the holidays, because the owner of the building got it inspected then), with its inner walls that Joe had called "birth canal pink," and the crumbly ceiling in the bathroom.

She remembered Joe's number. She'd surprise him. It had been at least two years since they'd talked. And now here she was, a block away from his place. She opened her cell phone and tapped in the number.

He picked up on the third ring. "Julie?" he asked. Caller ID had ruined her surprise.

"Hey, Joe," she said, feeling as if she were not midthirties but mid-twenties.

"Well, we thought you'd dropped off the face of the earth. How the hell are you?"

"I'm in the neighborhood."

"Want to come on over? Or we can go over to Starbucks."

"I just was remembering. Remember when we all got tickets for *Phantom*?"

"Oh yeah, that was great," he laughed. "We show up on the wrong night, and then Alicia manages to flirt with one of the ushers."

"And gets us the best seats in the house. God. We used to have such adventures. Some of which are not befitting a properly married suburban wife."

"I know. I'll be able to blackmail you in a few years." She could practically hear his good-natured grin on the phone.

"We were such good friends, Joe."

"Hey. I'll hear none of that. We still are," he said. "You don't sound so good. What's up?"

If I tell him, it'll lead to a long sad story and I'll cry and he'll cry and he'll insist on coming down here to comfort me and I'd have to look at him and feel as if my life were nothing but sorrow.

"Just a bad day," she said. "And I've got to get back to the kids."

"Well, don't be a stranger. Rick mentioned you the other day. He said he thought he heard your name somewhere. Couldn't remember where."

"It's always nice to be remembered. I miss you, Joe."

"Ditto, Jules."

After a bit more of the "let's get togethers" and "be sure and call back soons," she closed the phone and thought about calling her sister. Two skinny girls of eighteen or nineteen walked in Prada and Gucci shoes along the cracked sidewalk in front of her. "And so I was like, He's gay, you idiot, run for the hills," one girl said to the other as they loped along, uncertain in the stiletto heels.

Julie glanced at the cell phone, and then set it down on the step. She opened her handbag and dug down to her wallet, opening it up and sorting through a few torn small pieces of paper.

When she found the sliver of paper she had been looking

for, she stared at the phone number for a few minutes as if an entire world were within it.

Whomever her husband had been seeing, this was her.

This mysterious woman in the city who had some hold on Hut. Julie looked at the scrawl. Not Hut's handwriting. *Did you have a lover, Hut? A woman whom you met in the city? The one who kept you there some nights, not sleeping on the Aerobed or the cots at the clinic—someone whom you burned to see when Matt or Livy or I got to be too much for you?*

She wanted to call the number.

Instead, she called her sister to come get her and take her home.

3

Mel had other ideas. "You need a meal in you, and the kids'll be fine with Laura. She said they could spend the night if need be."

They drove to Benny's Burritos, and Mel got them a table at a corner window so they could have a little privacy. Mel ordered a chicken burrito that they'd split, and a margarita for Julie. "A little tequila never hurt anybody."

"Except a drunk. You shop for anything?"

Mel squinted her eyes slightly, as she watched her. "You really want to know?"

"Sure."

"I got a Pilates workout tape. I wanted some nice towels, but none of them seemed right. Some scented candles. They smell like blueberries. Oh, and I got you a gift. Just a little one. A terry bathrobe."

"Thank you," Julie said, managing a grin. She felt cold inside.

"Don't thank me too much. I just don't want to see you wandering the house in your underwear ever again."

When the chips and salsa came, Mel pushed them toward

Julie. "Start eating. I don't think you've had more than toast in two days."

Julie hesitated, then decided that appetite or no, she needed something. "It's good."

"It's always good here," Mel said. "So, why'd you keep me waiting?"

"I needed a hike."

Mel grinned. "Good. First sign of life from you."

"I'm running on fumes right now," Julie said. "I am so angry. Pissed off. At the fucking cops."

"You *never* swear," Mel said.

"I'm sorry. They're incompetent. I didn't want him moved from Rellingford anyway. Why can't they just do their dirty work at the Rellingford morgue? And that stupid sheriff out there, just . . . signing off on this . . . not even asking . . ."

"Can you just calm down a second?" Mel asked, dipping a tortilla chip into the salsa, dripping a little on her sweater. "Look. I'm the one who told him it was okay to move the body. You were down for the count and needed sleep. Julie, it's a *murder* investigation. Some psycho is out there killing people. Four people so far. They need help in this. And do not give me that look—you were out cold or crying, and when I talked to that detective and the sheriff, they both made it clear that my permission or yours didn't count. This is something that just had to be done."

"And so they lost his body," Julie said, grabbing her margarita practically out of the server's hands.

"They what?"

4

"Apparently, it's an ordinary screwup," Julie said.

"I can just picture you with those cops. Reading them the riot act."

"I don't know." Julie's voice grew faint. She looked out the window and saw a crowd outside the tea shop across the street. A lesbian couple walked by, arm in arm, looking as if they were happier than Julie had ever felt in her life. An elderly woman in a mangy fur coat walked an equally mangy little Yorkshire terrier, pausing at the window of the restaurant as if gazing at her reflection. "I don't know. I think I was too stunned to react. I should probably call Andrew."

"Hell, yes," Mel said. "The threat of a lawsuit might just do something. You know, if they don't find his body in the next twenty-four hours . . ."

"Maybe it's what Donati said."

"Who?"

"One of the officers. She said it happens now and then when bodies get transferred. They think all that happened is that he ended up in another morgue in the city. They're blaming the driver, who had several pickups and deliveries. It's all very . . . complicated."

"Well, they damn well better find him, that's all I'm saying," Mel said, biting into a slice of avocado.

"It's all too much for me. Too, too much." Julie continued to look over her sister's shoulder at the world outside, the world of smart young women parking their cars, a group of men in suits talking excitedly as if they just had made some corporate deal that would make them all millionaires, the woman in the ratty fur coat picking a newspaper out of the trash can on the corner.

She refocused on Mel's face. Mel looked at her as if trying to read her thoughts. *You can't get inside me, Melanie. You can't. I'm not that easy-to-see-through little sister you once had. Not anymore. I am made out of stone. I don't feel anything anymore. I am impenetrable.*

"It may be something else, though, Mel. It may be about the killer. The killer may come back somehow to collect the bodies. One of the other victims also went missing. It's just sick. I don't even want to think about it anymore."

5

A rundown Volkswagen Jetta was parked on the street in front of her house when they got home that night.

"How does she do it?" Julie asked, shaking her head. "She runs that crafts store in New Hope, gets her master's in psychology, and does crystal therapy . . . and has that awful boyfriend . . . and she still manages to get here this fast?"

Mel shrugged, as she turned the car into the driveway. "Toni Marino. AKA Mom. What more is there to say?"

6

If Julie were ever to draw her mother, it would be with nothing but circles and squiggly lines. Her hair was a bird's nest of jet black with glimmers of gray, her face was round, and she wore round glasses upon her round nose. Even the word "mom" seemed to be a round word. She somehow had lost the angular half-Italian look of her Connie Francis– inspired youth and had transformed into Earth Mother by the age of sixty-four. Her voice still was a strange hybrid of the Jersey shore and Pennsylvania clip. "I picked up the kids from your sitter," her mother said too quickly, as a shadow crossed her face. She hugged Julie while at the same time glancing around at the living room as if about to give one of her famous critiques. Livy was practically attached to her grandmother, clinging to her skirt like it was a security blanket.

"I am so sorry, my baby," her mother whispered, kissing the edge of Julie's ear.

Julie fought back her tears as she felt the intense warmth of her mother's cheek pressed against her own.

7

Mel made some coffee, while Julie and the kids sat around the living room as if they had to entertain her mother. "The one thing I've learned about life," her mother said with that wiser-than-thou voice. "The only thing, really, is that it's about accepting loss."

"We were talking about that in my coffee group," Mel said.

"Your *coffee group*?" Julie chuckled, with a little too much condescension in her voice. "God. My God, that sounds like 1950s with white gloves and cute little casseroles. You mean the church ladies?"

Mel must've been working to keep her patience. Julie was impressed. "The altar guild. My friend Elaine lost her husband to cancer three years ago. It was her faith that pulled her through. There really is no death."

"You're only in that group because you have the hots for Father Joe," Julie blurted, and then quickly apologized.

"It's not like Episcopal priests can't marry," Mel said, shrugging.

"We all go to heaven," Livy suddenly said, her small, wise voice a bit of a surprise.

"That's right, honey," Mel said.

"I don't know," Toni said. "A lot of people believe different. Death is just a problem of our vision. You know, how we see things upside down? How our eyes work? Our mind works that way, too. We go on. We just can't see it."

"Not your ghost crap again," Mel said, a bit under her breath.

Julie laughed. "If you have your sexy Jesus, Mom can have her spooks."

Mel shot her a look, then glanced at Livy, as if to say, *What kind of talk is that around your daughter?*

"Wait just a second, sweetie," Toni said. "They're not

spooks. And I'm only a lapsed Catholic, not a heretic. I believe in heaven." She motioned for Livy to come sit on her lap. Livy looked a little frightened, but Julie gave her a nod. Livy went over and climbed aboard the Gramma Express. "Spirituality doesn't start or stop with a church or a dogma. What is out there is out there. I'm not going to sit here and say that one group has cornered the market on the truth of existence."

"Is Daddy a spirit-chew-aliddy?"

Toni kissed her granddaughter on the top of the head. "Different people believe different things, sweetie. Some people believe we come back as newborns. Some people believe we go to heaven. Some people believe we never really leave. Some go, some stay, some come back. Like when babies are born. Maybe they're old souls. Who knows? I think you're an old soul, sweetie."

"Wow," Livy said.

"I bet in your last life you were a brilliant doctor like your daddy." Then Toni looked over at Matt. Matt had his camera on and it was aimed at her. "I'm on *Candid Camera*."

"I like when you talk about this stuff," Matt said, fiddling with the lens.

"Okay," Toni said. "I think I was a sherpa in my last life."

"Is that like a shepherd?" Livy asked.

"Mom," Julie said sternly. She felt a severe headache coming on.

"What? Reincarnation's as valid as anything," her mother said. Then she gave her that stern look that Julie hadn't seen in years—it was one of her "Take a life lesson" looks. "You want to live a happy life, Juliet, you start thinking about what comes after. It'll put a lot of things in place for you."

"It's like a nice fairy tale to tell kids," Matt said, "but the truth is, there's nothing after you die," his voice suddenly so harsh that it was like a shock through the room. He pivoted the camera around to look at Julie. "It's like the fairy tales about wicked stepmothers."

Matt put the camera down and stared at Julie and then her mother. "Talk talk talk," he said. "That's all anyone does. My father dies and it's all about blah blah blah." He got up and stomped out of the room as if he'd been insulted.

"Teenagers," Livy said, as if she'd heard this from her mother.

"Shouldn't you go to him?" Toni asked, hugging Livy. She had an expression on her face that was halfway between being aghast and ashamed. "That boy needs you."

"He'll be fine, Mom. Don't butt in where you don't know."

"Sometimes my daughters can be so cold," her mother said in a whisper meant to float over Livy's head. Then, more softly: "Children need to talk about death. About what happens afterward. About where we go."

"Where do we go?" Livy asked.

"Upstairs, sweetie," Toni said. "Upstairs. Only when we're alive, we don't know where upstairs goes."

8

Julie couldn't take her mother anymore, and left the room. As she went up the stairs to her bedroom, she heard Mel say something about sleep and shock, and Julie almost felt like going back down there and just telling them all to get out of her house and leave her and her kids alone. She wondered how much she could get away with—how cruel and mean she could get and still be forgiven later. How much slack did you get when your husband was murdered out in the woods by a psychopath?

She lay down on her bed, covering her head with the pillow, and submerged into sleep.

9

In a dream, his head was between her legs, and his tongue circled lazily. One circle wetly moved into another, opening her, with a kind of pressure of pleasure that disturbed her even while her body gave in to it. Hut whispered, his voice soft and vulnerable, like a little boy who has just discovered a new forbidden hideout, "Ah, yes. I love it. I love the taste. I love the smell. I want to be inside you. I want to dive into it. You're the lake, and I want to swim through you."

Her pelvis began to buck involuntarily, and she hated herself for the feeling she was having, which was not pleasure but some kind of mechanical movement as if she had no control over her body and it had no connection to her mind, but was a machine that just moved back and forth and up and down when someone put coins in—knowing that Hut was gone, knowing that this was not really him, knowing she was in a dirty, filthy dream where nasty words were said that she'd never utter in real life and nor had he, and shivery forbidden fantasies could exist, and the reality of the world, of death, was beyond this.

10

Sometime in the night, someone touched the edge of her cheek. Julie opened her eyes, feeling nearly out of breath from a terrible dream that she couldn't quite remember seconds after waking up.

In the bedroom, a small shadow before her.

"Mommy?"

"Oh, baby," Julie said. She scooted across the bed, allowing room for her daughter to climb up. The heat of her daughter's body pressed against hers was comforting.

"I have an idea. Let's ask God to get Daddy back."

She kissed Livy on her forehead.

"I mean it," Livy said, her voice wispy and full of wonder at her own idea. "Maybe nobody's ever tried, Mommy. We just ask. Maybe God feels bad for us and he'll send Daddy back. I can ask in my brain radio. I can."

"Oh, baby, honey, shhh," Julie whispered. "I love you so much."

"God can do anything. Matt said in the Bible God sent back a guy named Lazzus."

"Lazarus, sweetie. But it was different. That was a miracle."

"Nobody ever asked for their daddy back. Maybe," Livy said, getting louder, until finally she was yelling, "maybe if someone did, it would happen. God can do it!"

"I'm sorry." Julie couldn't control her tears.

"I just want God to send him back," Livy said, too loud. "I want my daddy back. God can do it."

11

Julie dreamed.

The day she met Hut. On the subway. He on his way to his residency, she with a day off, thinking about going to buy an air conditioner for her steamy apartment. The train was packed, and he gave up his seat to her. She could not stop looking at him. He was handsome in ways she'd never seen—not a pretty man at all, nor one that had a natural beauty to his face. He just had what seemed to be a chalk outline around him, an aura of something that made her want to know him. He had glanced at her a few times on the train, and then had leaned over and said, "You'd think the carnival was in town," which made her smile, as she glanced around at others on the train.

When they'd come up into a muggy afternoon, he said to her, "You know, you look like someone I'd want to get to know."

She had laughed. "That's the worst pickup line I've ever heard."

"It can't be," he said. "Surely it's only in the top ten of the worst. It can't be the worst of all."

From there, they'd made a casual date—to meet at the Empire State Building like Sleepless in Seattle. *"That way, if I scare you, you can have the safety of all those people, plus you can throw me off the roof if you decide I'm the wrong one. You can even give me a fake name if you want so I can't stalk you later. I'll buy the hot dogs."*

"I'll bring a parachute," she'd told him.

And then she dreamed of:

The face of the dead man in the morgue. It had not been Hut, even though it had been him. What was Hut had fled, and left the empty husk of flesh behind.

The face of the dead man with closed eyes.

In her dream, his eyes opened.

chapter seven

1

After a week, Julie felt herself rise up, a waking sleeper, from some dark place. She spent less time in bed. She began enjoying the taste of food again. Just a little. Less time avoiding phone calls from the detective. Less time avoiding her mother and sister and even her children. Livy started having bad dreams, but weirdly Matt was handling himself okay, and her therapist, Eleanor Swanson, said everything that was going on was all completely normal.

Within a few days, her mother went back to Pennsylvania, and as Mel came and went, Julie realized that it wasn't normal, not yet, and she felt as if she were hiding something, keeping a secret about how she wanted to scream and cry and yell and break things and kick walls in.

But she let some autopilot within her switch on, and focused on Matt and Livy, helping them navigate the slender canals of grief.

2

"Mommy!" Livy cried out from the backyard.

Some instinct kicked in, and Julie remembered the sharp

trowel she had left in the flower bed, and all she could think of was that her baby was hurt.

"Mommy, hurry!" Livy screeched.

Julie nearly flew out of the kitchen door, out to the patio.

Livy stood next to the low weeping willow tree at the edge of the lawn.

"Honey? You okay?"

Livy had a glow to her face—as if she'd been almost sunburned. She had her hands to her ears. "It's Daddy!" she shouted. "It's him!"

Julie went to her and squatted down in front of her so they were eye level with each other.

"He's on my brain radio." Livy grinned. "He's telling me he's okay."

Julie felt herself get all weepy as she lifted Livy up. Livy wrapped her legs around her waist. "He's in heaven," Julie said. "He's with God now."

"No, he's not," Livy said. Then, whispering in her mother's ear as if it were a big secret that nobody was supposed to hear: "Gramma was wrong. He didn't go upstairs. He's with us. Right now."

3

On the phone:

"Eleanor. It's Julie. I think maybe I'd like to ask you to talk with Livy."

4

Livy clutched her mother's hand as they stepped into the waiting room. Julie went to the assistant, a young man named Vincent who handled three of the psychologists in the suite of offices. Then Eleanor came out and gave Livy a warm smile. "It's good to finally meet you," she said. "I know your mom and brother Matt well. I've heard so much about you for so long, I feel we're practically neighbors."

Then Eleanor asked Julie to stay in the waiting area so that she and Livy could talk for a bit. Livy looked back at her, eyes wide, mouth a small tight O, and for a second, Julie felt as if she were giving her daughter away to a stranger.

5

Afterward, Livy came out, a grin on her face, and tapped her mother on the knee.

"How'd it go?" Julie asked, setting a magazine down on the chair next to hers.

Livy looked up at her, and for just a moment Julie felt a chill, as if her daughter contained some unknown well of anger and fury, and it was all in that glance.

"She's a nice lady," Livy said.

Later, when Julie called to ask about the appointment, Eleanor told her, "She thinks she sees her father. She told me that he started coming through her dreams, but one night, she saw him standing over her in her bedroom and he told her he'd come for her. Now, how are *you* doing?"

"Me? Okay."

"No," Eleanor said. "Not okay. Livy told me that you aren't talking to her as much. She said that you let things pile up."

"Well, it's been a little soon. It's not like I'm completely recovered."

"Julie, this is not something to take lightly. You are experiencing posttraumatic stress. Your husband was violently killed. It's a major shock—to all of you. You can't mask it. I want you to expect that your mind will be spinning around. I want you to expect that you're going to have nights when you're afraid of the dark. All of you will. I want you to come see me as often as you want. And I suggest that you try to get Matt in for sessions, too."

6

Late one night, Matt was in the den watching one of his homemade digital videos on the family computer.

Julie stood behind his chair. The video had been made six months before, around Thanksgiving, and Matt's voice on the video was generally happy as he narrated the world as he went through it. "Christmas shopping for Julie and Livy is nearly over," he said with a beaming exuberance that Julie hadn't heard from him in a while. He was in the city with his dad—there was Hut, oh my God, so close she could touch him by tapping the computer monitor—and they had just emerged from the Chelsea Market, Hut with a cup of coffee, and Matt with a Snapple that he waved in front of the camera as he turned the camcorder on himself. He looked so happy.

His father said, "Let's turn it off for a bit, Matty."

Matt filmed his father's face, a close-up, and then the video faded to darkness.

Julie leaned over to Matt and kissed the top of his head.

He reached up toward her, without turning around, and laid the palm of his hand against her cheek. "We can see him anytime we want," Matt said. "That's what movies do. They keep people alive."

7

She slipped into the bathrobe that Mel had picked up for her at Bed, Bath & Beyond, made some chamomile tea, and felt a little better. Julie sat up that night, late, after the kids were asleep and after Mel was asleep, and played Matt's videos on the computer, one after another. They were funny, or silly, and usually involved Matt after school with his friends, or Matt and Hut and Julie and Livy—ordinary happiness, as they all made supper together on a rare Saturday when everyone was free, Livy shredding Romaine lettuce for the salad, Hut chopping tomatoes and onions, and Julie sautéing the chicken in the round wide pan. Hut joked about crying over onions, and that got Livy giggling. Matt now and then said, "Now just act natural," and that got them all acting a little silly for the camera. Sometimes Matt turned the camera on himself, having watched too many episodes of *The Real World* on MTV, and talked about what he felt like, what he was going through. Nothing startling came through in any of this. Something within Julie ached for the normalcy of it all.

And then there were several Boys' Days Out, as they had called the Saturdays or Sundays when Hut would spend several hours exclusively with Matt. They'd go to a Yankees game, or fish out on one of the local lakes, or do what Livy called "boy things," which she demanded that her father take her on sometimes. Matt holding a big bass up to the camcorder and saying, "Julie, get ready to fry this up for supper!" or at the baseball game, Matt cursing as he videoed the game, and Hut's voice saying, "Now, Matt, let's not use those words again, all right?"

And then a video of an area of cobblestone streets, where half the block was sunlit and half in shadows. The city. Hut looking a little tense. Matt swinging the camcorder to the street and just videotaping his Reeboks as he walked along. "That thing doesn't always have to be on," Hut said a bit curtly.

Matt swung the camcorder up: a shot of his father's face, looking neither happy or solemn. Looking like he was angry at Matt. "Let's just turn it off, Matt. All right?"

Matt lied, "Okay, Dad. It's off. I just like looking through the lens."

A woman walked along the sidewalk opposite them, and then crossed the street as if coming right toward them. She was pretty, wearing sunglasses, and had pale freckled skin and shoulder-cut red hair that gleamed as she walked from shadow to sunlight in the street.

"Put it down," Hut said, and then the video went dark.

Julie stared at the computer monitor.

Then she heard a piercing scream.

8

It was Livy. Julie instinctively leapt out of the chair in the den and went running upstairs to her daughter's bedroom.

Matt was already standing in the doorway with the light on.

Julie looked over his shoulder—her daughter stood up on her bed, her back against the wall, shivering.

"What happened?"

Matt mumbled something, but Julie passed by him and went to Livy. "Did Matty scare you?" she asked, and then felt her face go red as she looked at Matt.

He glared at her. "She had a nightmare, Julie. I'm not running around scaring my baby sister. Jesus."

"I didn't mean that," Julie said. "I didn't. I thought maybe she saw you in the dark."

"Something's wrong with you if you think that," Matt said, and turned and went back to his room.

"Honey, what is it? What was wrong?"

"I saw a man," Livy said. "In here."

"Was it Matt? Maybe he was going down the hall?"

"No, Mommy. It was like a ghost. It was like a big shadow," Livy whispered. And then, as if it had just occurred to her, "Maybe it's Daddy. Maybe he came downstairs again. Maybe he was tired of being upstairs."

"Livy, there's nobody. But I think you were having a bad

dream. That's all. It's not real. If you want, I'll go check all the windows and doors."

"Ghosts get through doors," Livy told her.

9

In the kitchen, feeling a little spooked herself, Julie poured herself the last of the Sterling Vineyards merlot into a Dixie cup and sipped it as she walked around, checking the windows and doors to make sure there really wasn't the possibility of an intruder.

10

In her dreams that night:

The man on the table. Eyes opened wide. They were milky white. No pupil, no iris. It was Hut, but not Hut. His skin was translucent alabaster interrupted by blotches of bluish bruises. He rose up and reached for her. He had drawings all over his body—tattoos.

She couldn't move.

He leaned over and kissed the edge of her neck.

His lips were ragged and dry and kissed again, with a gentle suction against her skin.

His fingers crawled down her belly, lingering just above her pubic region, and then twirling the soft hair as his hand pressed down against her. All the while he kissed up her chin, to her mouth. She felt as if she couldn't move, push him off her. She wanted to get away from him, but his tongue parted her lips and flickered over her tongue and teeth.

And then she felt aroused and excited in the dream. Wet. Ready.

"Do you want me?" His voice came to her, but not from his mouth. "Do you want me inside you?"

She awoke, jerked from the dream so suddenly that when

she opened her eyes she wasn't sure if she was still dreaming or awake in her bed. A man stood there, a dark man against the darkness, and for half a second, she thought it was Hut. Her sleepiness was like a pillow smothering her, so that she didn't have the energy to flick on the light. Didn't even have the energy to stay awake for more than a few seconds. She felt the narcotic heaviness of deep sleep draw her back from fuzzy consciousness. She slipped back into sleep, and when she awoke well before dawn, she began shivering, feeling as if she had a fever. She kept looking at the doorway, half expecting someone to be there.

She remembered what her therapist had told her. About her mind at night. Fears. Thoughts that would keep her up. Even hallucinations. Thinking someone was in the house. Some stranger. Or that Hut would come home, just open the door and walk back in one day as if it had all been a dream.

Then she remembered a detail about the dream: The dead man, whom she could not completely think of as Hut, had those whorls and carving on him.

11

Julie flicked up the light switch in Matt's room. He rolled over, pushing back the sheet. The bedroom window was open wide. The room smelled like dirty gym clothes. Poster over his bed of Eminem. The place was a dump, but she never pushed him on it. *"I'll have to handle him,"* Hut had told her after an early battle of wills between Matt and Julie. *"He's always going to be like this, and it's up to me to handle it. It's his mind, Julie. He has some kind of block that won't allow him to handle conflict well. You shouldn't be in the middle of this."* Hut had even told her just to let Matt do what he wanted sometimes. She was the stepmother, and she had never felt completely comfortable stepping in and making him do things—even things as simple as picking up the clothes he dropped on his bedroom floor.

"Julie?" he asked, shielding his eyes from the overhead light.

Julie went to sit on the edge of his bed. "Tell me about the drawings you made. On your skin."

He squinted at her. "I'm sleepy."

"It can't wait."

He looked over at his clock radio. "It's four a.m."

"You're not going to school. You can sleep in."

He turned back over, his arms covering the back of his head as if defending himself. "Just let me go to sleep."

"I've been up half the night," she said. "It's important, Matt."

"Why?" He turned around violently, shooting her a nasty look, his face crumpled into a scowl. "Why is it so goddamn important?"

"Do not use that kind of language with me, young man," she said, feeling infinitely old as she heard the words come out of her mouth.

"You think I go around scaring Liv, and you wake me up when it's still dark out. God. You just go around sticking your nose in places where you shouldn't, Julie. You're not my mother. You want to see the drawings? Okay. Okay, Julie," he said, sitting up. He drew the long-sleeved T-shirt up over his head. His chest seemed scrawny, concave. Vulnerable. She winced when she thought of his mother— Amanda—and how she'd hurt him badly. How she'd tried to do terrible things to him.

She wondered if she was like Amanda to him now.

He showed her his arm, his chest. The carvings had faded, leaving only slight striations on his arm and shoulder.

"Seen enough?" he asked.

She tried to remember the patterns carved into the dead

person's back from the photograph the detective had shown her.

She didn't know what to say. She felt like crying but worked to hold back her tears. "I guess I'm a wreck right now," she said.

When he spoke again, after nearly a minute had passed, his voice was gentler than it had been. "You think I'm like my mother and I'm going to end up going crazy and hurting Livy or something."

"Matty," she whispered, touching his arm. "I don't think that."

"I'm not stupid," he said. "She's where they send crazy people. And I'll end up there, too, because I see things sometimes. I just don't tell you about them. You'll never understand."

"Do you want to visit your mother?" Julie asked, grasping for something hopeful to say. "I can drive you down there."

He turned over, facing the wall, drawing the sheet back up to cover himself. "Turn out the light," he said, his voice a monotone. "Go to bed. I'm sorry Dad's dead. I'm sorry you're stuck with me. I wish you weren't falling apart every five minutes. I wish everything was different. But it's not. And no, I don't want to see my mother. Ever."

She left his bedroom, and sat on the stairs in the hall, wondering if the pain and the pressure she felt in her head would ever go away.

12

Some nights, she stared at the wall of her bedroom and began imagining things, thinking that she heard Hut in the hallway. Livy had put the idea in her head—her bad dream about a ghost of a man.

His footsteps, heavy, coming toward her.
The bedroom door, open. Darkness in the hall beyond it.
Darkness seeping into her room.
His breath upon her face.
Do you want me inside you?

PART TWO

PART TWO

chapter eight

1

In the city: blue sky as far as he could see above the towering buildings. The sound of laughter and shouting and even some cussing from kids getting out of school. The harsh words, the tromping along, the hissing of subway steam. The shadows were still cool with the very last breath of spring, the sunlight beyond them warm and fresh. He felt a little bounce in his step as he bounded up from the subway steps into daylight.

Terry West had just gotten out of Harkness' lecture on the underpinnings of Jacobean tragedy, and was accepting the fact that he was going to get a D in the survey course. Terry was feeling damn good, and if that asshole Franklin hadn't fucked with his head that morning on the subject of his academic future, it would be the perfect day. He caught a bus uptown to meet Anne for a beer at her little studio apartment. When he arrived, she had on that sweater that was bright yellow that made him just want to pull it off. Beneath it, she wore nothing, and his cold hands trembled as he touched the edge of her nipples—each one receiving special attention from his fingers while his tongue slipped between her lips. She giggled when she felt his hardness, and he was thinking: *Life is better than anyone ever told me it was going to be.*

In the middle of it, when he had just slipped inside her, he whispered to her that he thought he was in love with her. But he wasn't sure if she'd heard him, and that was cool. After they had sex, he showered solo while Anne flicked on cable and watched the old *Match Game* show on the Game Show Network. When he got out of the shower, dripping, he went from tiny bathroom to tiny living area and sat down beside her and stroked her hair.

"I have to meet my mother in thirty minutes," she said. "She can't know that we're fucking."

"I thought she liked me."

"She thinks I'm still a virgin," Anne said, and squirmed a bit when he tried nuzzling her neck. "She's living in the twentieth century or something."

"I guess you're going shopping?"

Anne nodded. "That's all she does. That's all she ever wants to do."

"Your neck tastes good," he said, trying to kiss her one more time, but she pulled away and pawed the ends of the sweater arms over her hands like little mitts.

"Sex isn't everything." She shrugged away from him, got off the bed, and sauntered to the bathroom. "When I get out of the shower, you need to be gone."

"How about tonight? Maybe later?" he asked.

"Maybe."

Her hesitance did not ruin his good mood. He sat on the stoop of the brownstone next to her building, and lit up a cigarette, watching people walk by, checking out the pretty girls, feeling a little intimidated by some of the men in suits who looked as if they owned the world, wondering if he himself would ever own much. He grabbed a hot dog down at Gray's Papaya around two, and chowed down while calling up his buddy Rick, who lived in a loft in Soho with four roommates (instead of at home with his mom, like Terry still did), and asked if they wanted to go shoot pool at Fat Cats on Christopher Street in about an hour.

Then he got on the subway, and that's when he saw a man who was looking at him funny. Terry was used to gay guys giving him looks—after all, he was athletic and trim and twenty-two. But it didn't offend him in the least. He'd always felt complimented, whether it was a girl or a guy. But this guy was looking at him differently.

It pissed him off. He glared at the man. The man grinned, but then turned away. The man opened a newspaper and began reading it.

He wouldn't have thought anything more of it, except when he got off the train and began walking toward the exit, he accidentally dropped his keys, and when he squatted down to pick them up, he glanced back and noticed the guy was practically hovering over him.

Then the man passed by. Terry waited for him to continue up the steps to the street.

Outside, Terry saw the usual crush of people—and the man he'd seen wasn't anywhere nearby. He called up Anne and left a message on her machine that he was with Rick and some others playing pool and maybe she might want to meet up after her mother left and they could grab pizza at Ray's or something. "Or maybe we can do something after Bio tomorrow. Okay? Call me ASAP, babay-babay," he finished, their little in-joke. When he dropped the cell phone in the pocket of his denim painter's pants, he felt around for cash. He counted up about fourteen bucks in single wadded-up bills, and that'd be enough for a couple of hours of pool and air hockey, and with a few bucks left over for the kick-ass jukebox at Fat Cats.

"I'm like four blocks from Fat Cats," he told Rick via cell phone. "Are you down there?"

"Yep, me and Joe and Debbie. Deb's kicking my butt in air hockey. Want to say hi?"

"Fuck. Anne'll cut off my dick if she knows Deb's there. And I just told her to come down if she wanted."

"Maybe she won't," Rick said, and then the noise in the background rose as someone gave a victory yell and people laughed. "A lot of cute girls here, dude."

"Yeah yeah," Terry said, and as he turned the corner toward Bleecker to go get some more cigarettes—there was the man again.

As Terry passed him, the man said, "Terry? You're Terry West?"

He turned to face the guy, who didn't look strange or scary, just utterly normal. Kind of bland.

"What's it to you?" Terry asked, and felt he sounded wimpy.

2

More than an hour later, when Terry awoke, the first thing he did was cough.

Something about his vision was off. He couldn't quite see. Things were blurry, and he tried to reach up to wipe his eyes clean, but his hands were tied behind his back.

He tugged at them, but they wouldn't budge.

He didn't remember a whole hell of a lot since the man had started talking to him, talking about his mother, talking about some emergency, and talking to the point where something within Terry had felt a little tired and too confused to understand everything.

His breath returned to him, hot.

A plastic of some kind over his face.

Tied around his neck—a cord pressed at his throat.

He tried to make out the shadowy figure that stood before

him, but the light was too dim, and his own breathing had caused a fog within the plastic.

Soon the air around his face got warmer, and when he inhaled as deeply as he could, the plastic sucked up against his mouth.

He tried kicking out, but his legs were tied to the chair.

His lungs burned as he used every ounce of his energy to inhale what little air was left to him.

As he felt himself sink into unconsciousness, something—a man's hands?—grabbed his left arm and held it as if trying to pull him back from the brink of death.

chapter nine

1

Julie had arranged a little memorial service in May, just for close family and a few friends.

They had no body to bury—it had officially been stolen, according to McGuane, and they suspected the killer himself had some access to the morgue that they'd been trying to pinpoint.

Julie felt that for the children's sake, at least, there needed to be a service. She got Father Joe from Mel's church, St. Andrew's, to run through a liturgy just because Mel insisted on something religious. Hut's parents had made it for the weekend, and her mother had brought her boyfriend, and even two of Livy's teachers had shown up.

When Julie had a moment alone with Joanne Hutchinson, she asked her about Hut being an orphan until he was in his mid-teens.

"Steve wanted a son badly," Hut's mother said. "I can't tell you what it was like for us. We had tried to have children for years. And then our son died—our first boy. Before Jeff." She called him Jeff, not the nickname Hut that Julie had only known him by. Even hearing the word "Jeff" made him sound like a different person. She could imagine him as a sweet kid. Helpful. Generous.

"Well," Joanne said, "when the opportunity to take him in—Steve had been working with Big Brothers, and then got a call from a friend about some group home for kids who had been orphans all their lives—well, something got in us. It was like a gift from God. Steve loved working with teenage boys. He loved teaching them and guiding them. He's a man's man, I guess, and he loves camping out and woodworking and getting out with a football. Well, when he heard about Jeff's situation—about having lived as an orphan his entire life—he insisted we adopt him. Steve was raised in foster care. He knew the routine. When they met, they bonded immediately. You couldn't keep them apart." As she said this, Julie felt that Joanne Hutchinson was leaving something out.

"I'm sorry to even mention it," Julie said. "But there's so much about Hut I didn't know."

"He was quiet about his life, wasn't he?" Joanne said.

"I know this is a strange thing to bring up now, but when you adopted him, did you know much about where he'd been?"

"Somewhat. He had been in a group home for a year or so at that point." And then the tone of her voice changed—as if Joanne had guessed what this was about. "You mean the fire."

"Fire?"

"He never told you," Joanne said.

"No." But even as she said this, Julie remembered his nightmares. He didn't have them often, but he had awakened more than once early on in their marriage in the middle of the night, soaking the sheets with sweat. All he would tell her was that he had dreamed of something that happened when he was a boy, but he had never let her beyond that wall.

"I can't say I'm surprised. It must have been awful. He had been trapped in a building when a fire broke out that another student had set—perhaps a year before we adopted him. He got out in time, but some of his classmates died. He wasn't burned but had to spend time in the hospital for smoke inhalation."

"His asthma," Julie said.

"Yes, that and those night fears he had."

The mention of night fears reminded her of Hut waking up in the middle of the night as if he were a Vietnam vet experiencing posttraumatic stress disorder. He'd nearly leap out of bed, not sure where he was. But it had happened only once or twice.

"Was it some kind of government program he was in, as a boy? Some special school that tested him?"

"I'm not really sure. He got a good education, though. He was smart as a whip, and was a lot smarter than either of us," Joanne said. "Sometimes, well, sometimes it was like he knew what I was thinking. He was perceptive. My goodness, he probably told you more than he ever told us. He never talked about those years. We loved him so much, Julie. More than was probably healthy for Steve. When our son turned away from us . . . well, it's all in the past. None of it really matters, does it? He was our son. We loved him. Please, let's not lose touch."

Julie hesitated before asking the next question, but felt she had to, even though it seemed a betrayal of trust with Hut. "Can I ask you something that might be painful?"

"Go ahead."

"Did your husband beat Hut?"

Silence. Then Joanne said, "Julie, why would you ever get that idea?"

"Hut said—"

"That's *disgusting*," Joanne said. "That's the most obscene thing you could say to me. And now. *Now.* With Hut dead. No, his father never laid a finger on him. That man loved him to distraction. Even when Hut did bad things— boy things, I suppose. Even when Hut . . . well, that's all in the past. But my husband gave him everything he had and then some. His father is the kindest, gentlest soul on earth, Julie. How *dare* you."

Hut's mother turned and walked away.

2

The Hutchinsons were only in for the service and the weekend, and they were on a flight back home before Julie could talk to either of them again.

Julie let some things go. She just couldn't deal with housework, and she had the cleaning service that Mel had recommended come through, although every now and then, she let a week slip by and the laundry piled up and she'd see Matt wearing the same T-shirt for four days in a row. Sometimes she forgot to load the dishwasher, and too many nights, they ordered from Domino's or went to McDonald's or called up Chinese Gardens for carryout. Sometimes she cooked eggs for breakfast and left the pan on the stove and forgot about it. She accepted these minor infractions. Posttraumatic stress, she told herself. Shock. Death. Murder. The news of war overseas made her depressed, so she stopped watching anything but *The Simpsons* reruns and *Judge Judy*, as well as the collection of DVDs that they'd amassed— mainly rewatching screwball comedies from the 1930s and forgetting that there were too many half-used glasses of milk and soda and water sitting around in the rec room because the kids forgot to wash them out. She didn't let it bother her, even when she noticed. The cleaning service might take care of it. Or they might not. Her mind was elsewhere. She did gain a great sense of accomplishment from working through two entire *New York Times* crossword puzzle books before June first, a record for her. She had avoided putting Hut's things into storage or even sorting through all of his clothes that month. Sometimes, she just sat with his Burberry's raincoat and looked at it as if trying to find him there. Livy now had her own therapist and felt completely like a princess because of it. Julie began wondering if Livy liked having her night frights just so she'd have something to talk about. But Livy had been making a lot of progress since seeing Dr. Fishbain over in Ramapo Cliffs once a week. Mel had split up with her boyfriend and was thinking of buying her first house—at forty-one—not far away. Matt had kept to himself and refused the offer of therapy, and Eleanor had suggested that Julie not push him on anything yet.

Between days back at work (three days on, ten-hour shifts, with Laura Reynen and Mel both helping with the kids) and her three hours per week with her current therapist, she had managed to keep moving. Somewhere in there she'd gained twelve pounds and so she had started the Atkins Diet (lasted two weeks, cheated the whole time), then the South Beach diet (maybe three weeks, sneaking forbidden foods at two a.m. when thoughts of life and death sent her to the fridge) and settled into a modified version of those two diets with a little Weight Watchers and Dr. Phil on the side. She walked two miles every morning, and jogged twice a week with her sister. At least the quick weight gain had gotten her out of the house and enabled her to focus on something other than sorrow. She was moving forward, intentionally, away from death and Hut and murder and the ideas forming in her head about what life was about and why it should be lived at all. But the night fears continued—the dreams, the wakings, the sense that someone was there with her. She accepted a degree of insomnia, and afternoons turned into evenings too quickly.

McGuane drove over to the house once or twice for more questions, but her lawyer suggested that she not answer much until he could explain how a body got lost or stolen from the morgue. Once, she saw McGuane sitting out in his car, on the street, looking as if he couldn't decide whether to. get out or not. Finally, he drove away.

3

One afternoon, by herself, Julie drove over to the break in the woods where the gravel path went up to the place where Hut had been murdered.

She felt a little scared, but parked the car, got out and went up the path. It was a beautiful day, and the birds were making a racket in the trees. She felt as if she were walking to his true grave.

When she reached the plateau with its clearing, she glanced about. It was just land. Nature. There was no sign that someone had been murdered there.

No marker.

"Good-bye, Hut," she said out loud. "I'm sorry this happened to you. I'm sorry I couldn't protect you. I'm sorry we couldn't die together someday when we were old and ready for it. I'll take care of Matt and Livy and make sure they never forget their father. I know I never will."

And then she walked back down the path to the car.

4

"You look good," Mel said as they jogged the perimeter road along the lake.

"It's all the erotic dreams," Julie said, huffing and puffing as she tried to forget the slight pain in her left shin.

"That usually does it for me."

"I dreamed the other night that three strange men were just licking my toes. I felt kind of dirty, but I woke up laughing."

"That's so filthy it sounds almost clean," Mel laughed. "They call that a shrimp job."

"What?"

"Toe sucking."

"Shiver me timbers," Julie said. "I'll never order a shrimp cocktail again. I never had dreams like this before. It's actually a little disturbing." They came to a stop when they reached the small strip of brown beach at the lakefront along the dip in the road.

Mel lit up a cigarette. "Better toe-licking dreams than the kind where you're falling off a cliff."

Julie chuckled, catching her breath, trying not to remember the bad parts of the dreams. "I had one dream where . . . well, I kid you not, I was watching a man having sex with a woman, and when he, well, you know, when it got down there, three uncircumcised penises came out of her between her legs."

"Oh my God," Mel said. "That is the single most perverted thing I've ever heard. No wonder you see a therapist. And the best part is they're uncircumcised." Mel sucked back on the cigarette, and then exhaled a smoky laugh. "I never have dirty dreams. I wish I did."

Julie decided not to tell her sister that the man in the dream was Hut, and the woman was some red-haired young woman she'd never before seen except in a video of Matt's. Instead, she said, "God, this is the first day I've really smelled how good summer is. I can smell jasmine and honeysuckle. Even the lake's stink is good. I haven't noticed much of anything in weeks."

"You're getting back to life," Mel said. "That's great. I was getting a little worried. Now, tell me another dirty dream."

5

By the middle of June, she had received the first life insurance check, and it had a lot of zeros. She hated looking at that check, but she needed the money and thought how wonderful Hut had been to get such a major policy even when she had argued against it. She cried thinking about this, and felt guilt for not being a good enough wife, and that ate up a large chunk of a day. The check took care of some immediate problems, including paying off most of the mortgage, and since she felt the kids should have her for the summer, she called in some favors and got a few months' leave from the ER—until at least the end of September. She hadn't really accomplished much in her few days back at work since Hut's death anyway—they'd put her behind a desk and everyone had looked at her like she was the living dead.

Livy still had nightmares about seeing someone in her room, and Eleanor told Julie it was perfectly normal for a little girl to have dreams like that after losing her father. "I bet you've had some nightmares, too," Eleanor said in one of their therapy sessions.

In July, in the middle of the afternoon in the middle of the week, in her therapist's office, Julie leaned back, sinking into the cushy chair.

Eleanor had that look of God on her face. Julie thought of it as "God," because Eleanor projected a calming presence that made Julie want to open up about everything. Eleanor was a beautiful, radiant woman—overweight, but her girth only added to the Mother Earth aspect of her personality. Julie had once told Eleanor that she reminded her of a younger version of her mother, and Eleanor had said, "We can work out that problem, too, if you want."

The office was decorated in muted beiges and browns and always smelled of herbal tea. It was the most relaxing place that Julie knew—a genuine refuge when she needed to work out problems.

"I feel like I'm bad because I want to find things out."

"Why do you think that's bad?"

"He's dead. He was killed. My mind can't wrap around that and I still wonder if he loved me."

"Did you love him?"

Julie nodded. "I want him back so bad. I really do."

After she'd wiped the tears from her eyes, Julie said, "But I never really knew him. I thought I did. But I just don't think I did at all. There were those things that went unspoken. Those things I just ignored."

"You think he was unfaithful?"

Julie nodded. "But he's dead now. So it shouldn't matter."

"He may not have been. He may have been. Why do you need to know now?"

"I don't know."

"You do know. You just can`t say it yet."

"No, I really don't know."

"Marriage is based on trust, and what that means, really, is the opposite. You have to put blinders on to get through it sometimes," Eleanor said.

"My mother used to tell me that all men cheat."

"Your mother would only know that for certain if she'd slept with every married man on the planet, Julie. Are you really concerned that he was cheating on you, now that he's dead? Or is there something else?"

"You knew him. There was always something . . . unspoken . . . about his first wife," Julie began, fumbling for words.

"Amanda had problems that had nothing to do with Hut," Eleanor said. "Her violence didn't come out of her marriage to Hut, Julie. She had a long history from childhood, and what was going on with her at the point they divorced had everything to do with Hut wanting to protect his son. You are going through the grief process. Stage by stage. It seems like you're right on schedule. Didn't you read the Kubler-Ross I gave you? Allow yourself some time. Understand that sometimes ideas float around after a violent death takes place, ideas in the head of the surviving family members, not all of which are meaningful. But they may just be ways that we all work out the shock. I would guess you're experiencing dreams."

Julie nodded.

"Some good, some bad, some terrible."

Julie closed her eyes. Trying not to remember the dream where the man on the shiny metal table in the morgue opened his eyes. "A dream here or there."

"All right," Eleanor said, leaning forward slightly, chin in hand, her God look in full glow.

"Just little things. Memories."

"Any of them that make you angry?"

The white-blue skin of the dead man who could not be Hut.

Eyes opening.

Just milky-white eyes.

Looking up at her.

Down there.

His tongue thrusting between her legs.

"Sometimes."

"Does Hut hurt you in the dreams?"

"No. No, nothing like that." Julie could feel that she was blushing.

"Oh," Eleanor said, reading her. "Sexual dreams. What gives birth, also takes life. Tell me about them."

Julie nodded. "Really filthy ones. Like in porn movies." She quickly added, "Nothing like our sex life. Which was good. It was fine. But this is like, I don't know, cartoon sex. Ridiculous sex. Multiple . . . organs. Sex with women, sex with men, sex with . . . well, it's all disturbing to me. I've never had dreams like this in my life."

"You told me once, a while ago, that you didn't think you were much of a sexual person."

"I'm not. I never was. My sister is. She got the horny

genes. Me, I just like it now and then if I really care for someone." Her voice trailed off a bit, as if sorrow had returned with this thought.

"Sex and death are often intertwined in our consciousness," Eleanor said. "Erotic dreams after the death of someone close to us . . . well, it's not that strange. The French call the climax *petite mort*. Little death."

"I'm not even sure I could call these dreams erotic. There's this sort of outlandish element to them," Julie said. "Sometimes . . ." *The milky white eyes. The shiny maggoty white skin.*

"Sometimes?"

"Sometimes . . . it's just surreal."

"Your mind is going to work out all kinds of issues, Julie. Expect it to. You're lucky it's coming through as erotic. I had a patient once who dreamed his brother slit his throat. After his brother died." As Eleanor spoke, Julie shut her eyes. She imagined Hut coming toward her, as Eleanor's words created an image in her mind. "Just slit his throat. Every night, for fourteen weeks. *Imagine*."

6

The rain slashed the dark sky beyond the den window, a summer storm that was the last of a hurricane that had spun past out to sea, far beyond northern New Jersey, leaving heat flashes in the sky and a downpour to cool off the muggy evening. There was something comforting about the harshness of the weather. Julie clicked the mouse pointer around until she found Matt's video files. There were nearly a hundred of them, and she kept opening and closing the videos, lingering on some, depending on what they showed. The past year or so of Matt's life flashed by:

Matt and Livy at the lake. Livy splashing around the shallow end of the pool with her friends, while Matt's voice goaded her on to make bigger splashes.

Matt videotaping Livy trying to practice the piano—playing a little song called "The Bluebells of Scotland," and when she hit a wrong note, she turned to the camera and said, "You're making me mess up."

One day, out on the canoe with all of them stuffed in, Julie sitting at one end, the kids in the middle, and Hut at the other, steering. The lake was brownish, and the sky was dazzling blue. Julie's hair was pulled back in a ponytail that stuck through a tan baseball cap. Hut had taken his shirt off, and his hair was slick from sweat, and his skin had turned a light brown.

Matt kept surprising Livy with the camera: "I see you!"

"Shut up."

"Livy, do not talk to your brother like that."

"Yeah, squirt."

"Don't call me squirt."

"Okay, squishy."

"Matthew, let's not do this. Don't tease her."

"He's teasing me."

And then Matt had finished this brief video with a shot of his father passing him a can of Coke and saying, "Come on, kiddo, enough with the Spielberg act for now."

7

Julie clicked on other videos. There was a series of strange ones, and she wondered if Matt might be getting artsy with the camera. A static shot of a beautiful house on a lake—maybe the lake in Rellingford, or one of the ones nearby. The house was glassed-in on one side, reflecting the woods and the water.

Another was a shot of a chair. Nothing special about the

chair. Just a wooden chair. When Julie looked closer, she saw there was a bit of rope on the floor, beneath the chair.

Another video was of a wasps' nest. Must've been in the eaves of their house. It was like a small gray curled hand, with holes in it. The camera kept going in and out of focus as Matt got closer to the nest. Then the tip of his finger touched the edge of the papery nest and quickly withdrew.

A small yellow wasp came out, its feelers vibrating.

Then a video that disturbed her, although she chalked it up to childhood fascination with the forbidden. It was a dead dog in the road, hit by a car, apparently. Matt had kept the camera on the dog's body.

As she flipped the videos on and off, she began to dread some of them—he had filmed her sleeping once. From the light through the bedroom window, it must've been early morning. Matt touched the edge of her cheek with his hand, and then quickly withdrew it.

The face of the sleeping Julie flushed a slight red, as if the warmth of his hand had caused a reaction.

In another one, Matt had simply filmed himself, in the hall mirror. He looked as if he'd worked himself into some kind of frenzy—his face was pale and shiny with sweat, his eyes were encircled with dark smudges, and he began touching his face all over as if checking to see if there were something wrong.

One of the videos had Matt talking to a girl at school, roughly his age. Where were they? It might've been the bathroom. The walls were green, with some light from a nearby window. She was pressed against the wall, and he kept closing in on her face with the camera. She had tears in her eyes. "Don't make me," she said. "Please don't make me."

Julie sat there, stunned. Didn't know what to think. She glanced at the clock on the wall—it was nearly eleven.

After several more of these brief video clips, she found one of the videos that had the woman in it.

The woman in the city.

She was young, and she was beautiful, and she looked like the kind of woman in her twenties who would make Hut happy.

Julie felt an insane jealousy. She hated the woman. She wanted to know who she was. She felt she must be losing it if she thought a woman who happened to be at the edge of a video that her stepson had shot might be a woman who had been seeing her husband.

But still, her blood boiled a bit when she saw the red-haired woman, and her mind began imagining things.

She used the close-up feature to try to get a better look at the red-haired woman. Had she seen her before? She didn't think so. Surely this was just a stranger who happened to cross the street at the moment Hut had asked Matt to put down the camcorder.

Then she replayed other videos of the city trips on Boys' Day Out. She saw the street again. Rosetta Street. She wasn't sure where that was. Why would Hut and Matt be walking down that street more than once or even twice? Four times, over four or five months? Winter to spring?

Then, on the edge of one of the digital videos, she thought she saw a flash of red. She hit the close-up button and zoomed in. The woman? Was that her face? It looked like it. It might've been just some other person with red hair. But it looked like the woman.

She went back to the first video that Matt had watched in the den a few months ago. The Chelsea Market. Matt and Hut coming out, the camcorder capturing a moment when Hut took a sip from the white cup of coffee.

Just over Hut's shoulder, a handful of people. She had thought they were waiting for a bus or just talking at the corner with each other.

The woman with the red hair was there, too. This time without sunglasses. She was a bit indistinct, even in close-up. But she had glanced over to Hut and Matt and the camcorder's unerring lens just before Matt turned the camcorder off.

8

"Why don't you just ask him?" Mel asked. They went out for a brisk walk in the late afternoon sunshine while Laura looked after the kids for an hour. They were walking along the road in front of the house, then headed down the hill toward the lake.

"I can't. You know how he is. I just don't want to nudge him."

"Nudge him?"

"Push him. I saw some of his videos. Some are all sunny and bright and happy. But a few are just . . . strange. And he filmed me sleeping. And the one of his classmate. I don't know. It seemed . . . intrusive. Like he was making her do something."

"You're reading too much into it, Jules. For all you know, that was a drama assignment. Or it was something completely innocent. You won't know unless you ask him."

"All right. All right," Julie said, clenching her fists as she walked. "But those other tapes. In the city. Seeing that woman."

"Maybe you're looking for things to make yourself feel better about it," Mel said, her voice having a curious edge to it as if she were hiding something.

Julie stood still. Mel walked a few paces beyond her, then turned around. *"What?"*

"What did you mean by that?" Julie asked.

"Nobody would blame you. It's overwhelming to me that Hut's gone, too. That some psycho kills him in the woods not five miles from his home. But you have got to set your mind in balance fast, Julie. You have two kids who are depending on you. Who need you badly. I'm sorry to put it this way. I am. But you have to pull it together, slap yourself awake and forget anything you're afraid of from the past and move forward. You have got to get yourself together and not dwell. That's the best I can put it."

"What exactly do you mean by 'feeling better about it'? About what?"

"Hut. Being gone. Maybe if you think he was cheating on you, somehow you can deal with it."

"This is not little Julie weaseling out of anything," Julie said. "This is not me at ten years old not wanting to deal with Mom and Dad's divorce, Mel. I loved him. *I loved him.* I will never love any man like that again. I miss him. I ache at night knowing that I won't ever wake up beside him again. I am torn down the middle when I have a dream about him. I have to fight to keep from crying when Livy comes to me in the middle of the night because she wants me to help get God to send him back to us. I have to look her in the eye. She has nightmares three nights a week that a ghost is coming for her. She is seeing a psychiatrist, for God's sake. My six-year-old daughter. And Matt. Oh my God, Mel, Matt. I have to keep him from hurting himself and maybe anyone else. I have to keep him safe when his own mother would not. And I have to tell them that life is still good. That it's still worth something. Even if I don't feel it inside. Even if I'm not sure it's true. I'm not sure there's good in the world. I'm not sure that this life is worth living. I'm not sure that if the man I love can be torn from me by some—some obscene, insane, fucked-up human being who the police can't seem to catch, that I can look at my children and say, 'God loves you. The world is God's creation. We have a wonderful life.' I'm not sure I can ever, ever believe that. And I won't lie to them. But I want to know who Hut was. I want

someone else to tell me what I didn't know. I want to feel
that life is worth living. Do you understand me? Do you?
Can you?"

Mel had a blank look on her face. Nothing had registered.
"Julie. It's been months. It's not like you have this luxury
life. Your kids need you. I'll help out. But don't dwell on
every little unsolved mystery of his life. He was a man. No
one is perfect. You loved him. You're never going to find out
if he cheated on you. He's dead. Think of Livy. You have a
beautiful daughter. She needs you like she's never needed
anyone before. Put her first, and things will fall into place.
I'm not sure that therapist is doing you any good. If you
want to talk to a minister or priest . . ."

Julie felt an overwhelming desire to explode at her sister,
but instead turned around and walked back up the hill toward her house.

9

She went up to her bedroom, shut and locked the door.
She called the phone number she'd found in Hut's jacket so
long before that she couldn't remember which month it had
been. It felt disloyal to his memory to call it, but with the
distance of his death and perspective she'd gained from becoming a widow—suddenly, in a violent circumstance—she
reasoned that if he had been having an affair, maybe it was
partly her fault, too. Maybe she was too involved with the
kids and the ER and the idea of them as a couple instead of
as what he needed with all the stress he had at the clinic.
Maybe it was just the nature of men. "All men cheat," her
mother had warned her. Perhaps it was true.

*Mel's wrong. It won't make it easier. I don't want Hut
gone. I don't want to believe he's gone. I just want to know
something. Something true about him. Even if it was that he
wasn't in love with me anymore. Even if it's bad news.*

She whispered it aloud, as she thought it: "I don't want to lose him yet."

She gasped. She hadn't realized how overpowering the unspoken feeling had been.

Maybe no one will pick up.

She would tell the redheaded woman—whether real or imaginary—that Hut had died. That they'd both loved him. Blah blah blah, she'd say, being a wonderful and generous and forgiving widow.

Hang up, Julie. Just hang up the phone. You don't need to know who she is. You don't need to find out.

Someone picked up the phone on the other end.

Julie felt herself choke up. She couldn't even say, "Hello."

On the phone, the person who had picked up said nothing, but Julie heard breathing.

Julie waited a few seconds, glancing out to the golden afternoon beyond her window.

The breathing quieted, and then she heard a woman's voice whisper, *"It's her."*

Then the dial tone.

Julie tried calling back again, but the line was busy.

She tried again. This time, again she heard the breathing.

"Who are you? Did you know my husband? Did you?" she asked. She heard a faint echo, as sometimes happened, and it pained her to listen to her own stressed-out voice coming back at her: *"Who are you? Did you know my husband? Did you?"*

She closed the phone, set it down and began weeping.

chapter ten

1

The next day, she tried the number again, but it was disconnected.

2

Julie got an email from her mother:

Dear Juliet,
Melanie told me about the cops and the psychic stuff, and I don't know if you knew this but there were programs, sponsored by our own government, for special schools and testing projects for children who showed psychic ability. Maybe Hut was one of those? There was a fire at one, in Chelsea, in 1977. Seven children died. Four instructors. It was an offshoot of the Chelsea Parapsychological Institute, but was funded by tax dollars. I found all kinds of stuff online about it. What are the odds? Also, if Livy keeps having nightmares, you might want to get her another night-light. That might help. Tell her that Gramma loves her.
Love, Momma

Julie sent an email to Mel:

> *Mel—*
> *Please don't encourage Mom with anything you hear from me about Hut and the murder. She now is using search engines to find out every psychic program in existence to prove her point that Hut was psychic. The horror show that is our mother is set loose upon me and I want it to stop. SOS.*

Then, from Mel, she got this:

> *Julie—*
> *I didn't know any of this was off-limits. I'll call Mom off you. But do you think she's right? She told me once that Hut told her that she needed to get her brakes fixed, and how would he have known that? Maybe he was psychic.*
> *Love, Mel*

Julie shot off another email to Mel:

> *Mel—*
> *Stop it. It's upsetting me. Yes, he had those little intuitions, but he was an intelligent, well-educated man, and many people could guess that a woman who drove a twenty-year-old car and never took it into the shop might want to get her brakes checked.*
> *Between you and McGuane and Mom, you'd have Hut involved in some conspiracy theory with UFOs. You don't believe in psychics, do you?*
> *Jules*

Mel wrote back:

Julie—
Sometimes I believe in just about everything. Open
mind, sez me.
Mel

Then one from her mother that sent her over the edge:

Dear Juliet,
I found this online. Did you know that between
1970 and 1995, the U.S. government spent more than
$20 million on research about a psychic power they
called "remote viewing"? It was used to find weapons
and bunkers in wartime, during the Cold War and
after. They set up testing programs here. New York,
Los Angeles, Washington, and Chicago. I can send
you a link to the article if you want. Why don't you ask
his parents if he had any psychic aptitude? Or maybe
I can research some more. You know, I belong to a
group that meets sometimes. They know more about
psychic stuff than I do. I could call Alice in New York.
She worked on that psychic hotline. I bet she'd know
something. Let me know. I always knew Hut had more
to him than met the eye.

Julie deleted the email before she read the rest. Then she
just blocked her mother's email address so that she'd get no
more emails from her.

3

In early August, Julie got a call from Shakespeare &
Company, the bookstore in the city. She had forgotten all
about the book. Between the legal wrangle she'd been dealing with, getting the kids to settle in to a normal day without their father, and her therapy sessions, the last thing she'd

been thinking about was a book she'd ordered in some kind of fugue state after Hut's death.

"What's it called?" she asked on the phone.

"*The Life Beyond.* It's by the TV psychic Michael Diamond," the clerk told her. "It's been hard to get in stock because the publisher went under, plus he's pretty popular with his cult audience."

4

Before she drove into the city, she took the manila envelope out again, pouring its contents onto her bed. She lay next to them—wallet, watch, keys. Flipped through each key and could name them all—but two.

Two keys, one to a doorknob, one to a dead bolt.

Two keys, one with the name of a building in Manhattan engraved lightly into it.

The other with a number: 66S.

Sixty-Six-S. Sixty-Success. Sixty-Sex-ess.

She had not ventured into New York City since her third visit to the precinct where McGuane had met her.

Not for at least two months.

5

"Are you a fan?" the clerk asked as she passed the package over the counter to Julie.

"I've never heard of him. My mother recommended I read it."

"Oh," the clerk said. "I thought you might believe in that kind of stuff."

Julie glanced at the bag, then looked inside at the book. "He's a psychic?"

The clerk nodded. "I can't tell if he's real or it's all bullshit. He does readings with people on TV. Sort of like John

Edward or James Van Praagh, or—what's that woman's name? Sybil something. When I was a little kid it was Jeanne Dixon. Like them. Only not quite the same. Diamond's books never really go over big, but he's got that loyal following. His show's on really late at night—maybe at one in the morning, on cable. I guess he's not that popular. I saw the show maybe once. Usually the people who buy his books always look a little sad to me. But you don't."

"My mother." Julie grinned, shaking her head lightly. "Now she's the gullible one. She believes in practically everything."

She glanced at the display of books near the cash register. One seemed to jump out at her. "Oops, there's another one I want to get." She leaned over and pulled the book off the shelf.

"Oh, I love his books," the clerk said. "He's very funny."

"I'm an old friend of his," Julie said, smiling. "And this one, too," she added, grabbing a trade paperback off the counter. "I might as well buy up the whole store."

"Be my guest," the clerk said as she rang up the purchases.

6

It was a blisteringly hot, humid day, and she wore a skirt that felt too revealing. Without hose and wearing sandals and a light top, she felt less as if she were going to melt on the sidewalk. She strolled over to Washington Square Park and went to one of the green benches along its outer rim, brushed off the dirt with the edge of her hand, and sat down. The place was nearly empty, and there was something comforting about it. She opened the bag and drew the books out.

The first one was by Joe Perrin, her old pal, and she turned to the back to see his picture. He had used one from his late twenties—he had an ordinary niceness to him, and hair that was a little too long fell over his left eye in a Veronica Lake send-up. She grinned, thinking of him laughing at using the picture. The credit for the photo was Alicia Caniglia. Julie wasn't certain, but she thought she might've been there when Alicia snapped the picture. She recalled a day down in Battery Park, along the waterfront, and Joe saying he wanted to capture his youth while he had it so that when he became a famous writer, strangers would lust after him.

She missed him a lot, just looking at the picture, remembering days like that, of dreams of the future. Dreams of what was around the corner, of what could change in their lives in the twinkling of an eye.

She read the bio:

> *Joe Perrin is a thirtysomething writer who lives in New York City with his life partner, Rick Girardo, and a German shepherd named Dutch. His first novel,* A Perry Street Affair, *was nominated for a Lambda Award, and his second novel,* View from the Pier, *was optioned for the movies. He is currently at work on his fourth novel.*

She read the first line from Joe's book, aloud but quietly, as if she could conjure his voice from it. "In 1873, a surgeon named Edward Whistler walked away from his family and children and his successful practice of medicine in London's Regent's Row, and caught a ship sailing for a small island in the South Pacific, and there fell in love with a man named after a turbulent volcano."

She could hear Joe's voice in the words.

She savored the moment, and then closed the book, putting it back in the bag. She brought the second book out. This was a novel by one of her favorite writers, M. J. Rose, but she quickly put that one back in the bag, making a mental note to loan it to Mel first, who devoured her novels.

Then the third book.

A white cover, and a man's face. Michael Diamond looked like he had been a geeky kid who had grown up to put one over on a population of Americans who wanted to believe in anything, so long as someone made it all sound true. He was not cute, not attractive in the least, but there was something in his eyes—in the photograph—that intrigued her. She opened the book and skimmed the table of contents: "Who I Am," "The Spiritual Side of Life," "Death Is a Gift," "Cases of Speaking with the Beyond . . ."

She flipped to the opening chapter: "Exposing Lies, Seeking Truth."

7

From *The Life Beyond:*

I want to add a note here about phonies and grifters and con men who get involved in the schemes of the psychic world. I do not mean the well-meaning ones who believe they have ability. I'm talking about the ones who are getting rich by spreading a lie about the afterlife that they themselves know is false. Or at best, that they can't possibly know. They are too good at their jobs, frankly. They'll be on television or in front of an audience at some seminar, and one is hard-pressed to discover the trickery involved.

First, let me say, if there were a hell, they'd all burn there. Why? Because they're giving false hope to people, they're adding to the delusions people have, and they're intentionally doing it. I won't name names here, but you can guess who the culprits are. They can speak in front of an audience of a hundred or more people, and somehow they manage to know family names and seemingly secret things about these families. The truth is, they usually have done their home-work.

First, most people coming to see a psychic to talk to a re-cently passed loved one—or even someone who died years ago—are put on a waiting list to see the psychic. Why? Be-cause the supposed psychic or his research team needs to find out about the people on his or her list. If you have a rel-ative who died, chances are there's an obituary that can be tracked down. My own father died several years ago, and if you look up his name online or through public records, you'd eventually find out that he was a colonel in the army, that he served in Vietnam, that he worked in military intelli-gence and then as a liaison in Bosnia even in retirement. You'd know the name of his brothers, of his parents, of his children and even how he died, because contributions were made to the American Cancer Society. You'd know his date and place of birth. You'd perhaps have a handful of names to research further, too. The Internet today is so powerful that people can trace entire family trees going back centuries if they want to. How easy is that for a psychic? All the psy-chic has to do is spend thirty minutes or so researching one or two families who are showing up for his audience, and then he gets up in front of the audience and says, 'I'm talk-ing to someone who says he has a son here. He's showing me something about—a helicopter? Or a plane? Some kind of military plane? I'm getting the sense that he was a soldier of some kind. An officer? But there's something about Bosnia, too. Does this sound like anyone here?" And sheep that I am, I'd raise my hand and gasp and say, "It's my dad!"

Why would I want to expose fake psychics? After all, there will be those who believe I'm a fake as well.

Here's why: I believe it is the greatest human evil to de-lude a single human being with an idea that is known to be untrue. To play into another's delusion is equally evil. But to make a profit from that, well, some might say it's the American way, but I'd say it's the anti-American way, and no one should give people like that their business.

When I was a boy, I was poked and prodded by well-meaning people trying to understand why a kid of seven could predict the outcome of a card game ten times out of ten. Or how that same kid would be able to locate missing objects at a great distance. Or how that kid managed to understand what someone in contact with him had been thinking.

All I can tell you is: it wasn't through practice. It wasn't a trick. It wasn't a fancy way of cheating people out of their money.

It was a genuine talent, and based on my research, I believe it's an inherited ability. On my television show, I don't pretend to talk to the ghosts of the dead. I don't pretend to call up spirits and get them to tell Aunt Mildred that she needs to move on with her life.

I am not a mystic. If you want a mystic, go get another book. Find a guru to follow. Or a priest. I am not here to tell you about God. Or gods. Or goddesses. Or the Hereafter. The life beyond is about the life beyond the borders that you impose on your mind. It is about learning to tap into talent you may already have that has not been developed. The brain is the most underused muscle in the body, in my opinion. We lift weights, we do aerobics, we go for jogs, or we swim, but we do not take our mind and exercise it, stretch it, allow it to grow.

I was born with an ability. It may be like an ability you have—only you don't know how to switch it on. It is not magical. It is not a religious experience. It is an aspect to human life that has been untapped for centuries because the very thing I most believe in—Reason—has decreed that anything that does not make immediate sense is impossible. Yet we know now, via science, of the subquantum realm of existence—of being able to divide molecular structures to the left, and find that similar structures to the right respond at the same time, though they are untouched. Is this magic? At one time, it was considered such. Now it is part of scientific inquiry.

The human mind is an untouchable realm. We can test it, zap it, watch it disintegrate, observe those who suffer from its disorders, and recognize a first-rate mind, but the one thing that we have never been able to do is define its limits.

Well, my friends, there are no limits to the human mind. It is a frontier of infinite proportions. And it's time we began exploration of it.

I mind hunt. And what that means is: I sit with someone, I get to know them as quickly as possible, and I delve into their thoughts briefly. Perhaps this is a molecular occurrence. Perhaps it's simply a strong intuition. I would guess that 5 percent of the U.S. population has this talent. Perhaps it's as low as 3 percent. I suspect a thousand years ago, it was a stronger talent in the population. I suspect that despite the cloud of superstition over the ancient world, one of the reasons for the miracle-makers, the professional fortune-tellers and witches, may have been that this talent existed in gene pools and among families, and predetermined a certain unusual life for the bearer of the talent.

I have known others with similar talents. I have worked beside them. To us, it is simply ordinary. It is not supernatural. It is no more remarkable than if one of us were left-handed, or redheaded, or had one eye flecked with blue and the other with green.

But I've yet to encounter a talent that could genuinely speak with the dead and the dearly departed. I believe, truly, that these are the phonies of the psychic world. I wish I could deliver kinder, gentler news than that.

Beware of these fakers and con men. I want you to believe, but not in something that I tell you to believe. Never believe in dogma for which you must pay. If you believe it, if you have your faith, that's your decision. But don't accept the easily paid for delusions of another.

I want you to go on the journey of your life and find your own treasure.

Do I believe in the life beyond?

Perhaps. I am not all-seeing, all-knowing. I don't make claims to fake authority. I am a seeker after wisdom and truth, as you are. I am living life as anyone would, but with an ability that arrived with me at my birth that might provide some insight for you, I hope.

But by naming this book *The Life Beyond*, I wanted to suggest the freedom each of us needs to feel from the chains of the past—whether the past is something tragic that occurred, or whether it is looking forward to the end of our lives and planning for a spiritual awakening. I do believe in spiritual awakenings. I believe in souls. I believe that there is something sacred about the threshold that exists between life and death. And I have been at the deathbeds of people, and I have seen what mystics might call miracles but I would call natural phenomena when the soul leaves the body.

Where that soul goes is not within my field of understanding. I am not out to prove or disprove your God.

I truly doubt the afterlife is within any human being's understanding. To the religious, it may be the peace that passes all understanding. To the nonreligious, it may be that the door that shuts us off from this life is enough to know for now.

As you continue reading my book, I hope you will travel with me on the journey of what I know from my psychic readings, from my experiences with remote viewing, and from my understanding of how to move from this life to what I hope will truly be, for you, the life beyond—beyond the petty anxieties, the wasted efforts, the small-mindedness of the everyday problems.

An interviewer once asked me: Do you believe in an afterlife?

I have to say: it's not a matter of belief. I know there is one. Centuries ago, men dreamed of flying, but could not. And now they can fly. So that means that in dreams, we can see all that is possible. Nothing within the limits of the human imagination and mind is impossible. If it were, we could not imagine it or dream it.

But what is the afterlife? I haven't yet been there—that I know of—but perhaps in exploring the human mind more fully, we can find the questions to ask of ourselves, of each other, as to where our journey continues, in the life beyond.

8

Julie closed the book. She put it back in the bag and folded the edges over. A woman across the park, elderly and with a large, mean-looking mastiff, walked slowly, taking deliberate steps, as if she might fall at any moment. A long-haired young man of about twenty or so played guitar near the fountain rim, two or three friends sitting near him, singing along.

Julie felt inside her bag for the keys.

Finally, she went to find the building on Rosetta Street.

chapter eleven

1

She'd narrowed it down to the block in Matt's videos, on Rosetta Street, which was near Chelsea, but toward the water. With the heat turned up full blast, she was drenched in sweat by the time she wandered down to the end of the Village, and then just beyond it, made a left onto James Street, and then a right onto Rosetta.

She had that feeling of déjà vu, remembering Matt's video, the cobblestoned street—it was not quite as lovely as it had seemed in the video, for most of it was taken up with meat-packing plants, and there was that awful smell in the air of raw beef and something uglier. The sidewalks outside one of the buildings had just been hosed down. A few people walked along the opposite sidewalk, obviously using the street as a shortcut from one business meeting to another, or to a lunch, lives that she could only imagine.

Then she came to the sunken doorway of the building she had been dreading since she had first found the phone number and the keys.

She tried each key on the door of the building, but neither worked.

She sat on the edge of a stone pediment, just at the edge of the steps down to the front door.

She was about to leave when a young overweight woman with a bundle of groceries stepped off the sidewalk, heading for the door. "Forget your key?"

"I'm apartment sitting." Julie thought it up quickly. She held up the two keys. "A friend's cat is inside there, very hungry at this point."

The young woman looked at her warily. Too innocently, she asked, "Which apartment?"

"66S."

"Ah," the woman said. "I already put in a complaint about your friend. Last week it was like a herd of elephants were dancing up there. I hope you don't mind my telling you. Nobody does anything about anyone here, and I'm tired of it."

2

The smell in the building was like a pure blast of just-sprayed Lysol mixed with the undeniable warm bleachy odor of a nearby laundry room.

"This weather, can you get over it?" the woman said. "I hope fall is nice. Fall is usually nice for about three weeks. I could use those three weeks about now. Hell, I could use three days. I can't stand winter and I can't stand summer. I should just live in one of those plastic bubbles."

The elevator was small, and Julie helped the woman with her groceries as she shut the outer blue door so that the elevator's inner doors would shut properly. "I don't want you thinking I normally call the super when anyone has a party. I don't mind that kind of thing," the woman said. "Parties or whatever. I mean, sometimes I feel like the people in 53R have a disco going on. It's just that this was pretty bad. I was trying to sleep. I work weekends and the noise was bad. Press five, would you?"

Julie pressed the buttons for the fifth and sixth floors, and the elevator lurched, shook slightly, and then moved upward with a slight whine.

"Do you know the people in 66S?" Julie asked hesitantly.

"This building is the unfriendliest in the city," the woman said, with the kind of cadence that made Julie think she'd used this line before. "I don't even know my next-door neighbors. But you know, sometimes that's a good thing. God knows I hear them enough. And someone on my hall has the yappiest dog alive. I love animals, but not that damn dog."

After the woman had stepped off the elevator, she turned slightly, smiling. "I'm not saying your friends are bad. They just get noisy sometimes."

"A herd of elephants." Julie nodded. "I'll tell them to take their shoes off next time."

The woman laughed. The elevator door shut again. The woman's pale round face, her dark hair, were all that Julie could see in the round window of the outer elevator door.

Julie drew the keys out of her pocket, clutching them tightly.

At the sixth floor, she got out, fully expecting a long hall with many apartments, but instead there were only six.

At the door to 66S, she pressed the key into the dead bolt, and it turned.

She drew the key out.

She hesitated a moment, and then rapped lightly on the door. Then she pressed the bell.

She waited for what seemed an eternity before trying the other key on the knob. It went in easily, and she turned it.

3

She stood in the doorway.

The air-conditioning in the apartment was on high, and it was chilly. She could see a foyer that was made up of closets on either side, and a narrow hallway. Her first impression was that the apartment must be a fairly large one. The walls were white and off-white. There was an unshaded window at the very end of the foyer, allowing a smattering of light through its casement-style windows.

"Hello?" she asked.

She stepped inside, closing the door behind her. She felt strangely comforted by the plastic bag with the books in it beneath her arm. She felt as if she could just say that she thought it was someone else's place, if caught. She could say something like, "I was given the keys—see? My husband gave them to me." She felt her heart beating as if it were in her throat as she stepped across the floor. She took each step forward carefully, trying not to make a clicking sound with her sandals on the parquet.

When she got to the window, the apartment turned to the left, and beyond the wall that divided the foyer from the rest, it was enormous. It became a loft that seemed to be at least two thousand square feet or more, with exposed brick along one long wall, and a huge skylight above. It was oddly furnished—the lamps all seemed to be huddled at one end, while a broad leather sofa, love seat and two chairs were arranged alongside the far wall. The furnishings seemed years out of style and pushed around as if intended for storage. Copper pots hung from the ceiling along the kitchen area, above a central marble island, and there was a bright rectangle of clean wall where the refrigerator should have been settled. There was a long butcher block table just under the enormous loft-length opaque window that was divided, factory-style, into several casements.

For just a second, she thought she heard a noise behind her, and she glanced back for a second in case the woman who owned the apartment had come home—*What the hell are you doing here?*—but there was no one. She turned back around the corner of the hall, to the foyer, but no one had entered.

"Someone's here," she said aloud, as if it would make her feel safer.

What the hell are you doing here?

It was not her voice, within her mind, saying this.

She couldn't identify the voice, but she had a sudden feeling as if someone nearby had whispered this.

What the hell are you doing here?

And then she smelled something. Something that became overpowering—not just a smell. A stench. It was of a smell she knew from childhood, when a dead animal had lain in a ditch for days. Her mind flashed on the image from Matt's video of the dead dog in the road. The smell was growing. She glanced at the walls of the apartment as if they held something threatening, as if she half expected to see bloody handprints.

Then she was sure she heard something move in the room beyond the living room. Someone was in the bedroom.

Something moved there.

She heard the tap, tap, tap of shoes on a floor.

Someone was coming.

Her heartbeat seemed too noisy, as if it were not inside her at all, but outside of her body, a clock, ticking too fast.

The voice in her head grew louder, pounding within her mind: *What the hell are you doing here?*

She saw the shadow of the person, first, in the open doorway across the room.

Then she saw a man standing there. Only something was wrong. Something must have been messed up about her eyes, because it was as if his face was a blur of movement.

Julie took one step backward, then another.

He stood in the doorway, his face fuzzy and indistinct, his hands moving in what seemed like slow motion.

She turned and hurried into the foyer and out of the apartment, shutting the door behind her, not bothering to lock it. Her heart beat rapidly—it felt as if it were thudding against her rib cage—and she pressed her back up against the hallway wall, looking back at the apartment, while she waited for the elevator to arrive.

She didn't feel safe until she was out on the street again, out among the throngs of people along Hudson Street, moving as if they were fish in a murky sea.

She went into the Chelsea Clearwater movie theater, and just sat through a movie she barely noticed, trying to erase the image of the faceless man from her mind. Then she felt that maybe it had been her mind playing tricks, that it had been her fear within her perhaps building something up— and she was sure that there was no man there at all. That it was like a flash of seeing something. Not a person at all. It was impossible for it to have been a person.

"The human mind cracks more easily than we suspect," Eleanor had told her, in her first session after Hut's death. "You need to be aware of it. Your brain is opening and closing doors. Some of them get slammed. Some get torn off their hinges. You bottle up too much, Julie. If you don't find a healthy way to let some of this out, it'll rupture inside you. Just be prepared for when it happens."

4

She left the movie before the halfway point, and, feeling better, called up Joe Perrin. They met over at the Starbucks on Eighth Avenue. She felt as if she'd calmed down, finally, from that awful feeling she'd had. *That face that was not a face.*

And finally, she told Joe about Hut's death.

"Oh my God, Julie. Julie," he said. He brought his chair around the small round table and wrapped his arms around her. She wept into his shoulder, forgetting the world of the coffeehouse, forgetting anything but the comfort he offered. "My poor baby," he whispered.

5

Her tears dry, she drank some of her cappuccino. "God, you'd think I'd be all cried out by now. It's been months."

"Tears are one of those self-renewing resources. And it's only been a few months. Healing takes time." He pushed a small plate with a big black-and-white cookie on it toward her. "Hungee?" It was their joke word from years ago.

She broke off a piece of the cookie, and took a bite. "Mmm. Reminds me of all our adventures."

"Most of which are best forgotten."

"Oh, Joe. I feel . . . I feel like I've lost my soul or something."

"Well, I think your soul's intact. It's your mind that's a bit scattered." He looked up to her with those warm brown eyes that seemed both playful and a little sad to her, like a boy playing peekaboo.

"I'm sorry I've been distant. All these years."

"It's okay. It's only been a few years, really. I saw you when Livy was, what, two and a half? It wasn't that long ago. Life takes over," he said. "Rick and I are practically hermits since we tied the knot. If he didn't get me volunteering at the Center, I'd probably just live in my little office."

"I bought one of your books today," she said, brightening. She brought the package from Shakespeare & Company up, opening it.

"Ooh, which one?"

She drew out the book, *Dr. Notorious.* On the cover, the torso of a young man, and just a sliver of his chin.

"I hate that cover," Joe said. "The book is about a guy in the nineteenth century who goes to the South Pacific. And they put a twenty-year-old gym bunny right out of the New York City Club on the cover to sell it. I could write a book about measles, and they'd put a cute guy's butt on the front of the book. But that's showbiz, as they say."

"Speaking of showbiz—you sold a book to the movies?"

"Sure. Everyone does. They pay you a few grand and you get to say maybe it'll be a movie. But Hollywood is never making that movie, believe me. When my friend Chris Bram wrote *Father of Frankenstein*, it got turned into the great movie *Gods and Monsters*. Why? Because it's a great story that people can relate to, whether it's about being gay or not. Me, I sell them *View from the Pier* and they will never make that movie because no actor is going to want to play a guy who knows he's gay, falls in love with a guy, and then stays in a marriage to destroy his wife and children and the guy he loves. It's too . . . dark, I guess. Even my editor called it unsympathetic, and she liked it. You can't make a movie about that and expect to sell tickets."

"Sure they will. It sounds wonderful. Joe, I'm so happy for you, for all this. And I can't wait to read this one. I haven't kept up with your career as much as I should've."

He shrugged. "It's not exactly a career. What's the other book?"

"It's some psychic book. My mother pushed it on me, and in a weak moment I ordered it."

"You believe in that stuff?"

"Not really."

"I do," he said. "Since my dad died. The day he died, I dreamed that he came to me and told me that he loved me. He had never said it before. Not in real life. He was a military bruiser, basically. He didn't want to have a kid like me. Even when I was on the football team in high school, he thought I was too soft. He blamed Mom's family because my uncle was gay. He said it ran in families. But in the dream, he said he loved me."

"Oh."

"When I woke up, I saw him. I saw him as clear as day. He was at the foot of my bed and he said, 'I'm glad you found love, Joe. You have a lot to give. I love you, Jojo.' And then he faded." His voice cracked a little, and she thought she caught a glimmer of a tear in his eye, but his smile belied any sadness. "Maybe it was, you know, a cobweb of wishful thinking. Or one of those hypnogogic things, where you're still half-asleep and a dream seems real even when you're awake in your bedroom. But it was some kind of gift. I believe it. Maybe I choose to, because it makes it all easier. It didn't change my core beliefs. But it showed me that there's something else out there. Something we don't yet understand. He was as real as you are, right here. I think maybe we have these kinds of experiences all the time, only we don't know how much of a gift they are. And it made me remember all the good things. All the things about him I'd pushed aside because of our differences. All the wonderful things he had been to me, despite his worst nature." Then he gave her a look she thought of as his "wait a second!" expression. "You must've had some kind of . . . unusual experience, or you wouldn't be picking up books on the afterlife, right?"

"No," she said, thinking of what she saw in apartment 66S. The face that was not there. The blur of movement that was the face of a man. *But I am losing it now. I am seeing things that are not there. I won't mention this to Joe. Not yet. He'll look at me sweetly and sadly and tell me that it's normal to see faceless men after a tragic death.* "I think Mom wants me to feel better. She's got the hots for this psychic." She brought *The Life Beyond* out and showed the cover to him, with Michael Diamond on it.

"Oh, him," Joe said. "He's so serious looking, isn't he? Like the Professor from *Gilligan's Island*. I've caught his show a couple of times. He's a complete fake. He has to be.

His stuff is too good. When a psychic's that good, there's some trick going on. I don't think psychic stuff is like a Mc-Donald's: I don't think one psychic can serve a billion customers. I think it's more personal. You should have a psychic reading sometime. They can be really good. I know this woman who does them. It's not creepy at all, believe me."

6

After coffee, they walked through the old neighborhood. Joe updated her on each window—who lived there before, who had moved, who was turning into the cat lady, who had become the neighborhood watcher, and what had happened to the little old man in the fedora who used to feed pigeons on the rooftop, pissing off everyone who lived on the block because of the increased birdshit on the street. They wandered over to a bakery renowned for its cupcakes and split one, and then went over to another bookshop nearby called Three Lives & Company. It was a small, quaint bookshop packed with books. "Remember this place?"

She drew a blank. "Sure."

He made a face that she could only classify as dimwitted. "*Julie*. It's where we met."

"Oh," she said, clapping her hands together. "How could I forget *that*?"

"Yeah, some strange chick coming up to me telling me that I shouldn't read Mary McCarthy because she claimed she was a fascist, when in fact it was Cormac McCarthy's *Blood Meridian* I had in my hand."

"I don't know why I was so hard on Mary McCarthy. She wasn't a fascist at all. I loved *The Group*."

"And I told you that Ayn Rand wrote books for humorless Sarah Lawrence girls who wanted to get laid but still feel smart afterward," he said. "And then you said that I was sexist and probably racist and probably homophobic. And I said—"

"You looked at me as if I had just slapped you hard in the face and said, 'I can't be homophobic because I'm a homo,'" she chuckled. "Whatever happened to those two stupid young people?"

"I don't know, but I read *Atlas Shrugged* all the time and it never helped me get laid," he said.

Finally, he walked her to where her car was parked and kissed her on the cheek. "You need anything, I'm here. Rick and I can be out in the burbs on a moment's notice."

"I thought you were anti-suburban?"

"For you," he said, "I'll brave the wilds of Jersey. I miss my old buddy. I miss you. I want to see Livy, too. And Matt."

"We blocked you out, didn't we?" she said, sighing.

"Not really."

"No, we did. Hut didn't like you. I guess I can say that now. I think he thought you were a threat in some way."

Joe grinned big and broad, just like he was a wicked kid. "I am the all-powerful Oz."

"I can't throw all the blame on him. I went along with it. I should've fought. But I was busy with the kids, and I was busy with the house and my job. And I just let it all go."

"Well, none of that matters. We kissed and made up. You're my old buddy, Julie. And don't read that Michael Diamond book. Okay? He's full of it. Go get a John Edward book. Or even Sylvia Browne. She's good. Diamond has something wrong with him. I've seen his show. He just gets pretty nasty. I don't think he helps people at all. He does more damage than good."

Another kiss, and Julie was in the car and driving out to the Westside Highway, to the Lincoln Tunnel, and then north up to Rellingford, the city vanishing as she entered the suburban wilderness.

7

"What do you know about this?" Julie asked, dropping the keys to apartment 66S on the table between them.

Outside, with Matt, on the picnic table in the backyard.

"They're keys."

"Keys to an apartment on Rosetta Street. You used to go there with your father."

"That's crazy," he said, looking up at her.

"Matt, I know this might not be easy for you. I know we've had our ups and downs. But I want you to tell me about this. It's important."

"Important to who?"

"To me."

He didn't look her in the eye. "You're nosy."

She glared at him. "Just tell me."

"I feel sorry for you, Julie. I really do. Sometimes I hate you. But I feel bad for you because you're too much like my mother. You stick your nose in where it doesn't belong."

It stung when he said it. He'd never said anything like that to her before. *He's been through hell. Cut him some slack.*

"All right. Well, you can hate me. It's okay by me. That doesn't answer my question."

"I don't remember," he said.

"What does that mean?"

"It means: I don't remember. Maybe Dad took me there. I don't know. I can't remember."

"You mean you don't want to tell me," she said, trying to remain calm.

"God, you are such a *fucking* bitch," he spat, his face suddenly going red. This wasn't the first time he'd gotten this over-the-top angry. She'd understood—from Eleanor and from Hut—that Matt had something wired in his brain that just didn't stop him from taking things too far. Knowing that helped her deal with it. "Why don't you ask my mother about those keys? Why don't you fucking ask her? She knows everything. She's the one who knows it all. Quit fucking bothering me."

Julie leaned forward, touching the edge of his hand. "Oh, honey. You know I love you. You know I'm not trying to upset you."

"You know I love you," he mimicked. "Love love love. Fuck this. Just ask *her*."

Julie sat there, stunned. She knew from her sessions with Eleanor that Matt needed to feel safe. That he needed to act out. That he needed to say things that might be hurtful sometimes. *It's part of what he's dealing with. He's working out past abuse from his time with his mother.*

"Ask her. Ask her whatever you want. Just leave me the hell alone, bitch." He swiveled around on the bench and got up, shot one last look of contempt her way, and then stomped off into the house.

Then she heard something that Hut had only referred to from the past but Julie had never seen—one of Matt's fits of rage.

First, the sound of breaking glass.

And then shrieking as if he were hurt.

8

In therapy.

"I can't convince you not to pursue this?" Eleanor asked.

Julie shrugged. "Maybe."

"What do you think you will accomplish?"

"Closure?"

"You don't sound sure."

"I'm not. Matt won't talk to me. Not right now. He'll yell at me, but not talk. I haven't heard him swear in a long time. I'm not a prude about language. But it shocked me. It was so . . . sudden."

"Violent?"

Julie frowned, nodding. "I didn't feel threatened. He broke a couple of plates. He tried to slam his fist into the wall. No real damage. He was fine ten minutes later, but he didn't want to have anything to do with me. Just turned sullen and quiet and I figured I needed to leave him alone for a while. It just seemed . . . out of the blue."

"Anger is normal. You're being very confrontational, Julie. You must acknowledge that. You know that Matt has limited resources within himself. Whatever happened when he was young can't just go away. A lot is going on inside him, and his father's death probably left him afraid that you'd abandon him, too."

Julie raised her eyebrows slightly.

"I'm not here just to tell you what you want to hear. Look, give him a break. He's had too much loss in his life. He's probably afraid that you'll give him up. You're not his natural mother. With his father gone, it's normal for him to have that kind of fear. Plus, you're digging, and he doesn't like it."

"I feel it's important."

"To whom?"

"To me."

"Why are you asking my permission for this trip?"

"You're my therapist."

"I'm not your mother."

"She wouldn't sign my permission slip."

"This woman has attempted suicide three times in her life. She has a history of violent behavior. God knows what she did to her son in that short period of time when she raised him, but I doubt she was a fit mother for a child. I just think you're playing with fire here."

9

Julie called the psychiatric center that afternoon and set up an appointment to see Hut's first wife.

chapter twelve

1

The psych rehab center was just outside Philadelphia in a lovely suburban world called Greenwood. The area was surrounded by woodlands, and she barely saw it in time to make the turn off the highway onto Beacon Drive. It looked like an old mansion that had been grafted onto a nursing home and its bright neoclassic exterior, with pergolas and balconies and colonnades, belied the monastic sparseness of the interior of the building.

"She lives in West," the clerk at the front desk said. "I need you to hand over that bag." She pointed to the handbag. "Any keys, pens, anything sharp, too."

Julie passed her handbag over. "My appointment was at three."

"It's all right. We know traffic can be bad. She probably just had a nap at this point. Go down through the double doors, elevator on right—the red elevator, not green—and take it to the third floor. Make your first left—two doors down is the social worker's office. That's Gigi Kaufmann. She'll take you to see her."

2

The social worker was in her mid-fifties, wore thick glasses, and her hair, nearly white, was wrapped around her squarish face like cotton candy. She spoke in a loud whisper, making Julie feel like a kid in a library. "She was doing great up until the news in April. I'm afraid it caused her some agitation. But she's better now, I think."

"Is there anything I should know? A way I should talk?" Julie found herself whispering as well.

The social worker strode down the hall as if she were in a hurry to get this over with. The halls were painted a muted pastel yellow, and they passed other patients' rooms, which seemed uniformly dreary and white. A woman in bed, her hair a bird's nest tangle of white, sat up and stared at Julie as if she'd brought bad news. Two men, orderlies, stood at the end of the hallway by a barred window, one sipping coffee, the other gesturing as if toward a third person who was not there.

"She's not dangerous to anyone, if that's what you mean," the social worker said. "She's really a model patient. The medication helps, of course. It grounds her in reality a bit. You'll find her quite chatty."

"Is there anything I shouldn't mention? Any subject matter to avoid?"

The social worker grinned. There was something uncomfortable in the overfamiliarity of the smile, like she was sharing a joke. "Well, all I can say is, don't talk about sex. She has some hang-ups, as they say."

Before Julie could figure out what that comment meant, they were at the doorway marked AMANDA HUTCHINSON. The social worker stopped, checked the clipboard that hung next to the door, and scribbled something across it in pencil. Stuck her head through the open door and announced too loudly, "Hello, Mandy. We've got a visitor."

3

"Come over here, sweet pea," Amanda Hutchinson said, motioning with her hand. Her voice betrayed her southern accent, something that Julie was surprised hadn't faded away over the years. Amanda had been born in Georgia and had moved with her family to New York, where she and Hut had been together as a couple. She sat in a cushioned chair, near the window. There were ornate scroll-like iron bars across the window, as if the institution wanted to disguise the fact that this was to keep patients from jumping.

Julie noticed that mental illness had been kind to Amanda. She didn't have the look of the others on the hall. She had retained her beauty—at forty—and her mane of jet-black hair was shiny and neatly arranged around her shoulders. She wore a minimum of makeup, and her face was a pure white. She had the formal air of a deposed princess that Julie remembered from a previous visit, before Livy was born. Although, back then, Amanda had been more heavily sedated, and the right meds had not yet been found for her, so she had looked haggard. Now she positively glowed.

Julie stepped into the room. It smelled clean and fresh, with a faint pine scent lingering.

Amanda held her hand up. "Come on, I won't bite, even though they say I do."

Julie grinned and went to her. Took her hand. "Hello, Amanda."

Amanda squeezed her hand a little too tightly, and Julie felt intense heat in the palm of her hand. "Aren't you just the picture of delicious? You got balls coming here, Mrs. Hutchinson Number Two. Big hairy balls." She said it in a southern singsong voice, like she was the mistress of some great plantation.

"Call me Julie. Please."

"I like calling you Wife Number Two. I'm Wife Number

One. Mother to the heir apparent. You're just second in the harem." She finally let go of Julie's hand. Julie noticed that there were faint scars on Amanda's hands, as if a cat had scratched her up.

Amanda rubbed one hand over the other unself-consciously. She seemed to enjoy the attention. "Tell me, sweet thing, you have any contraband?" She said "contraband" like it had seven syllables.

The honeyed southern thing was growing a bit old for Julie. It felt like an act. She tried to keep the slight smile plastered on her face, but it was getting difficult.

"I just mean cigarettes, dear *gaw-ad*," Amanda said, "you look like you thought I was asking for cocaine or something."

"Want me to go get you some?"

Amanda's eyes twinkled. "He must've loved hearing you ask 'How high?' whenever he asked you to jump." She motioned toward a wooden chair in a corner. "Pull that thing over. Just throw all the magazines off."

After Julie scooted the chair closer to Amanda's, she sat down and hesitated before saying, "I'm really glad you agreed to see me."

"Why wouldn't I? I have nothing to fear now. I'm dispatched like a queen to the *Tow-uh*. Look at all this," she laughed, pointing to the TV set on the wall and the narrow bed. "I suppose I'll be here until the day I die. I'll be moved downstairs where the little old ladies push their walkers around and talk about how life turned out awful for them. But it's better than being out there where the wild things roam."

"You're not in here against your will," Julie said.

Amanda Hutchinson smiled broadly. She looked down to Julie's feet, then up her legs, her hips, her waist, her breasts, settling on her face. Julie remembered something that Hut had told her about Amanda's ambiguity. She had always thought he'd meant her indecisiveness, but now wondered if he hadn't meant that she was bisexual. Amanda certainly seemed to be checking her out the way crude men sometimes had in the past.

"I completely volunteered for this, believe me." Amanda turned and looked out the window: through the bars, the beautiful lawn and the neat rows of boxwoods around a central stone fountain. A bitterness entered her voice. "I have been diagnosed, my dear. It's a diagnosis that keeps me safe in the Tower, away from the dreaded executioner. I wonder if Anne Boleyn longed for the sword to the neck by the time she'd lived in the Tower long enough. I don't. I don't want my head to roll. I keep that one awful thing alive. That one terrible thing. Hope. Hope that maybe I'm insane and all these meds will help me. That these Tower walls will keep me safe."

Then she shot a sharp glance back at Julie. "To what do I owe the pleasure of your visit, Wife Number Two?"

"I thought maybe there'd be pieces of Hut's life that you . . . well, that we could discuss."

"How's my son?"

"He's doing good."

Amanda gave her that catlike look, as if she were playing with her. "I'm surprised."

"He's a . . . a wonderful boy."

"That's more of a surprise. I haven't seen him since he was six. He was a pretty little boy. But he's dead to me, isn't he? Does he ask about me?"

"Sometimes."

Amanda laughed full-throated, with something malevolent in the sound. It made Julie nervous. "I bet it's not good when he does. I bet he gets violent. I bet he curses my name. As well he should. I'm a monstrous mother." She said this as if it was of no consequence. "He's a little brain-damaged boy." She watched Julie for a reaction. "I dropped him on his head when he was a baby. I suppose that's what Hut told you. I beat him until he just got to be damaged goods."

Julie was ready. She reined in her reaction. *Don't give her ammo.* Julie fingered the edge of her chair. She looked at her own hands. At the ring on her left hand. *Do not react to her poison. That's what Hut had called it. Her poison.*

"You knew Hut when he was young," Julie said slowly.

"We were kids. It was the last good time of my life. Under the age of twenty. After twenty, it was all downhill for me. Nervous breakdown city. Hallucinations. Seeing . . . ghosts." Amanda grinned wickedly. "But I don't want to bother your pretty little head with any of that. So, now that he's dead, you want to know about him? Why's that, Wife Number Two? Because when he was alive, maybe you never knew him at all? That doesn't surprise me. You think he didn't pick you out of a lineup of possibles. He did. I know him. I've known him since he was younger than Matt. You know, he's still with us. He may be in the backseat of your car right now, for all I know. Just waiting to surprise you."

"I don't find this funny at all. This kind of talk."

"Sensitive pretty little Wife Number Two. All right, fair enough. You want to know what Hut was like? I knew him before he was adopted out. I knew him when he was seven years old, and he was a bad little boy. Worse than Matt, and you think Matt's horrible."

"Matt is an angel," Julie said, feeling defensive.

"You're good. You're really good, Wife Number Two. You can lie with the same look in your eyes as when you tell the truth. My foster mother used to call it the clear blue eyes of a born liar. They say it takes a criminal mind to do that well."

They both were quiet after this for several minutes. Amanda glanced around the room as if she were taking mental photographs of the moment.

Then Amanda broke the silence. "Did he ever tell you about when we were children?"

"Only a little," Julie said. Then she added, "You were in a school together?"

Amanda kept a Cheshire cat grin on her face. "The drugs I get here stunt me a little. In the brain. They turn off things that hurt, and they seem to turn on the warm fuzzies. But I can't get used to it. Not being able to figure things out, the way I used to. Like why you're really here. It's not about my son, it's not about Hut. It's about something else, only the warm fuzzies have taken over my brain and I can't quite pinpoint it. You're pretending it's about remembering Hut in all his glory, the doctor to the poor, the wonderful man who gave you a daughter and me a son. But you want something from me. What is it? Let's just get this over with. Fish or cut bait, as they say."

"I'm not really sure why I'm here."

Amanda gave a low growl of a chuckle. "It's because your poor pathetic little life is a big fat lie, Wife Number Two. It's because he never let you in on his secret. His deep dark wound of a secret that would destroy you if you knew it. And I can't even tell you about it. Even if I wanted to. Even if I dreamed of doing it. The warm fuzzies have me. You found out about Rosetta Street, didn't you? That's why you're here. You found out about 66S. You are so warm, Wife Number Two. Warm and getting warmer. But you get too warm, you burst into flames. I did. I got too warm. I got too hot. I burned up there, in 66S. I dream about it now. It's a nightmare from hell, but I dream about it and what happened, and you want to know why a mother hates her own son, Wife Number Two? Why my little baby Matthew is dead to me? Just go ask them. Ask 66S. You can get burned, too. Or if you're smart, if you're a genius, you will walk out of this room, and go home and pick your daughter up and get as far away from 66S as you can, before it happens to you, too. Because eventually we all burn, Julie. All of us. We burn eternally."

"I'm sorry," Julie said.

"Do you believe in heaven? Do you? Or hell? Or anything?"

"Maybe."

"You should. There's something else out there. Something beyond this life. Something that's worse than dying. Worse than suffering. Worse than the torture of being alive." Her voice took on an undertone of growling sensuality, and Julie felt as if she were being hypnotized by it. "It's not beautiful heaven. It's not even beautiful hell. It's a thousand times more terrifying than anything you can dream up in your feeble nightmares. The apartment on Rosetta Street is a burning place, Julie Hutchinson, Wife Number Two. It is a torture chamber, and you will find yourself on fire if you ever go there."

"I've been there," Julie said.

Amanda looked at her as if just seeing her for the first time. Her eyes widened, and the smile crept up wider than before. She gave a full toothy grin, and her face seemed to gleam as if it excited her to hear this.

"It's a place of impossibilities. If you'd really been there—really been in 66S—we wouldn't even be having this conversation."

"There was nothing there."

"Oh. There was *something*. You just didn't look hard enough."

Julie briefly closed her eyes. Remembered the blurred gray face of the man in the bedroom doorway.

"Open your eyes," Amanda said. "You *were* there. You saw something. Only you left. Fast. Fast as your pretty legs could carry you."

Amanda went silent, and looked down at her hands, wiping them against each other as if washing them clean.

When Amanda spoke again, it was in a whisper.

"I'm sorry," Julie said. "What?"

Amanda whispered again. Something playful in the curve of her lips, in the way her eyes flashed.

Julie smiled back, almost involuntarily.

Something about the way Amanda leaned forward made Julie get up and move closer to her. She sat on the edge of the bed, and Amanda leaned closer to her from the chair.

Julie tried to make out the words forming silently on Amanda's lips. Something in her went cold—something about being so close to Hut's first wife—and yet she felt nothing but heat emanating from her.

"He's trying to contact you. They do that, you know. After they're gone. They try to. That's why you're here. You want to know. But I can't tell you. The warm fuzzies have me, they have me, have me, have me," Amanda said softly, so softly that Julie could barely hear her. "You want to know who lives in apartment 66S?" Amanda reached over to touch a strand of Julie's hair—Julie gasped for a second, her nerves tingling—then gently placed the strand of hair back behind Julie's ear like it was a flower. Her touch almost sexual. Almost threatening.

Julie felt something at the center of her being—no, lower—something that was like a gentle tickling from the inside. Her breathing slowed.

Amanda's breath—warm, musky and sweet.

"Pretty Wife Number Two. So beautiful. So sad. So wanting."

Julie looked into her eyes. Amanda's eyes seemed endless to her—deep pools of darkness.

"66S," Amanda whispered, letting it become a hiss.

Then Amanda leapt toward her, and for just a second, Julie felt as if she were watching some wild animal sprung loose from its cage.

4

Julie scrambled backward, and her legs went in the air. Amanda Hutchinson was on top of her, swinging her fist down on the side of her head.

Once hit, Julie felt as if she were losing consciousness. She wasn't sure, but she thought she felt a strange warmth— as if Amanda's hand were now going down between her legs, down to touch her, beneath her skirt, the edge of her panties.

Amanda's urgent whisper in her ear: *"Does he come to you at night and touch you, only it's better than he ever did before? Does he make you moan, Wife Numbah Two? Does he try to get inside you?"*

Julie took a deep breath and brought her knee up, knocking her attacker in the arm, pushing her hand away.

Fingers had just grazed the skin beneath her panties.

Then an orderly was running in the room, shouting, "Mandy! Get off her right now! Holy shit, Jimmy, get down here!"

5

After Amanda had been subdued, Julie stood just outside the doorway to her room. She briefly glanced inside. The orderlies had not yet righted the overturned chairs. They had just finished tying Amanda's restraints to the edges of the mattress. Although she'd been given a shot of some kind of sedative, Amanda continued to struggle in the restraints. One of the staff nurses bandaged her fingers where the nails had torn.

The social worker touched Julie's arm. "She'll sleep now. It's all right. Sometimes there are flare-ups. Let's get you down to the nursing wing to look at those cuts."

6

"She jumped me," Julie said, as a young male nurse daubed a Q-tip soaked in hydrogen peroxide on the slight cuts on her arm.

The nurse grinned. "You're lucky. She took someone's eye out last winter."

"My God."

"It happens now and then. Mandy is docile as a lamb for eleven months of the year, and then one day—or night—she snaps. Sorry for the gallows humor. I know it can be pretty scary. She went Lizzie Borden on me once, too. Right after I started."

"I just didn't expect it," Julie said. "We were . . . well, I hope I didn't do something to provoke her."

"Probably not," the nurse said. Then, noticing the cuts on her knee: "She didn't . . . do anything else, did she?"

He means "Did she touch you down there?"

"No. Well, I mean, she sort of scratched me up . . . all over."

The nurse nodded, as if considering all of it. "Sometimes she does some inappropriate touching."

"I'm sure that's not what it was."

He shrugged. "Business as usual," he said. "You probably just upset her a little, and that's enough for her to go full throttle. Ever since her son's death."

"Her husband," Julie corrected. "Her ex. My husband."

"Oh. I'm sorry," the nurse said. "I'm sorry to hear that. I can't believe I got it wrong. Well, it really gets her going sometimes. You probably just reminded her of some bad stuff. And she never really sleeps much. She wanders sometimes, at night, and thinks someone's following her. She thinks someone is trying to kill her."

chapter thirteen

1

That night, Amanda Hutchinson awoke from a deep dreamless sleep. She found that the restraints on her wrists had been loosened, and she easily slipped out of first one, and then another. Then she sat up, working on the restraints on her ankles.

Her room, dark except for the patch of light from the hall, her door just half-shut, had been cleaned up, and overturned chairs had been righted. She listened for orderlies or nurses in the hall, but there were none.

She got out of bed and went to the window, looking out on the moonglow across the lawn and trees.

And then she heard the voice in her head. A voice that the warm fuzzies had blocked and that she had thought would leave her alone.

But it was that woman. Julie. Coming to her. Pushing at her. Making her remember things that were best forgotten.

2

After she'd written the note, she went into the small bathroom and took off her clothes. She turned on the shower, making sure it was as hot as she could get it. She got under the water, and let it burst against her scalp, trying to wash memory from her, clean the past out.

Instead, his face came back to her, inside her mind, opening her up for other memories, breaking down doors she had let the warm fuzzies seal up.

She slammed her head against the tile of the shower stall.

Again.

And again.

Until she felt the blood dripping down along her face, down her shoulders and breasts, into the drain at her feet.

She kept it up as long as she could, bashing her head into the tile, trying to unlock every door she had before someone tried to slam them closed with medication.

She heard one of the night nurses calling out, trying to open the bathroom door, but she had jammed it so it couldn't open. Amanda drew her bloodied head back and slammed it as hard as she could against the tile.

The last things she heard were a sharp crack, and the cry of the nurse as the bathroom door flew open.

Amanda sank down in the shower stall, resting her head on the cool floor by the drain. Her vision weakened, and the throbbing in her head went from burning pain to a frozen numbness.

She felt her consciousness fading. She tried as hard as she could to open one last hidden door within her mind, and let go of the flesh.

chapter fourteen

1

"You went to see *who*?" Mel nearly shrieked.

"Take off the sister hat and put on the friend hat," Julie said.

"I'm wearing the *smart* hat. What in God's name were you doing there?"

They were driving around looking at real estate listings in Forest Lake, because Mel was still thinking of buying a place nearer Julie, "but not so close that I see you every day," Mel had said.

"Look at that one." Julie pointed at a small house at the edge of a hillside. "Look, it must have a view of the lake in back. Write down the Realtor's number."

"Why the hell did you go down there? What good would it do?"

"Quit yelling at me."

"I am not yelling."

"I didn't think it would turn out like it did. I thought maybe . . . I don't know. I thought maybe she'd know something I didn't."

"She's insane, Julie. He divorced her because she tried to kill her own son. Isn't that enough for you?"

2

She dreamed that night of Amanda Hutchinson, stun-
ningly beautiful, dressed in one of Hut's business suits. Julie
lay on a bare mattress on the floor of an auditorium. She had
the sense that people were watching her. She struggled, but
her hands—though not tied down—wouldn't move. Nor
would her legs.

Julie became aware of her nakedness only when Amanda
bent down and touched her foot. Amanda licked the edge of
her foot and took a toe in her mouth.

Then, on all fours, Amanda climbed on top of her, bringing her face within an inch of Julie's.

"Does he touch you like this?" she asked, her tongue
flicking out and lapping at Julie's lips. "Like he's more alive
than he's ever been?"

In the dream, Amanda's hair was no longer black, but
bright red. Julie noticed that there was a chair above her,
hanging suspended from the sky as if by a wire that went all
the way up to heaven.

Julie felt a hand on her belly, fingers moving down toward the thatch of pubic hair.

Amanda Hutchinson's face became a man's face, blurred,
but with the same long red hair.

He had carvings all over his skin.

It was Hut. Hut with tattoos all over his body. Holding her
arms down at her side while his enormous penis pounded
her. And she felt herself opening in that space, between her
legs, opening herself to his sex, to his forced entry, unlocking the doors for him, letting him through.

In her dream, she whispered, *I want you inside me, Hut. I*
want you inside me.

3

She awoke, thinking she'd heard Livy cry out. It took her a minute to adjust to the darkness. She was used to the routine of Livy's nightmares. She rolled out of bed, putting the terry bathrobe on, and padded down the hallway through the veiled darkness punctuated by the numerous night-lights she'd scattered in various outlets so that Livy could see her way to the bathroom without getting scared.

Right on schedule, Livy was standing in the hallway, her back against the wall. Julie flicked up the hall lightswitch. "Honey," she said.

Livy looked up at her, her eyes wide. "I'm sorry, Mommy. It just scared me. I know it's just dreams. But it seemed real."

"Well, you're fine, now. But doesn't Dr. Fishbain talk to you about this?"

Livy nodded.

"Does it help?"

Livy nodded again. "But Dr. Fishbrain doesn't have to sleep here."

Then Julie had an idea. "What if I could prove to you that there's no ghost?"

"How?"

4

Julie enlisted Matt to help set up the old NannyCams that they'd used when Livy had been younger and before they'd discovered Laura Reynen as a sitter. Julie had loved the NannyCam—Mel had convinced her that all babysitters were potential child abusers after Livy had been born.

They set up one of the NannyCams along the stairs, and then the other one at the entrance to Livy's bedroom. Matt brought up the VCR from downstairs, and then Julie got the old one that was in the storage closet next to the linen closet. They tested them, since none of them ever watched VHS anymore, having gone to DVDs. Both machines worked fine. He set up the wires and cables and put some tapes in each machine. "See, Livy? This one"—he pointed to the NannyCam in the hall—"goes to this VCR. And that one, in your room, goes to the other one. If anyone comes in, we'll catch it on the cam."

Livy added more night-lights, pulling them from the three bathrooms in the house, and then the ones that Julie had bought at Home Depot. "They're like little soldiers," Livy said.

"See? We'll catch the ghost," Matt said, attaching the NannyCam to a small block of wood to steady it.

"There's no ghost." Julie crossed her arms, a bit annoyed with Matt for saying it in front of his little sister.

Livy seemed thrilled to think that her bad dreams might finally end.

5

The first morning after they'd set up the NannyCams, Julie sat down with Livy in the rec room and fast-forwarded through the resulting videotape. The hall tape showed nothing but the sentry line of night-lights, occasionally punctuated by Matt coming out into the hall and walking sleepily to the bathroom. "He pees a lot!" Livy giggled.

She and Livy laughed while Matt sped up, walking like a fast-paced Charlie Chaplin down the hall to the bathroom. For fun, Julie showed it backward and then forward.

"See? Nobody."

"Matt was funny," Livy giggled. "Let's make him walk fast again."

"Okay," Julie said. Then she sped through the rest of the

tape. "See? Nobody's in the hall. No one in your room other than you."

Livy shook her head. "He didn't come last night."

6

They repeated this morning ritual for the next several days, and Livy was thrilled to see Matt—or even herself—wander to the bathroom in the purple light of night. One tape had Julie looking right into the NannyCam and singing a silly little made-up song. She played the tape for Livy, and Livy laughed and told her to turn it off before she exploded. Then she let Livy watch herself sleeping in bed. "I snore!" she cried out with glee. "Just like you do, Mommy!"

One morning, Julie woke up and Livy was in bed with her, pressed against her back.

"I had a bad dream again," Livy said.

After they'd been up a bit, Julie got out the videotape and said, "Let's watch the NannyCam and see."

"No," Livy said.

"Come on. We can laugh about how Matt waddles down the hall."

"No. Mommy. I don't want to see him."

"I promise you won't," Julie said, playing with Livy's hair. "I promise you, Olivia Hutchinson, that you will not see a single person on the videotape unless it's you or Matt going down the hall to the bathroom."

Livy reluctantly agreed, and they went to watch the tapes. Julie sat in the rec room and fast-forwarded through the NannyCam tapes. There was Matt on his nocturnal trip to the john, and then she saw a blur of movement. She stopped the tape and froze on the picture.

"That's him!" Livy cried out, pointing at the screen. "That's the ghost!"

Julie shushed her and told her that it was nothing. "It's

just shadows, baby. It's not a ghost." But she shut the tape off and tried to get Livy to think of something else. She took her out into the garden and they planted some seeds from packets that they'd bought at the local nursery. Now and then, Livy mentioned the ghost, and Julie did what she could to talk her out of it.

But later in the day, when Livy was reading in her room, Julie went back down to the rec room to watch the tape.

It wasn't much. Might've just been a problem of the tape. She played it in slow motion.

She held her breath for a moment, surprised.

It was a blurred figure moving down the hall, but in weird jumps of motion. Then she played the video at regular speed, but it was impossible to see it. She could only see it when she slowed the tape down or watched it in fast forward.

She played the tape backward and forward.

The hallway with the night-lights in a row like luminarias outside Livy's bedroom.

It wasn't that it was a blur—it was that whoever was crossing in front of the night-lights darkened them in such a way that they created a blurring effect. There was no way that it was Matt. It was a large person. An adult.

Then she put in the tape for Livy's bedroom NannyCam.

Fast-forwarded through the night as Livy tossed and turned, throwing her American Girl doll from the bed (where it should not have been in the first place), and pulling her pillow down to her chest. Julie paused the tape, freezing the picture.

It looked like a dark movement near Livy's bed. For just the flash of a second.

Then it was gone.

After it moved back into the shadows, Livy's eyes fluttered open, although it was hard for Julie to make out much about her face in the darkness.

Livy sat up and looked as if she were watching someone in her doorway. She clutched her blanket and pulled it up around her shoulders, and then shut her eyes tight.

7

Julie got Matt to watch the tape with her, and he said, "Wow. I wonder what that is?" He squinted. "It's hard to make out in the dark. Sometimes video sucks."

"Do you think it's a person?"

"It has to be, Julie. Look at that—the way it moves around. That has to be an arm—right?"

"I don't even know what this means."

"Maybe it means someone is coming in our house at night," Matt said.

8

She showed the tapes to Mel, but she told Julie she wasn't sure it was a person at all. "I don't know. I don't want to jump to conclusions," Mel said. "I think it's just shadows and stuff. I don't really see anyone." But she suggested that Julie get some kind of protection system in place. Julie decided to go all out: She got a burglar alarm system that was wired to the windows and doorways. A security company installed it within a week, and although it cost a small fortune, she decided it was well worth it. She made Matt memorize the code, but she kept it fairly simple. "At least until it gets cool, we keep the windows closed, and go in and out only through the front door, okay?" She told both of them not to play with the alarm. Then she tested it once to see how fast the local police could get there.

She had a nice talk with the cops who showed up and told them about the tapes. One of them volunteered to sit down with Matt and fast-forward through the tape to see what he could make of it. When they came back up from the rec room, Matt said, "Julie, you must've erased the tapes last time you watched them."

"Yeah," the cop said. "It looked like *Seinfeld* reruns on one of them."

"Mel," Julie said.

Matt turned to the cop and said, "My aunt Melanie. She loves *Seinfeld*. She taped over my movie of last year's Fourth of July parade, too."

9

Julie kept taping the hall and the bedroom for several days, but didn't see the shadowy movement.

And Livy began sleeping through the night.

10

On the phone with her mother:

"Did you read it?" her mother asked.

"Read what?"

"That book. *The Life Beyond.*"

"Some of it."

"Well? Did you love it?"

"Mom, you know I don't believe in that stuff."

"I've seen him twice. He's fascinating."

"I am not going to delude myself, Mom. I'm not going to pretend that there's someone out there who speaks to the dead."

"No, it's not like that. He doesn't do that," her mother said. "He just picks up things about you. When I was there a year ago, he told a man that his brother was looking for him. And within a month, it turned out the brother he thought was dead was actually alive. And a woman who had blocked childhood memories suddenly recalled that she'd witnessed her mother and her uncle making love. And that's why she'd hated her mother so much. It's halfway between psychic and therapy."

"I have a great therapist."

"Anyone can be a therapist," her mother said. "Michael Diamond is a psychic. A real one. Read the whole book. He's not like those others, sweetie, believe you me. I've researched them all. He's not as flashy, maybe, but he delivers the goods. And we have tickets to his show. I've been waiting for them to come through since mid-May. And guess what? It must be fate. They came through today."

"I am not going," Julie said, and clicked the phone off.

chapter fifteen

1

"I don't know how you roped me into this," Julie said. It was a lie: she knew how her mother had done it. Julie's interest had been sparked by Michael Diamond's book, and by her curiosity about Hut's childhood and how it might be connected to psychic ability, whether that existed or not. She didn't believe in it. But people did. Even the U.S. government, for God's sake. Even homicide detectives in New York City, the city that wasn't exactly the city of gullibility. Detective McGuane had even told her that while he didn't wholly believe in it, he had seen psychics consult on murder cases once in a while, with impressive results.

She sat sandwiched between her mother and sister in the television studio with its uncomfortable chairs and blinding overhead lights. The place was packed, but Julie guesstimated that there weren't more than two hundred seats. The stage was round and small. Three large cameras and their operators moved around on it. And various lights came up and down. Taping wasn't scheduled for another twenty minutes.

"I can't wait to get his autograph. I loved his new book," her mother said. She had a small cloth bag stuffed with paperbacks. "Melanie, you really should read some of them."

"I prefer to stick to the classics," Mel said, grinning, poking lightly at her sister.

When the show began, Michael Diamond came out onto the stage. He was tall and looked like a gawky high school kid who had just hit his mid-forties. His hair was a little too long, and he had the sheen of one who has just been made up to look fantastic. Julie was unimpressed. He looked slick and sort of comfortably nerdy at the same time—not her type at all, although Mel raised her eyebrows a bit, her signal that she thought he was cute.

He spoke more to the cameras than to the audience, but within several minutes he stepped off the stage and went into the audience. He asked about someone who had lost a child, and a woman in the back raised her hand.

He jogged up the steps to where the woman now stood. The woman was short and stout, had a mullet-style hairdo, and wore a sweatshirt and jeans. Diamond went to her and took her hand. One of the cameramen followed, trailing thick electrical cords up the steps.

"What's she saying?" Julie's mother asked.

"Quiet," Mel whispered.

"Here's what I'm getting," Michael Diamond said. "You have been beating yourself up for years about the event. Do you have an item?"

The woman nodded, producing a small shoe from a wadded-up brown paper bag.

On the monitors that hung over the stage, the cameras went in close on the small red sneaker in Michael Diamond's hand.

Diamond closed his eyes. He said, "His name was Jimmy. He was four. No, five. You lived on a. . . . cul de sac. In . . . somewhere in Connecticut."

"New London." The woman nodded.

Diamond opened his eyes. "Please, don't tell me. I don't want to know. Let me tell you, and you can tell me if I'm wrong."

He closed his eyes again, pressing the shoe against his left ear as if the sneaker were a seashell and he was listening to the ocean. With his free hand, he pressed his fingers into the corners of his eyes, rubbing at his eyelids.

Then he opened his eyes and passed the shoe back. "I'm sorry. His name was Dennis. You lived separately from his father. A woman with the name of M. Mary? The name Miranda is somewhere in there. Or a name like that. Mary Anne? Marianna. That's it. Is it?"

The woman nodded.

"You need to forgive her," Diamond said. "She's not at fault. It was an accident."

The woman took the sneaker back, staring at it.

"If he were here, he'd want you to forgive her. That's really all I can say," Diamond said, touching her gently on the shoulder.

The woman's head slumped against his chest.

"You need to get some rest. You can't put yourself through this. You've relived that car accident for two years. Dennis wouldn't want it."

"I hate her," the woman whispered, her voice barely audible in the microphone that hung suspended from a boom one of the TV crew held overhead.

Michael Diamond pulled sharply away from her and put both his hands on her shoulders—more to separate himself from her than to console. "You need to look in the mirror, Alice. You need to see what role you played in this. Accidents happen. You need to forgive Marianna. She was only a girl herself. She had just gotten her driver's license. You could as easily blame yourself. But Dennis would not want you to do that. Dennis is gone."

Julie touched the top of Mel's hand. Mel looked over at her, a question forming on her face.

Julie whispered, "He seems a little harsh."

2

After two more readings, Michael Diamond went to the stage and said, "Someone is here who recently lost a husband. Someone named Jewel?"

"Julie!" her mother called out, pointing to her daughter.

"I'd like to do a one-on-one this time," Diamond said. His face was enormous on the monitor that Julie watched. She felt she could count every pore in his skin. She saw flecks of yellow in his brown eyes.

Then she looked from the screen down to the man in front of her. He half smiled, and for some stupid reason she instantly felt comfortable with him, as if she'd known him all her life.

"Okay," she said, and just before she got out of her chair, Mel leaned over and whispered, "Sit on his lap."

3

The one-on-one was a segment of the television show where the subject sat with Michael Diamond on the low-backed curved sofa at the back of the stage.

"You're still grieving," he said.

"Yes," Julie said. She was about to say: *And I don't believe in psychics, thank you.*

"It doesn't matter if you don't believe in me," Michael Diamond said. His words sent a shock through her. "Belief has nothing to do with it. Tell me about the brain radio."

"What?"

"The brain radio." Michael Diamond grinned. He kept his

hand on her forehead. She felt a warm gentle pressure from his palm and the headache she'd had began to dissolve.

"It's what Livy—Olivia—my daughter—calls it when she hears things." Then Julie realized that was inadequate as an explanation. "She thinks she talks to people with it. Or hears songs on the radio even when the radio isn't on."

"She talks to your husband. Sometimes."

"When he was alive. They had a pretend game like that."

"Do you listen to what your daughter says about it?"

"It's usually silly. Fun stuff."

"Your husband was murdered."

Julie gasped. She glanced toward her mother and sister, who sat at the far end of the couch. The bright lights and the anonymous eye of the camera seemed to wall her in. "Yes. He was."

"It's terrible," Michael Diamond said. "You've been fumbling through life since then. You've seen movies? Movies of some kind. There's a place. A place in the city. A number and a letter. You won't face what others want you to face. You . . . you haven't listened. No. No, that's not true. You've tried to listen. You just don't know what it is you're hearing. Your daughter needs you. She needs you. Someone else needs you. Needs her. Someone needs both of you. Someone desperately wants you. Male. Someone male. Someone wants you to understand. Badly. But death is all around you. Fear of death is inside you. Ah!" He said this last part as if catching his breath upon seeing something—something that left him awestruck.

And then she felt it.

No longer in the studio, no longer with lights and camera and mother and sister and audience and sofa.

She felt as if he had pressed his warm hand beneath her breast and rested it just along the thumping halo of blood encircling her heart—as if he had reached within her and emanated a strange warmth that took her back to her dreams of Hut:

Making love to Hut in the warm bath, candles glowing all around the tub, Hut pressing into her as she gasped and felt love in a way she had not thought possible—

Giving birth to Livy, the way Hut had clutched her hand tightly, had breathed with her, and kissed her on the forehead as Livy arrived into the world—

Holding Livy for the first time, a bloody, hideous baby that was the most beautiful human being she had ever seen, and Hut there, his happiness extreme as he laughed with her, with the exhaustion at the end of labor, with the surrender that childbirth demanded.

And then a moment in time that had been long forgotten, but it came to sudden life within her mind as she felt an electric shock—seeing Hut in the shower, water cascading over his body, his muscles taut, drawing back the shower curtain and seeing the look on his face, the seething anger, and he turned to face the tile wall, and then seeing the scratches along his back and wondering if he had been in an accident, and then she realized it was something else—something about why Hut hadn't been home in three days.

And then her vision turned red, and Hut—not vibrant Hut, but the dead man from the metal table, milky eyes, shiny maggoty skin—his arms around her, pummeling her with his hips, driving himself into her, turning her over onto her stomach, taking her like that. And she felt ecstasy as he whispered filthy things, his lips pressed into her earlobe, his tongue etching fire as he said things she'd never heard a man say.

Julie felt as if her consciousness were shot out of the barrel of a gun—it hurt to open her eyes. She had to force them open, feeling as if heavy weights kept them closed, kept her in the darkness of her own mind.

Open. She saw the others there. The watchers. The audience.

She flushed with embarrassment. She felt shame the likes of which she hadn't felt since she'd been a child, caught naked with a little boy, playing doctor. She felt as if all her secrets had been announced on loudspeakers, and the people in the audience had used what was in her mind as entertainment, something for their amusement: her shame.

Her breathing felt labored. It was as if she'd been running and had suddenly stopped, unable to catch her breath.

She was in the television studio. On the sofa.

Michael Diamond's palm was warm and moist against her forehead, and he was whispering something to her . . . to the others. The audience. To the world.

Some secret about her. Something she had harbored.

"You want him to be alive," Diamond said. "You feel guilty because you stopped loving him. And then when he was killed, you wanted more than anything for him to be alive because . . . because it meant that you could leave him. But now you are stuck remembering only love. You've forgotten the winter that settled between you both. The fighting. The arguments. The dislike. The indifference. The lack of trust. You were in love with him for two years, and then you caught him in too many lies. You stopped trusting him. You were planning on leaving him. One day. One day soon."

Michael Diamond's face shone with sweat. It looked as if in the few minutes he'd been doing the reading of her, he'd been up for nights. "I'm sorry," he said under his breath. Then, more loudly, "Love and death are strange companions. Those whom we were conflicted about in life, we now are tied to in death."

Julie felt as if she had been invaded. As if someone had crawled inside her, and taken, forcibly, things from her. She felt icy inside, and burning on the surface of her skin. "What the *hell* did you just do to me?"

She pushed herself up from the sofa but felt the room—
the watchers, the cameras—spin around her.

Her knees buckled beneath her, and she collapsed.

4

Julie lay on the couch in the green room—which was not
green at all, she noticed, glancing around at the pale walls—
and finally took a sip of the orange juice that had been offered by the assistant who had rushed in after they'd helped
her out of the studio's auditorium.

She looked up at her mother, who stood nearby. "Why did
you set this up?"

"Honey, I didn't. I really didn't. I'm sorry," Toni said. Her
mother's eyes were red from crying.

Julie closed her eyes and tried to push away the conscious
world. She had to force herself to breathe more slowly.
Counting four seconds in, four seconds out. For the first
time in her life, she understood what a panic attack might
feel like.

5

Once Julie felt strong enough to sit up in a chair, her
mother left to go wait in the car. The television people
brought some sandwiches in, and Mel cajoled her sister into
taking a bite "for energy."

"I can't believe he'd . . . he'd lie like that," Julie said.

"That's showbiz," Mel said. "Don't worry. I don't believe
a word of it. He's a con artist. Cute, but still a con artist."

"Did Mom set this all up?" Julie asked. *"Did she?"*

Mel shot her a harsh, unforgiving look, as if Julie had just
said something terrible.

6

When she was feeling better, she demanded to see Michael Diamond, and Diamond's assistant rushed her into his office, which was a suite of rooms down the long corridor.

He looked different to her than he had in the studio. He seemed older, and perhaps exhausted, as if he'd been up for several nights in a row. His hair was slicked back and his forehead had speckles of sweat. Something about his face reminded her of a hawk. She remembered the cover of his book, where his face seemed geeky-sexy. Now it just seemed tired. He sat on the edge of his desk, his hand extended for her to shake.

She kept her arms crossed.

"If you're so psychic, tell me what I'm thinking," she said.

"I'm sorry that was so harsh," Michael said. "I know you're in pain. Look, we'll cut the segment. Don't worry. It won't be televised."

She said, "What did you do to me in there?"

"You don't believe in psychic ability, Julie. I'm not here to change your mind. I'm sorry what I said hurt you in some way. I can't take it back. It happened. It's what I picked up from you," he said. "You know, sometimes I feel things that are terrible. I pick up images and words from someone on the show that I couldn't possibly verbalize. It would be too awful. It would be too painful for the person to hear. But something inside you wanted it to come out. What I said, what I saw inside you, Julie, wanted to come out."

While he'd been speaking, she felt as if she were being drawn to him. As if he had a level of charisma that went beyond normal charm or attraction. She felt she trusted him the way she trusted her therapist. When she took a deep breath, she tried to analyze the feeling, but could not.

"What was inside me?" Julie asked. "What did you see?"

"Just a glimpse," he said. "Of something terrible. I . . . I don't know what to tell you."

"If you're psychic, read my mind."

"It's not like that," he said. "Mrs. Hutchinson, you've got an aura of death around you. I'm sorry to say this. You've been touched by someone who died."

"That's easy enough to figure out," she said, feeling a bit harsh but happy to throw it back at him. "My husband died in April. That's what you were so glib about in front of your audience."

"No, this is a woman," he said. "Somehow, she's connected to you. She had answers for you but couldn't let them out."

7

She went out and got in the car. Mel was in the driver's seat, her mother in the back. "Don't talk to me," Julie said. "Just drive. I want to go home."

She could feel them making concerned faces to each other, but she was pissed off at everybody and fighting back the urge to cry like a baby. *I am not a two-year-old. This is all bullshit. Hut was not part of some psychic program. Michael Diamond is a grifter with a camera in his face and probably six ghostwriters writing his bullshit books. It was all a guessing game. He had seen Hut's obituary. He might've even heard about the murder. He had exposed himself already: in his book, hadn't he said about how, if a show had a waiting list, the psychic could research the people in the audience? He'd have their names, a phone number, an address. How hard was it to find Hut's obituary?*

8

That evening, Julie had another argument with her mother on the phone and accused her mother of setting her up for

Michael Diamond's show at a particularly vulnerable time in her life. As soon as she'd hung up, it rang again. Thinking it was her mother, she picked up and said, "I am not changing my mind."

"Hello?" a woman said on the other end.

"I'm sorry," Julie laughed. "I thought you were my mother."

"Mrs. Hutchinson?"

"Yes."

"I'm calling about Amanda Hutchinson," the woman said, and Julie placed the voice: it was Gigi Kaufmann, the social worker with the owl eyeglasses. "I'm afraid something tragic has happened."

Julie held her breath, waiting.

"She died. It was . . . well, she left a note. For you. Once the certificate is signed and everything has been put in order, we'll send it on to you."

chapter sixteen

1

A week later, after she got home, she checked the mail.
Bills for Comcast cable and Sprint, and there was some invitation to a health care forum in Montclair. Then a letter,
with the name Kaufmann on the return address.

She opened it up. It was a photocopy of the note that
Amanda Hutchinson had written the night she had killed
herself.

Dear Wife Number Two Julie Hutchinson,
If you're reading this, it's because my plan to some-
how jump out of this body worked. It's the warm
fuzzies. They fucked my brain up too much. They made
me think different. They made me remember things
wrong. Say things I don't always mean.
You knew Hut. But you didn't know him. You
thought he loved you. But I knew he didn't. It was all
because of the hand. Five fingers, all separate, but
they are all part of the hand. You can put your hand
down a garbage disposal and turn it on, and it can
tear into you and make your blood spurt up out of the

sink. But when you pull your arm out, the hand is still there. Do you understand?

You will see Hut. He will haunt you. He haunts me. Even in the warm fuzzies I see him. He has come back now and he will never let you or your daughter alone. Do you understand? Do I make myself clear? Don't hate the one who killed him. Sometimes, death is not the worst thing.

It's not that you can ever bury someone. Julie, there is no death. There is no death.

I am going to try to die. If I don't, you'll never see this note. If I do, you'll read it. Consider this my warning to you.

Worse than seeing Hut, Julie, is you may see the other ones, too. The fingers. They may be all around you, grasping. Because from you, something has come out. I knew when you visited me. Something is inside you and it's coming out, and they want that. It's something they can't have because of who they are. They are not dreams, Julie. They are real.

We kill our children so they can wake up, only they wake up somewhere else. And they shouldn't wake up. I should've killed Matt the night I tried to. I wish I had. He was already dead to me.

If I wake up from this, you'll know. But if I don't, thank God.

Love,

Amanda, Wife Number One.

2

Julie put the note down, folding it over. She had the urge to throw it out. It seemed obscene—insane and evil in a way she had never thought the written word could be. She felt a lump in her throat, thinking about Matt's mother. And how she was going to tell Matt. She had to do it.

She knew that if she didn't do it now, she'd lose her courage.

She found him at the kitchen table, with a microwaveable macaroni-and-cheese snack bowl, a carton of Jersey Farms milk next to his half-empty glass, and a jar of Ovaltine beside it.

She sat down next him.

"Yeah?" he asked, looking at her suspiciously.

"Matt, I've got some bad news." She felt her eyes tearing up.

"It's my mom," he said. "I know." He took up a forkful of mac and cheese, slipping it between his lips. "They called here earlier."

"I want you to know—" she began.

"Fuck it," he said. "She's been dead for years as far as I'm concerned. She tried to kill me. That's something you don't forget. She tried to set me on fire, Julie. She poured gasoline all over my body and tried to light me up. Do you think I'll ever forget that? Or how I was crying and asking her not to do it, and she just kept telling me I was from the devil and needed to go to hell. Do you think I care if she finally died?"

Julie couldn't control herself. "It's your *mother*," she said.

Seconds passed. He stared at her, his mouth a small O.

"I hate you, Julie. I hate you. Hate you," he spat. And then he began weeping, his shoulders heaving, and she drew close and held him tight, and no matter how he struggled, she wouldn't let go.

She whispered, "I'm sorry, I'm sorry, I'm sorry," and finally he stopped crying and kissed her on the cheek and told her he prayed every night that she would be his mother but was afraid that she'd leave him now that his dad was dead.

"You're my son," Julie whispered. "You and Livy are my children. Don't ever be afraid that I'll leave you."

3

Julie got in her car and just drove off. She knew she shouldn't leave Livy and Matt home like that. She knew that she should turn around, ten minutes into the drive, and go back home. What if something happened? Something unexpected? What if there was a gas leak? What if she'd forgotten to turn off the stove? What if . . .

Didn't matter. Drive. Just drive. Drive and be free.

She sped along the winding roads of Rellingford, down into the darkness alongside the lake, taking the curves too fast, unconcerned about pedestrians, windows down, her hair blowing back, feeling as if she were sixteen again and free of every obligation, every weight, every care.

She parked near the gap in the woods that was the beach. She took off her shoes in the car and walked barefoot out onto the grassy dirt patches that became fine sand, and then her bare feet felt the welcome chill of the lake as she waded in. Across the lake, the lights of houses. The richer people of Rellingford lived on that side of the lake, in houses that cost a fortune. It was like seeing a string of pearls along the throat of night.

She unbuttoned her shirt and took it off, then unzipped her dress, slipping out of it, getting it wet in the process.

Then her bra, and finally her underwear.

She tossed them back to the shore.

The mugginess of the evening clung to her naked form. She felt alive in a way she hadn't in months. She stepped forward deeper into the water.

Another step.

Another.

She put out of her mind the snapping turtles and the fresh-water eels and snakes and any of what Livy would call the squirmies, and went farther into the water until she was up to her neck. It was so dark that she felt as if there were no separation between the water and the woods and the sky, and she dipped her head beneath the surface of the water.

Coolness.

Up again to breathe, to gasp.

The lights across the water.

She saw the faint prickles of stars in the dark sky above, and as she kept watch on the sky, they seemed to come out by the hundreds and thousands.

It had been years since she'd looked up at the stars. Years since she'd swum in this lake that was less than a quarter mile from her house.

Years since she'd felt young.

And she remembered:

She and Hut had been talking divorce. Well, she had been—he had ignored her. He had told her she needed therapy. He had told her that she needed to start taking antidepressants. He had told her she needed to quit the job at the ER and be a better mother.

They had been fighting.

The last three years had felt like hell to her, but she'd put up with it for Livy. For Livy and Matt both, and for the shred of memory of love she still carried.

Somehow, it had all been wiped away in the murder.

Somehow, her mind had changed the bad memories to good.

Somehow, she'd turned Hut into a saint after his death.

He was a difficult, complex man. And she'd loved him as much as she could, until he had turned mean, and cold, and unfeeling.

And the day she saw him strike his own son, she had been planning to leave him and somehow get Matt away from him.

All pushed aside, blocked, when he'd been murdered.

And the touch of one man had opened it, like an old Christmas present at the back of a closet, forgotten, hidden, pushed aside, and then drawn out into the light of day, its wrapper torn back. Michael Diamond. He was a bullshitter. But he knew things. How had he known? How had he been able to know about Amanda's death?

Julie walked back to shore, dressed, and hurried back to her car.

At home, in bed, she stayed up late, reading Diamond's book *The Life Beyond.*

4

She had an eleven a.m. with Eleanor Swanson, who wanted to meet at Julie's house. "My office is being redecorated by the group," Eleanor explained when she arrived.

"The group?"

"The Seven Arts Medical Association. Every five years they decide they need a different look and redo the offices, and suddenly I'm paying more in rent."

"Oh." Julie smiled and set a cup of coffee down on the table in front of Eleanor.

"Thank you, dear," Eleanor said. "I'm glad we could meet here. I'd have suggested my house, but it's a mess right now."

"It's nice to do this here," Julie said. They talked a bit about the heat and vacations, and then Julie said, "I have to talk to you about these sexual dreams."

"Still going on?"

"They've intensified, Eleanor. I mean, they're full of perversions and things that I'd never do."

"Hut's in them?"

"Sometimes it's Hut. Sometimes not."

"Well, what's disturbing about them?"

"It's like I close my eyes. And suddenly they just begin. It's a roller coaster."

Eleanor nodded. "Maybe you need a little something to help you sleep."

"I've tried sleeping pills. I have a prescription. But it doesn't take them away."

"I'm not much of a conventional therapist. I'm no good at just sitting and listening. If I think I can help, I'll try to bring my insights to this. You're in your mid-thirties, you lost your husband. By your own account, you don't consider yourself to be very sexual. Now I think your subconscious is making up for lost time. Sure, there might be disturbing or—as you put it—perverted elements to the dreams. But all of us have them. All of us have pent-up fantasies that now and then become unleashed in our dream life. Women peak sexually after thirty. You're right on schedule. Part of this is you're horny. The way every adult human being gets, particularly when they're lonely."

"But it's not as if I enjoy them."

"Don't you?"

Julie stared at her. "They're horrible. Some of them."

"But you've told me all along they're erotic."

"Yes, but . . . there are things in them . . ."

"What things?"

Julie hesitated. She crossed one leg over the other, leaning back in her chair. She looked up at the ceiling. "There's a kind of cruelty to them. There's a meanness. In them, Hut is dead. I mean, dead. A corpse. His eyes are . . . well, they're not human. And there's a woman—with red hair—who . . . who . . ."

"Ah," Eleanor said. "You've been holding out on me."

"I couldn't say it before. I just couldn't."

"You experience pleasure in these dreams, but you feel

guilt because Hut is dead, even in the dream. And jealousy, too, of this other woman. Thus, they're cruel and mean."

"Even when he's making love to me," Julie said. "It's like necrophilia or something." Suddenly, she asked, "I'm not some nut who thinks he's trying to speak to me from the great beyond or anything. I mean, you don't believe that kind of thing, do you?"

Eleanor wore a half smile. It was a God smile, and her eyes were God eyes. "Why would you ask that?"

"I . . . well, my mother took me to this psychic . . ."

"Oh." Eleanor wrinkled her nose as if she smelled a fart.

"He told me that someone who was lost was looking for me. And that doors in my mind were locked, and needed opening . . . and other stuff."

Eleanor smirked. She lifted her cup and took a sip of coffee. Glanced up midsip, like an amused parent. "Sometimes mysticism helps people get through grief. Did it help?"

"I don't know. I just . . . these dreams feel like . . . Sometimes, I think it's like he's not really gone. Until I wake up."

"Julie, dreams are just dreams. It's the mind sifting through things. We can do some more work here, if you want. But recognize that you're working through guilt and anger and shame and fury and fear. All the things that accompany the death of a loved one."

"Did I really love him? I'm not even sure."

"See? Even now you're expressing a perfectly normal anxiety. Don't fight the dreams. Don't fight what you're going through. Follow it. Go on a journey. Celebrate life when you can, but let your subconscious work through what it needs to. Now, tell me about this visit to the fortune-teller."

Julie told her about the TV studio, and Eleanor said, "Oh. Of course! One of those TV people. It's great showbiz to do what they do. Do you know the technique? There's a way to anticipate what people will say next, just from eye movement and very minor facial movement. But you can't believe that nonsense. It's not rational. Do you believe it?"

Julie frowned. "I don't think so. It just seemed . . . true."

"Maybe there's something to it. I just can't say. My favorite is John Edward. He's adorable." Eleanor grinned ear to ear. God and Earth Mother converged for a moment. "Do you ever watch him? I don't often, because I just hate seeing mysticism being promoted like that. It's not my thing. But you can believe what you like. I don't mean you're wrong. Or even that they're wrong. I just don't think it's true myself. Did you learn anything valuable from this guy?"

Julie shook her head. She didn't want to talk about it anymore. It felt too private, even for Eleanor.

5

Julie went online that night and ordered a few of Michael Diamond's books on tape from Shocklines.com, a bookseller that sold occult, horror, and other strange books. She also found his book called *Unlocking Dreams*, and ordered that one, too.

Within three days, the tapes and book arrived. She went out jogging with her Walkman hooked up, listening to his book called *The Mind's Journey*. When she drove Livy to Dr. Fishbain's in Ramapo Cliffs, she kept the book on the tape player in the car and sat in the parking lot, listening, while Livy had her appointment.

6

From *The Mind's Journey*:

"Some have called this astral projection. That, to me, implies mystical, magical places and other dimensions. Remote viewing is something that seems anything but magical to those who do it. Your consciousness roams. At first, it just rises up from your body, after meditation and relaxation of the body have been achieved. It remains near you, mainly because you fear this new ability. Then, as you get used to it, your mind—or your mind's eye, as I like to think of it—moves outward, exploring. As you become braver, it goes farther. Then the view is like a wide-angle lens. Peripheral vision is out of focus, but the central vision is nearly normal, with some distortion. I liken it to being slightly drunk—you swing around a bit, you move in fits and starts. But it is simply consciousness, projected outward."

7

In the night, Julie awoke to the sense that someone else was in her room. She half expected it to be Matt, because she was sure it was a man.

After several minutes, she was wide awake enough to sit up. She flicked on the bedside lamp to dispel the shadows. No one there.

She turned the lamp off. Pressed her hands into her forehead. A terrible headache had come on.

She rose to go to the connecting bathroom to get some aspirin and a glass of water. In the dark, she fumbled through the medicine cabinet for the aspirin, and when she shut the cabinet mirror, she saw Hut.

His face.

He stood there.

She was too terrified to turn.

Her throat went dry, and she dropped the aspirin bottle into the sink.

She leaned over, clutching the rim of the sink, staring at him in the mirror.

His eyes were not the milky white that they had been in

her nightmares. They were normal. Even in the dark she could tell that.

He looked just as he had the morning before he'd died.

She raised a fist and slammed it into the bathroom mirror, cutting the edge of her hand. *Don't believe. Don't. It's a dream. It's a nightmare. It's your mind fucking with you because some part of you doesn't want to look at his death. Some part of you is resisting the idea that he's gone. Some part of you feels guilty because you didn't love him enough. You didn't make yourself available to him enough. You weren't a good enough wife. You're not a good enough mother. You are punishing yourself.*

She felt a panic—a sense of insanity inside her mind, of hallucinations brought on by stress and grief—or else it was some trigger inside her that had been pulled tight and then released. For a moment, she felt as if she were dreaming, because that would seem all right.

But it was no dream.

She struggled to reach the light switch by the door, sure that at any second, the dread she felt would somehow stop her heart from beating.

The light came up in the bathroom.

The only thing behind her was the photo collage of their first few years together, with Matt and Livy at the tidal pool in La Jolla, with Livy with her gramma, and Matt's sixth-grade class picture.

No one.

She was alone.

The mirror on the cabinet, cracked like a spider's web.

The blood on the edge of her palm was real enough.

She opened the cabinet again and brought out the brown bottle of hydrogen peroxide. She got a cotton swab and dipped it into a capful of the peroxide, and then pressed it lightly on her cut. She washed it off, then swabbed, then washed, and then pressed toilet paper against it to stop the slight flow of blood.

She couldn't sleep the rest of the night. The following night, she stayed up reading more of Michael Diamond's books and re-reading sections she'd only skimmed of *The Life Beyond*.

8

Joe Perrin and his husband came out to the burbs one Sunday when the weather was perfect, and they had a little barbeque out on the patio. Burgers and corn on the cob, and Rick brought some great French wine from the store in the Chelsea Market. Their big friendly German shepherd, Dutch, which both Matt and Livy took to right away, had come along, too. After the meal and some retreading of old memories, Julie sent the kids to play with the dog in the front yard, and Rick opened the wine.

Joe and Julie and Rick hung out on the picnic table, blue plastic cups in hand, looking over the back lawn, beyond the neighbor's house to the dip down the hill and the bit of lake they could see through the trees. They talked about anything and everything, and eventually, the third or fourth cup of wine in, Julie brought up Michael Diamond and Amanda Hutchinson.

"Joe, he said I had a connection with her. A woman. And then, Hut's first wife is dead."

"Sounds psychic to me," Rick said, grinning.

"Oh, you," Joe said. "Rick doesn't believe in it."

"It's nonsense. Julie, if we could get into each other's minds, wouldn't we have solved the greatest problem in the world?"

"What's that?" Joe asked.

"The distance between two human minds," Rick said. "If we could really get inside somebody's head, would we have wars? Would we need territory? Wouldn't we understand each other so well that we'd just support and help everybody?"

"Rick's theory of the benevolent universe," Joe laughed. "No, Ricky, I think if some of us got inside the heads of people around them, we'd probably try to manipulate things. Take control. Turn people into, I don't know, love slaves. I mean, I'm saying this as if I were single, so don't take it personally, honey, but if I could get inside other guys' heads, I'd just have them take off their clothes and dance around for me all day long and do my wicked bidding."

Julie grinned, having drunk a little too much wine. "If I could get inside people's minds, I'd probably try to get them all to give me a dollar. All I'd need would be a million people, and then nobody would be hurt, would they?"

"You think people are greedy," Rick said, nodding.

"No, I think *I'm* greedy," Julie said. "My point is, if I were psychic, I'd do all kinds of things. And I think I'm a nice person."

"So do I, baby," Joe said, lifting his plastic cup in a toast. "Just imagine if the people who aren't so nice could do this. Well, maybe they'd all become the Michael Diamonds of the world."

"I just don't buy it at all," Rick said. "It's like believing in ghosts. Once you open up yourself to that kind of magical thinking, you'll swallow anything."

"I believe in it," Joe said. "With some restrictions. I don't believe that a psychic can really see anything you don't want them to. I think our own minds can block things."

"Hon, I love you, but that's magical thinking," Rick said. "That's like, if I think about flowers, suddenly I'll get flowers."

"It is not," Joe said, ticked off. "Maybe you should consider things outside of your narrow view."

They got quiet too suddenly.

Julie reached out and touched Joe's hand. "I don't know if I believe in this stuff or not. But I could've dismissed everything that happened with Michael Diamond, except that he told me that Hut's ex had died. I don't know. I feel like I'm becoming surrounded by all this psychic crap. From the whole thing about the school Hut went to, to this."

"What school?" Joe asked.

"Oh. God. I feel a little awkward talking about it. My husband was tested for psychic ability as a kid. In some program. It's all been news to me. I guess that's why I was willing to see Diamond. Hut must've wanted to put it all in the past. He did that a lot. He put his first wife in the past. He put his adoptive parents in the past. I think he may have even been ready to put me in the past. It all gets confused in my head. I see things sometimes now. I have these . . . delusions. Hut's death may just have been too much for me. But . . . he was who he was. And I need to get on, right?"

"Right," Joe said.

"But give yourself a lot of time to heal, Julie. Don't short-change this process," Rick said.

"You sound like my therapist."

"Dr. Rick," Joe laughed, swatting his partner lightly. Then he said, "So Hut had secrets. I knew it. He was a man of mystery."

"He was. I'm not even sure how much to believe. My mom sent me some stuff. Our government sometimes gave these aptitude tests when kids showed some unusual ability."

"The remote viewing tests," Joe said. "I read about them. In the *Fortean Times*. They were cut off around the Gulf War in the nineties. But they go back a ways."

"Really? You read about them?"

"It never amounted to much. But a lot of tax dollars were spent."

"Wasted, is more like it," Rick said. "Just like I don't believe God came down from the sky and made a virgin get pregnant and I don't believe that vampires get up out of their tombs at night to suck blood, I don't believe this stuff. I think human life is rough enough without these . . . popular delusions."

"You told me you were skeptical," Joe said. "I didn't know you thought I was delusional."

"Baby, not you. I respect your beliefs. I just don't believe this stuff."

With this social stalemate threatening to bring storm clouds, Julie suddenly got the idea that they should get the croquet set out and get the kids playing in the front yard. It helped break the brief, slightly drunken tension between Rick and Joe, and Dutch, the dog, loved chasing after the croquet ball.

9

Rick and Joe were staying in the guest room, and when everybody was getting ready for bed, Rick pointed to the little night-lights in the hall. "What's with all the night-lights?"

Julie was in the bathroom with Livy, both of them brushing their teeth in the mirror, Livy standing up on the footstool that allowed her to get up high enough for the sink and mirror. After Julie rinsed, she said, "It's because it's too dark at night."

"It's for me," Livy said. "I see a ghost sometimes."

10

Right on schedule, Julie's erotic dream took her over when she fell asleep.

The dead man who was not quite Hut turned her on her

stomach. He began licking from the nape of her neck down to her shoulder blades, following the slight knobs of her spine, his tongue wet and flickering as he tasted her skin. He held her wrists back with his hands, and he went lower, and when he reached the dip in her back, just before the rise in her buttocks, he made a slow long circle there and bit slightly down on her cheek before his mouth went between the cleft.

She moaned into the pillow, but she was not in her bed but on a dirty mattress in what seemed like a dungeon, with gray stone walls around her and what looked like metal instruments of torture hanging from the ceiling.

He licked her inside and out, up and down. Every part of her below the waist grew moist and warm with his ministrations.

Then he rose over her, hefting his weight onto her back until she felt crushed and her breath came hard to her, and then he entered her from behind, first in one orifice, then another. She felt a burning sensation. Oh, but it felt good, and the dead man whispered in her ears, his spit sliding just inside her earlobe, "Do you want me inside you, Julie? Do you? Do you want me all the way in? Every way? I want to open you. I want to open you up, Julie."

And she opened her mouth wide to say yes, but a muffled sound came from her that was not quite her voice.

Then, someone said, too loud, "Julie? Julie?"

11

Julie looked up in the dark. A man stood there. Her eyes adjusted, and she reached for the bedside lamp, fear pulsing through her.

Flicked the light up.

It was Joe, wearing a San Francisco 49ers T-shirt that went all the way to his knees. "Are you okay?"

"Joe? Joe—what's wrong?"

"You were screaming," he said. "In your sleep."

Then Julie realized that she lay there naked, the covers thrown off the bed, her pajama bottoms pulled down around her ankles. Quickly, Joe looked away, and Julie reached for the bedspread, pulling it up over herself.

chapter seventeen

1

After Rick and Joe and the dog left for the city again, Livy asked to talk to her in private. Julie went with her to her room, and Livy shut the door behind her.

"What's up?" Julie asked.

"He came into my room last night," Livy said.

"Who?"

"Daddy."

"Honey, it's not Daddy. You know that."

"It is," Livy said. "But he told me you wouldn't believe me. He told me he was going to come for his family and that he loves all of us and not to cry."

"Livy, it was a dream you had."

"Maybe," Livy said, looking at her curiously as if she didn't believe a word that her mother said.

"There's nothing to be scared of. We have the burglar alarm. We have the NannyCam. Don't be frightened by these dreams. You're safe."

"I'm not scared anymore," Livy said. Then she opened her bedroom door again and went down the hall to the bath-room, shutting the door behind her.

Julie sat down on Livy's narrow bed and looked up at the

NannyCam on the bookshelf by the door. She grabbed the videotape from the previous night.

2

She fast-forwarded through the tape of the hallway Nanny-Cam. Joe and Rick stumbled back and forth to the bathroom at the end of the hall. Matt got up to use it. And then nothing. Nothing. Nothing. Empty hall. Bedroom doors either shut or slightly ajar.

And then a movement through the hall.

Julie felt her heart leap into her throat. Adrenaline pumped through her veins. She paused it, looking to make sure that it wasn't somehow Joe or Rick. It was someone else.

It was a dark shadow moving in the hallway, obscuring the night-lights as it went.

It passed Livy's bedroom.

It kept going down the hall.

Straight down the hall to Julie's room, pushing the door open slightly.

Then the shadow passed into her room.

It could not have been a shadow, she knew. It was someone. Some man.

Some stranger had gotten into her house and had gone into her bedroom.

And then the NannyCam's videotape went to static as if it had shut off prematurely.

3

She checked the burglar alarm, made sure it was operational. Checked all windows. Double-checked the locks on the doors. Grilled both Matt and Livy when they got home from school, but she didn't tell them what she'd seen.

Then she asked Matt to move the wires and the videotape equipment for the NannyCam to her bedroom. They put it all on her dresser, to the left of her bed, and aimed for a shot of her entire bed. Then the other one on the doorway. When Matt asked what it was about, she told him it was just an experiment to see when she snored because she had to see if it was sleep apnea or not. He didn't quite get it, but he didn't ask her too many more questions after that.

She didn't fall asleep until five a.m., because every time she started to close her eyes and drift off, she thought she heard a noise and woke up. She ended up sleeping all day, and then getting up that night to try it again.

The next night, she had trouble sleeping again. She took an Ambien, and had a glass of the wine that Rick and Joe had left behind. *Sleeping aid and booze*, she thought. *Nice descent into pathetic, Julie.*

That night, she had the dream of the dead man again, lifting her up, her legs around his waist as he pierced her, and she opened for him and he entered her deeply and she felt as if she had been plugged up, that she had no opening, and he took his fingers and pushed them into her mouth and she tasted his skin and in the dream she kept telling herself it was a nightmare and she had to wake up, she had to wake up right now!

4

Later the next day, she fast-forwarded the video, watched herself finish off the glass of wine and lie down.

And then, when the clock's display read 3:00 a.m., a shadow moved into the room.

She could not see more than his dark form—his body was so much like Hut's, it shocked her—and his face was darkness. He came to her bedside, putting his face near hers. Then he slowly slipped a hand beneath the covers and drew it back, exposing her in her pajamas. Then he ran his hand down along her breast, squeezing lightly. She shivered as she watched it.

Slowly—it might've taken him a half hour—he unbuttoned her top and unlaced her bottoms, pulling them both off while she slept, moving slightly.

When he had her naked, he pressed his mouth against her forehead while his hands roamed down over her breasts, and then farther down, between her legs. He pressed his hand into her, and the sleeping Julie lifted her hips to him.

"Fuck," Julie said aloud, watching this, not believing it, her mind spinning out of control.

Then he brought his hand back up to her mouth and pressed his fingers between her lips. It looked like the sleeping Julie sucked at his hand. Then he went to her breasts, taking each nipple in his mouth. For the flicker of a second, she was sure that he was looking straight at the NannyCam lens, knowing that he was being watched.

Then he kissed down past her navel and went to her pubic hair. He moved around so that he crouched over her. He was naked. His penis was hard and long and poised over her mouth as his own face went between her legs.

Julie paused the tape, freezing it. She felt as if she were having a heart attack. She felt as if she had been raped, but wasn't sure if she could really believe what she was seeing. It was like this was a tape not of her bedroom, but of her dreams, of what she experienced in them.

She hit PLAY, and the tape continued.

The man's head went between her legs and moved around in circles as he dipped and wiped his penis across her face. Sleeping Julie opened her mouth and took him inside her. His buttocks began pumping against her face while he lapped at her.

Then, after minutes, he drew out of her mouth and sat up beside her on the bed. Looking straight at the NannyCam, he rolled her over onto her stomach. He got down on all fours and began licking down her back, to her buttocks—as she had remembered from the dream—and then he pressed himself deep into her, and sleeping Julie cried out into the pillow, and he had his face next to her, against her ear, and she cried out again, and his buttocks pounded harder into sleeping Julie.

And then the tape went to static.

PART THREE

chapter eighteen

1

She rewound the tape several times and watched it slowly and quickly and backward in parts. She tried to get close to the Sony Trinitron to see if she could make out a face. At first, she'd felt horror at watching it, then she was fascinated and confused. She cried on one viewing of it, because though she felt raped she didn't understand how it could be because she looked as if she were going along with it. After all, although her eyes seemed closed—she couldn't quite tell—it looked like the sleeping Julie opened her mouth on command for him. It looked like the sleeping Julie was fine with rolling over. There was no struggle.

Watching it, she grew increasingly angry, and finally turned it off and drew the tape out. She called up Mel and told her about it, and Mel suggested that she call the police. "What if it's the man who killed Hut?" Mel asked. "What if he somehow drugged you."

"With Ambien?"

"You never know how this stuff works," Mel said. Then she regaled Julie with the story of a teenaged daughter of a friend who was drugged with something called the date rape drug and was conscious through the whole horrible ordeal.

The family brought charges, and the boy responsible was behind bars. Then Mel interrupted herself: "I'll be over in half an hour."

Mel came by, and Julie reluctantly popped the video into the machine and pushed PLAY on the remote control. When the video played, everything was the same as before—with the clock reading three a.m.—but there was no dark figure coming into the room at all. Instead, Julie threw off the covers and began taking her nightclothes off. Once she was naked, she began stroking her nipples. Then, she licked her left hand and reached down between her legs.

"Oh my God," Julie said, and turned off the tape.

Mel sat there and stared for a few seconds at the television screen. She looked over at Julie.

"Mel, I swear to God, that is not what was on the tape before."

Mel offered up a warm look, and she looked too much like their mother at that moment. "Julie? What's going on?"

"That was not what I saw. I saw a man. I saw . . . Hut," she said it aloud finally. Something in her mind cleared. "I slept through it last night. But I know I saw him."

"You know what we both just saw on that tape," Mel said in a too-sympathetic tone. "Why would you tape yourself like that?"

"Mel, you know I'd never do that."

"All I know is I didn't see Hut in it, Julie. Hut is dead. He was murdered. I know that's hard to face. Look, I love you. You're my sister. We're best friends. I have nothing against anyone getting their jollies from innocent stuff, but . . . I didn't expect this. Are you doing okay? Is that therapist helping you through all this? I've seen the house. I know it's a lot to keep up with, but have you looked around? I can only come over and help so much, Julie," Mel said, her hand laid gently on Julie's arm.

2

Mel told her to rest, that she'd take the kids for a few days, but bring them over after supper so Julie could get some peace and do whatever it was that "will make you whole again." She lectured her that she needed to somehow face herself, deal with life as it was, "the hand that fate dealt." Mel talked a blue streak about shirking responsibility and getting back on your feet, about her work at the hospital and planning on the future happening even if Julie wanted to remain behind, and it just went on and on. Julie listened, nodded at the appropriate times, but began to resent Mel, resent her family, resent Hut and his death and the cops who couldn't catch the guy who'd killed him, and even resent Rick and Joe and their oh-so-perfect coupledom. Finally she just told Mel to leave, that she was getting a headache and they could talk about this later.

Then Julie wandered the house, room to room, looking at it in a way she hadn't in a long time. There was dust and dirt where the kids had brought it in from outside. Hadn't she cleaned up for Joe and Rick? Perhaps she'd been preoccupied. The kitchen was filled with dishes and glasses piled in the sink. There were three dirty saucepans on the stove, some stains around the counter, and empty soda cans near the toaster. That wasn't too bad. She wasn't much of a housekeeper, but she hadn't even called in the cleaning service in weeks to help out. She saw piles of clothes on the washing machine, and more piles as she passed the kids' rooms. In the corner of Livy's room, her T-shirts and shorts from the summer lay in a heap. The whole house seemed dull and gray.

She went into her bedroom and for the first time felt as if it were stuffy. She went to open the windows and then saw her own clothes on the other side of her bed. In her bathroom, the medicine cabinet's mirror was still broken. She hadn't even thought of going to Home Depot to get another one. And she had done so little shopping in the past week that she wasn't even sure if the kids had snacks or if they had what they needed for the first weeks of the schoolyear. Mel had taken up the slack, and she supposed Matt had done some of it, too.

What was wrong with her? She looked at her cracked image in the mirror and wondered what it was that made her see a man who in the dark looked very much like Hut, having sex with her while she slept, forcing himself into her and against her body. And yet somehow later she instead saw a video of herself masturbating. What had brought her to this? she wondered.

She lay down on the bed, but could not stop looking over at the NannyCam's metal eye, watching her.

How can someone put an image in my head like that? Make me see it on a video that changed when someone else saw it?

She got up and tried calling her mother, but couldn't reach her. Next she called Michael Diamond's office, but tracking him down was next to impossible.

Julie couldn't bring herself to watch the tape again until after she'd had more wine. She watched it again, and this time it was exactly as she'd seen it with her sister: she was masturbating alone in bed, and the room seemed to have more moonlight in it, for she could tell that her eyes were not closed. They were open. She felt disgusted with her own body, watching this. She felt as if a nerve were pinched inside her mind as she tried to make sense out of this—out of the dreams, out of the tapes, out of seeing things that weren't there. Seeing things that could not be there.

She had two choices: she was either losing her mind, or this was something else entirely that she couldn't fathom how to explain.

3

Her laptop open on her bed, she connected the cable and went online. She pulled up some search engines—Google and Hotbot and Yahoo—and began searching for the terms "school," "psychic," "remote viewing," and "1977," hoping this would come up with something. In each case, there were pages upon pages of listings, and she scrolled up and down the screen, taking a stab at each listing or mention. None of it seemed to point to anything helpful.

After about an hour of searching, she nearly gave up, but came upon a link to a Web page that didn't have much on the surface—mainly just a mention that there had been a sleep study for psychic ability in the 1970s in Los Angeles, and it had been completely unsuccessful. In the brief article, the writer referred to the "legendary scandal of Project Daylight."

McGuane had said that Hut went to the Daylight Project.

Julie saved this page, and opened a new browser window, looking up the words "Project Daylight," "remote viewing," and "New York."

Nearly one hundred references came up for these search terms. It completely surprised her.

She began clicking links. All seemed to go to conspiracy-theory-type sites. Some of the sites dealt with paranormal phenomena, some with urban legends, some with UFOs. When she found mention of Project Daylight, she also found mention of a sleep study of children with sleep disorders—whether "night fears" or general insomnia. Each Web site she visited seemed to have a different piece of this puzzle about Project Daylight. Brief mentions, like "Nobody really knows about Project Daylight, other than that a fire destroyed the house where the research took place." That was really the most definitive statement she could find. There were at least twenty children in the program, and many of them had come from the foster care system. One of the children had shown what was called an "advanced PSI ability." She wasn't quite sure what PSI meant, other than psychic and a variant on the acronym ESP. In due course, she found its definition, and it did, indeed, refer to paranormal ability such as clairvoyance, telepathy, psychometry, and psychokinesis. She knew the first two terms, but was unsure of psychometry or psychokinesis, but she could take a wild guess.

The Chelsea Parapsychological Institute kept coming up as a connection with the Daylight Project. She looked it up, too, and found that the institute had shut down in the early 1980s, although it gave their old address.

It was the building on Rosetta Street.

Sixth floor of the building.

66S. Sixth floor, sixth apartment, letter S.

And she found out something else about the Chelsea Parapsychological Institute.

It had been run by a retired colonel in the army who had once worked in military intelligence. A man named Alan Diamant.

She remembered something in Michael Diamond's book about his father.

4

She sat at the kitchen table, with Diamond's books open. She skimmed pages, trying to remember where he mentioned his dad. Then she remembered. It was the first thing she'd read. She opened *The Life Beyond* and scanned the introduction.

She found it:

"My own father died several years ago, and if you looked up his name online or through public records, you'd eventually find out that he was a colonel in the army, that he served in Vietnam, that he worked in military intelligence and then as a liaison in Bosnia even in retirement."

5

Back at her laptop, Julie did a search on terms she thought most likely to come up with an obituary of a man named Alan Diamant. It took her three tries, adding search terms each time. Finally, an obituary from 1982 showed up as part of the online archives for the *Journal for Paranormal Research of America*. It had all the particulars: colonel in the army, Vietnam, went from military intelligence to applied research to parapsychology to founding—and funding—the Chelsea Parapsychological Institute (CPI) for the decade of its existence. Married, divorced, remarried, divorced again, mention of the closing of the CPI, mention of two children. No mention of cancer, as Michael Diamond had indicated in his book, but rather his death was attributed to "the result of an accident." There was a picture accompanying the obituary of Alan Diamant in his late twenties, in uniform. The obituary turned into an article about founders of various paranormal groups, and there was mention of government supervisions of certain programs.

That was it.

"It doesn't mean it's his father," Joe Perrin told her when she called him up. "Even if it is . . ."

"If it is, he might know about Hut. If Hut was there. If any of this matters," she said. "Joe, you told me you believe in this kind of thing. I've experienced something recently."

"A ghost?" His voice carried with it a half joke in the word, as if he were uneasy mentioning it.

"I don't know. A phenomenon of some kind that would make any sane person start drinking and any insane person start jumping out windows," she said, completing his joke to keep it light.

"I believe in ghosts," Joe said. "And I know about our government-backed programs for remote viewing. I've read too many articles about it not to believe it. It's tough believing they might've used kids, but if it was a sleep study, maybe they did."

"I'm going to ask him."

"You got balls." Joe laughed, but she didn't. His comment reminded her too much of something Amanda said to her.

"Well, even if it's not his father, he told me that I should come talk to him. Maybe he's psychic. I'm just beginning to push to that side of things."

"Belief?"

"Or being open to this. Given everything that's going on. And maybe Alan Diamant knows something. Maybe he was there. If your dad runs a parapsychological foundation, it's pretty likely that you may grow up to be a psychic," she said. "Right?"

"I don't know. Maybe. But Diamant is a different name than Diamond."

"I don't know. It's not so different," she said. "Maybe he's ashamed of his father. Or maybe the name Diamond is just more . . ."

"Hollywood," Joe completed her thought. "He's cubic zirconium. Diamonds are not always a girl's best friend."

"Ha," she said.

"Don't forget me when you're in the city," Joe said before they hung up. "I'll do some snooping around in all these books and magazines I've got piled up. Do you want a psychic reading? I can ask my friend Lauren. She's excellent."

6

She decided to tape one more night. She went to Matt and asked about his camcorder. Could it be set up with a timer? Yes. Could he set it up so that it could shoot a reasonably de-

cent video in the dark? Yes. Could she then take the DVD
and put it right into the computer without him seeing it? Yes.
This time she intended to be drugged out of her mind with
whatever substance could knock her out. She had an old bottle of whiskey in the liquor cabinet that she and Hut never
drank, but she knew it was the good stuff. She took a few
swigs before going to bed, very late, and then lay down on
her bed. This time she kept her clothes on—her shirt and
jeans and a sweater.

She drank three small glasses of whiskey and sat up late
into the night and when sleep came, it was deep.

In the morning, she took the NannyCam tapes and
watched them, and there was nothing. Same for the camcorder's DVD. She tried it for three more nights. Nothing.
Nothing.

The fourth night was the charm.

7

Although the visuals were too shadowy in the NannyCam
tapes, Matt's camcorder had night-vision technology, and
she saw the dark of her room with greenish glows. And the
green-black figure of a man. His face so much like Hut's it
made her gasp.

As she watched, she again had the feeling that the man
was looking at her watching him. Knowing that she would
watch him hours later. Knowing that she would see this
videotape.

He went to where the camcorder was set on the tripod and
looked directly into the camera. It was Hut. The video was
dark and glowing green and grainy, but there was no doubt
about it. He seemed to be trying to say something, but there
was no sound on the video. Then he fumbled with the camera. He lifted it up, and now he had it in his hands and was
filming the bedroom. Filming her. With one hand, he unbut-

toned her sweater, and then unbuttoned her shirt beneath. He spread the material apart and pressed his hand in the brief gap between her breasts. He kept the camera focused on where his hand went. He delicately drew back each side of her shirt, exposing her breasts, and then put his fingers around the nipple of her right breast and twisted it slightly. He cupped her breast in his hand, then drew the camera back.

He continued to undress her with dexterity, filming each movement he made.

When he had her completely naked, he put his hand between her knees and pushed them apart. Then he put the camera there, close enough that she could see herself—and he began stroking her there, between her legs, all the while keeping the camera focused where his fingers played.

She couldn't watch it anymore. She shut it off. Covered her face in her hands. She couldn't even conjure tears.

8

"I'd like to speak with Eleanor Swanson," Julie said, holding the cell phone close to her face.

Eleanor's assistant told her that she was out for a few days. "Just a brief holiday," he said. "If it's an emergency, I can make sure she has your message before the end of the day."

Julie paused, and then said, "No, it's all right. I'll call her when she gets back."

Then she made a call to Michael Diamond's office. They gave her the runaround and put her on hold twice before she gave up. She made sure all the doors and windows were closed and locked, checked the burglar alarm and got in the Camry and drove to the city.

In the backseat of the car, she'd tossed copies of *The Mind's Journey* and *The Life Beyond.*

chapter nineteen

1

"I'm sorry," the woman at the front guard desk said, looking at her with what Julie assumed was the kind of sizing up security guards needed to do if they smelled a stalker. "His show tapes Mondays and Tuesdays. If you'd like to get tickets, the ticket window is—"

"I'm not here to get tickets," Julie said, and then left abruptly. She got a bagel and bad coffee from a street vendor, and stood on the corner of Fifty-third and Sixth Avenue, wondering when she had transitioned from a widow to a stalker.

On her cell phone, she dialed the studio, and got a recording, and on the recording was an 800 number for buying Michael Diamond's books and tapes. She called it and got an operator.

"I need to reach him," she said.

"I'm sorry. We're a warehouse fulfillment service," the man said on the phone.

She hung up.

Then she opened the book and looked at the last few pages. Diamond was shilling his tapes and books and seminars and . . . consultations.

She called the number listed for the consultations. "I'd like a consultation. But I want it immediately."

"I'm sorry," the young woman said, her voice practically a chirp. "Mr. Diamond has a waiting list. The consultation price is two thousand dollars for one hour, and I can put you down for . . . how's October twelfth?"

"Listen. I don't care about his schedule. You tell him—or his handlers—that this is Julie Hutchinson. The woman he had on the show recently. The one who he told that someone would die. That person died. You tell him that if I don't see him, and fast, I'm bringing a lawsuit down on his head that will ruin him forever."

2

He agreed to meet her at a restaurant called Pastis that was just outside the Village, toward Chelsea, in the meat-packing district. They sat outside, the restaurant's awning shielding them from the sun. She ordered steak frites, and he ordered beans on toast and a glass of white wine.

"So, you're threatening me," he said.

"I had to see you."

"I know."

"What . . . what was that all about?"

"In the studio? It's what I do. I viewed you."

"Viewed?"

"Call it a Vulcan mind meld. That's how I thought of it when I was a teenager. I go inside people sometimes. It's like possession, I guess, only I'm not a ghost. It's my mind—it's not magic. It's a genetic mutation, I think. My grandmother had this, too. You know, I thought you hated my guts after our session."

"I did. But . . . you said things that . . . well, they were accurate. I had buried them, but they were true. I've never admitted them to anyone. Not my mother, my sister, not my kids."

"I know."

"You know all?"

"No, I don't. I know very little in fact. What you consider normal intuition—I've got zero. Truthfully, if I didn't have this ability—we call it Ability X—I'd be a bum on the street. In fact, I was, for several years. It goes in and out, depending on a host of factors. But it's come on strong in the past six years. I've had to make hay while the sun shines. So, you need my help with something you don't really understand. Is that right?"

Julie nodded. Their food came, and Julie picked at her French fries.

"But you don't really believe," he said.

"I thought you said belief doesn't matter. There are things I need to know."

"About your husband."

She nodded. "I know it sounds crazy, but—"

"You've seen his ghost," Diamond said.

"I wish that's what it felt like. I think I've been losing my mind since he died. I think my mind is flashing on and off or something. A few nights ago, I thought I saw him. As close as you are. I thought I saw him, but when I turned on the light, he wasn't there. And then there's a video I made. He is in it. But the video goes bad. All the videos went bad."

"I have to tell you, Julie, I don't believe in ghosts. Not like you're saying. I don't believe there are physical manifestations of spirits where you can see them."

"So I guess I'm halfway to the psych hospital," she said, and tried not to imagine Amanda Hutchinson.

"I didn't mean that," he said. "I meant, sometimes what

happens is our brain gives access to projections—so what we see isn't a ghost, so much as . . . well, a movie. A movie our mind creates, influenced by either our own psychic ability, or someone nearby who has that ability. Your daughter, for example."

"Livy?"

"Well, you told me about her brain radio. She thinks she communicates with her dead father."

"I didn't tell you that."

He grinned. "For all you know, you live in a psychic household. Let's assume your daughter has some psychic ability. Anyone else in your family have this?"

"My mother thinks she does. But she doesn't. Believe me, she doesn't."

"It's usually genetic."

"Ah."

"I can tell by that 'ah' that you think this is one loony bin candidate talking to another. Think what you want, just stay with me on this. You've read my books. You know what remote viewing is. That's why you're here. You know about the Stream, don't you?"

She nodded. "From your book. It's what connects consciousness between people."

"It's fluid, and just because physics hasn't yet described it, doesn't mean it won't eventually be mapped out just like DNA. I believe it's the connection between entire species. Ants have it—and it's obvious they do. Birds that migrate have it. As we go up the food chain, it seems to have been weeded out. Who knows why. Now it just shows up as a genetic burp. That's what I think I am: a burp."

She laughed, and for just a moment forgot her headache—the one that hadn't disappeared in days.

"I am here," she said, "to find out if you know about something called Project Daylight."

3

A strange look flickered across his face, as if he were deciding on something that might affect her.

"It was your father who ran that program. Am I correct?"

He nodded. "Yes."

"It was on the sixth floor of an apartment building on Rosetta Street."

Again, he nodded. "It began as a sleep study for children with certain disorders. My father hired several medical people to oversee aspects of it, but this was a cover for what it was really about. He had received funding from the army to find out if there was a key to turning on Ability X in people. Children with the ability seemed to have an easier time of it. My father was misguided. He assumed all children were good. But they are not. Some children had come from abuse and were angry and had the seed of something more in them . . . Well, the place was badly ventilated, apparently, and when the fire broke out—caused by faulty wiring—many people died. Project Daylight was a disaster, it cost too much money, and the army wanted to hide it once the fire happened. So it got buried."

"My husband was in Project Daylight."

"Then your husband was psychic. Or had some level of ability as a child."

"He never told me about his childhood," she said.

"Given what happened in Project Daylight, I doubt he would," Michael Diamond said.

4

Although she wanted to open up to him, Julie became worried as Diamond spoke to her that she would sound too crazy. She wanted to unleash everything, to ask a thousand questions. But it all came down to one question. The one question she had never known during her life with Hut. "Do you know who my husband was?"

Diamond put down his fork and said, "I'm not sure. All of us in that program, Julie, lost memories."

"You were in it?"

"My father had some psychic ability, and I inherited it. My mother had it, too. People with Ability X often seek each other out. I'm surprised you don't have any."

"Well, I don't."

"You don't really believe in it, do you?"

"I believe that people believe. And maybe I want to know more," she said. "Did you . . . did you know Hut? Well, his name was Jeff. I don't know what his last name would've been. He was a ward of the state at the time."

"Well, memories were lost, believe me," he said.

She nodded. "A boy was burned."

"He died," Diamond said.

She remembered something that Detective McGuane had mentioned. "Died? I thought he lived. The cops think that the man who killed my husband might have been that boy."

"Do they? They think a dead boy killed someone?" He let the question hang in the air. Then, he said, "I can show you the few memories I have of it. But they're vague. They're out of focus."

"Show me?"

"Whether or not you believe in Ability X, Julie," he said, "doesn't matter. I can bring you inside myself. I can show you what I remember. At least fragments."

"How?"

"If you really want that, I need total access," he said.

"What does that mean?"

"It means, I need to delve into you—into your psyche. I need to unblock and open doors in your mind. I need to let things out that you don't want to get out. It's not selective. I can't pick and choose which door to open. I'm just the locksmith. I can unlock the door, but I can't prevent things from spilling out. Do you understand?"

She squinted as she looked at him. "I guess I'm still skeptical. But, when you touched me in the studio that day . . ."

"Ah. The laying on of hands. In religious mysticism, it's the most important way to the Stream. To move from my consciousness into yours. Once you've let me inside you, you can slip into me." He took a sip of wine, and grinned like a teenage boy who just shot off a bottle rocket. "It's like I feel everything the other person has felt. It's like unleashing impulses. It's like . . . well, pardon me for saying so, like an orgasm. And it's scary." He touched the tip of her fingers as she reached for her water glass. She withdrew her hand.

Maybe he's just nuts, she thought. *Maybe you need to get out of this lunch. Maybe whatever little bullshit ability he has isn't going to be what you want. You're smart, Julie. Eleanor told you that you might hallucinate and see Hut. That it was the normal grief and stress and longing. That it's not some supernatural event. It's just the human mind with a few cracks in it.*

"Maybe I *am* nuts," he said, too easily.

"You read my expression," she said. "You wrote that in your book, about the con artists. They know how to read people from body language and even the looks on their faces. My therapist said it, too. Things most of us don't even notice, but you've trained yourself to do."

"But you don't believe that, do you?" he said. "Not after recent experiences. You didn't seek me out because of lack of belief. When I viewed you, Julie, I was there, with you, *inside* you, Julie. The birth of your little girl. Making love to your husband. I was there, with you, in your memory. As creepy as it sounds, it's not. It's a beautiful experience. It's a connection of souls. It's like a spiderweb inside each of us, and each strand of that web is a different world within us, and each strand shoots out and connects with strands of others outside of us. A few of us are lucky enough to go inside. We need permission to do it. We can't just slip into someone else. They have to want me inside them."

His words made her shiver slightly. Reminding her of words the dark figure had whispered to her in her dreams: *Do you want me inside you?*

She closed her eyes, made a brief wish, opened them. His face seemed open and warm and unassuming.

It was like stepping off a cliff, stepping into his world of psychic "reading."

A world of illogic and mystical crap and all the things she'd fought her whole life never to believe.

"Can I trust you?" she asked. "I mean, really trust you?"

He nodded without hesitation.

"I saw his wounds after he died. I was at the morgue. He is dead. But I see him. I think . . . I think I'm being haunted by him. Look, I'll pay you whatever it takes just to find out if I'm sane or not."

"I don't want your money," he said.

5

His apartment was less impressive than she'd expected. It was a three-flight walk-up on Perry Street, in the Village. When he opened the door, she saw a place that looked like it had only been lived in for a few weeks.

"Most of my money goes to organizations I believe in," he said, noticing her raised eyebrows. "It's the main reason I write the books and do the show. That's the carnival aspect of Ability X. My income mostly goes to nonprofits that deal with, oh, the usual."

"Animal rescue groups and homes for wayward girls?"

"Something like that. When you live mainly in your mind, you have modest needs."

6

"On the table," he said, directing her to what looked like a massage table near the window.

He drew the shades. Then he sat down in a chair beside her.

"This'll seem awkward. Just try to relax. All right? This is called body work. Just think of it like a massage. I need you to loosen your shirt. Would you mind taking it off?"

"Why?"

"Trust me or don't trust me. You've had massages, I assume."

"Yes. But usually . . . in a spa."

"Tell you what, keep your cell phone on autodial for 911 if you're afraid of me."

She was about to pull out her cell phone. Everything had begun to frighten her, but she started feeling a certain numbness inside. She remembered the video of Hut looking at the camera, saying something, and then filming her in the most obscene way. *Is this what insanity is? Is this what Amanda felt like? Is this how it crawls inside you?* Finally, she said, "I'm not afraid of you."

The look on his face was of utter seriousness.

"Clothing interrupts the Stream." He said it so matter-of-factly that she felt as if any threat had been removed.

He wasn't even interested in her in that way. She could sense it.

"If I were a doctor, you'd have no problem removing your clothes. If I were a masseur, you'd be naked before I could say, 'Get on the table.' Think of me like that."

She fought an internal battle, wondering if she had gone off the deep end. But finally she unbuttoned her shirt and drew it off.

"I'll get you a towel," he said. "For modesty."

He got up and went toward the bathroom. When he returned, he tossed a large white fluffy towel at her. It smelled fresh, as if he'd just done his laundry.

"I'll go make some tea." He gestured toward the boxcar kitchen.

After he'd gone over to the sink, she slipped out of her skirt, but kept her underwear on. She wrapped the towel around herself, and it managed to cover most of her, breasts included. She had an awful feeling that she was stepping into a trap. That she had let a dream rape her, and now she was setting herself up for a man who was a virtual stranger to do the same. And yet she had to see where this went. She had to know what was in his mind, his memories. She had to know more.

After he poured himself some tea, he returned to the living room and sat down beside the table.

"Are you comfortable?" he asked.

"Mmm." She stared straight ahead: her view was of the bathroom door, which had a long mirror hanging on the outside. She saw her face, saw Michael Diamond in the chair beside the massage table.

"I want you to know that you are safe. I won't be touching you, but your mind will think I am. Have you ever gone to a Reiki therapist? They hold their hands just so, above certain points of the body. They believe they're directing their healing life energy to the subject. This is somewhat similar. My hands will be this far from you the entire time. I want you to be aware of it, because there will come a point when it feels as if I'm touching you. Do not break the Stream. I Stream into you. I want you to close your eyes. Now. All right. Think back to a time when you first remember seeing a flower. Yes, a flower." He said the words slowly, carefully, and she felt his hand on the back of her scalp. As he kept his hand there—barely touching her hair— she began to feel an intense heat, as if his hand emanated an aura of warmth. He guided her through looking at the first flower, then the first friend, then the look on her mother's face when it was Christmas, and each time he took her mind somewhere new, she felt the presence of his hand again— not his hand itself, but the warmth beneath it as it hovered at the back of her neck, between her shoulder blades, down her spine, as he parted the towel, to the base of her spine, and then slowly back up again.

She remembered other things from her childhood, remembered a fight her parents had, remembered when she and Mel had dressed up their pet schnauzer in baby clothes, and then the memories came forward as if, by touching her, he had begun opening doors in her mind that she'd been shutting behind her.

Soon, she had lost even the sound of his voice but still felt him there, his hand no longer moving just above the surface of her skin, but inside her in some impossible way—beneath the surface of consciousness. His hand guided her along through doors of memory that opened, one after the other. Then more than memories—fantasies began coming to her: of flying in the air, of swimming like a fish through the water. And then she felt as if she were butting up against some door that wouldn't open, but his hand was there, with her, and finally it flew apart as if smashed, and behind it was a bloodred room. She was there with a man without a face, and he caressed her and touched her, parting her legs as he parted her mouth with his tongue, and in this red room, she felt no shame and had no care that they were being watched by the outsider, by the psychic who chaperoned her journey into her subconscious. The faceless man against whom she twisted and bucked in a sexual fantasy of frenzy and animal lust now took on the form of Michael Diamond himself for a flickering moment—but then, as if propelled by pathways of the pulse, she was ejected from her inner fantasy and moved again to a new image—to a row of iron doors that looked as if they were locked, bolted, and bound by some kind of interconnecting bloodroots. But she heard the distant sound of a series of pops, and the doors opened, all of them, and it was as if she were spying on herself, spying on her life with Hut, on the life they'd built, only she watched it like it was one of Matt's movies. As she watched, she saw Hut for who he really was, not the man of her fantasies and not the man of her illusions, but a man who was cold with her, and brusque, a man who was selfish with his time and displayed little love even for his son—a handsome, vain man who watched her at times as if she were not entirely human to him . . .

She heard Michael Diamond's voice, "Let's move beyond all of this. There's another place we need to go. You may be afraid; you may not want to go there. But fear isn't what it seems. Fear awakens us to our abilities, our senses that have been hidden. Fear is the key to the final door inside you." She felt as if someone had taken her wrist and tugged on it, pulling her into a dark place inside her mind, a dungeon where some beast growled in a corner.

"There's a place inside you," Diamond whispered. "A place where you've been, but you don't remember. It's been hidden from you. But you know it. I want you to face your fear and venture there again. With me."

7

Julie moved as if swimming underwater, with dark vines moving slowly as if pushed by some unseen tide, and the doors were there, before her.

One of them began to open.

When it did, she saw Hut.

His eyes milky white, his grin impossibly wide.

His arms outstretched.

His penis erect.

And she moved to him, as if that invisible force pushed her toward the dead man.

8

Julie's eyes opened suddenly.

She got her bearings: she was in Diamond's apartment. It was mid-afternoon.

There was an overwhelming pounding behind her eyes, as if she had a terrible headache that had just erupted.

She glanced straight ahead at the long, vertical mirror on the front of the bathroom door. Her flushed face, her bloodshot eyes—as if she'd been crying—and Michael Diamond in a chair next to her. He looked up at her staring at his reflection.

Only it wasn't his face in the mirror.

It was a blur of grays and blues.

It was the face of the man in apartment 66S.

And his body was different. She saw him as if he were naked, standing in the mirror. Covered with burns. Covered as if most of his body had been consumed in a fire.

chapter twenty

1

"You're the boy," she gasped. "You're the boy who burned. The boy didn't die. He didn't. He lived. It's *you*." Her throat clutched as she said it, and she pushed herself up on the massage table, drawing the towel more tightly around her.

"Julie?" he asked.

She looked at him, and he was normal again, then she looked into the mirror and there he was also Michael Diamond, dressed, rising now from his chair.

She dressed quickly, feeling a pulse of horror within her body. Diamond may have been speaking, but she didn't hear a word. She just knew that if she didn't leave his apartment, she would scream or jump out a window. She felt the urgency of it, as if something was coming toward her, some shrieking insanity swooping down from shadows. She thought of Amanda, with her caged animal beauty, her fierce attack, and wondered if she hadn't experienced what was going on in her mind. If she hadn't begun to see people's faces as blurs of gray and blue. She felt as if she'd been infected with something, some awful poison, something that had begun eating away at her sanity.

She raced down the stairs, not caring if she tripped and

fell, and out into the street. She was disoriented and couldn't remember where her car was parked. She wandered through the Village, her heart seeming to beat a thousand times a minute. She felt as if she would die at any moment, and she was about to let it happen, about to let the anxiety and breathlessness within her win.

As she rounded a corner at Bleecker and Cornelia, she saw a crowd gathered around what must have been an accident. She felt drawn to it and went to the group of people, who all stood still, watching a delivery boy lying on the street, his bicycle mangled. Several feet ahead, a taxicab, with its driver standing half in and half out of the car, door swung open, looking shell-shocked.

The boy had been knocked off his bike, and his head was twisted unnaturally around. His left arm was bent over his right shoulder. He looked as if he were no more than seventeen years old.

The Chinese food he'd been delivering lay in mashed white cartons beyond the small crowd.

The sound of the ambulance rounding the corner.

She looked in the boy's eyes. She had to, she wanted to see what death was again, she wanted to believe it was final, and that whatever had been that boy was now gone, irretrievably.

Then she felt a tender cracking, as if inside her skull, and for a moment she wondered if this was what a brain aneurysm began with—a slight cracking sound—and then she heard her husband's voice.

"I would never leave you, Julie," he said. *"Death is everywhere. But not where I am. Do you want me inside you?"*

2

She dropped by Joe and Rick's place.

"Jesus, Jules. You're white as a sheet. And that's a cliché

I never thought I'd ever get to say out loud," Joe said after he opened the door.

"I'm losing my mind," she said.

3

After she told him everything, Joe said, "He might as well have raped you, Julie. He told you to take your clothes off? You did it? You went along with it? How do you know he didn't hypnotize you or something and then do something awful to you while you were under? You've got to be more careful. God, should we call the cops?" Realizing his tone, he calmed a bit. "No, we call them, how is it going to look? Julie, do you really think he killed Hut? I mean, you happen to read his books. You happen to go to his studio. You happen to—"

"I know it sounds crazy, Joe. But you believe in this stuff. What if he had psychic talent to draw me to him? I mean, what is the extent of this thing? What about the burns I saw? In the mirror?"

"I don't know," he said, and for the first time ever in their friendship, she thought she detected a flicker of distance in him. As if he were looking at her in such a way that he thought she was damaged. Deranged.

"Joe, I'm not crazy. I know I'm not. I saw him. I think he did what he said—he streamed into me. And when I came out of it too suddenly, I saw him for a split second. He told me that I couldn't be inside him unless he first opened me. He said it. And that's what it was. I saw inside him. That's what I saw with the burns. But . . . if he were burned as a kid, how could he look so . . . normal?"

Joe thought a moment, and said, "I worked with a woman once who had been in a car crash. Eighty percent of her body had been burned. Five years later, with a lot of surgery, she looked better than she ever had. I guess, maybe if you saw him naked, you'd see the burn. If . . . if you really saw something that was real. Julie, now don't get pissed off at me or anything, but if you saw this for just a second, couldn't it maybe have been some kind of hangover from what he did to you? Like waking too fast from a dream?"

"Joe," she said. "I saw things. Things I've forgotten. Things that . . . he unlocked inside me. And then I thought I heard him. Inside me. Maybe it was crazy. Maybe it was my mind on hyperspeed. But I saw him."

"Diamond?"

"No," she said. "Hut."

4

Julie finally opened up about the apartment on Rosetta Street.

"I know that block. It's creepy. I had to walk through there at night one time, and I swear the ghosts of all the cows they killed down there are wandering." He grinned. "You still have the key to the place?"

Julie nodded.

"Let's go," he said.

5

This time, to get through the building's security door, Joe buzzed one of the first-floor apartments and pretended to be the son of an old lady on the sixth floor. It took three tries before he got buzzed in—"It's not the nicest way to sneak into a building, but it works sometimes"—and when they got to 66S, Julie reached for her handbag, but Joe said, "I guess we didn't need the keys after all."

The door was ajar.

"What if someone's in there?" she asked.

He smiled. "We say we had the wrong apartment and we

back out slowly. Gee, makes me feel like I'm one of the Hardy Boys."

6

Inside, the light switch didn't work. It was growing dark outside, but there was still some light from the large factory-style windows of the apartment.

"Hello?" Joe asked, his voice booming. He turned back to her. "Open the door wide so we can get more light in here."

She pulled the door back, and a rectangle of white from the hall light illuminated the foyer.

"Stinks," Joe said, pinching his nose, stepping through the doorway.

"Where are you going?" she asked.

"There's bound to be another light around the corner," he said, holding his nose from the smell that emanated from within.

She watched his silhouette as it melted into the grayness.

Then a light flicked up in the next room. She went down the hall and into the living area. It was now almost completely empty of furniture, as if someone had moved out.

There was one high-backed wooden chair at the center of the room. It reminded her of a chair she had seen in a dream. Somehow she'd seen it, but she didn't mention this to Joe.

"I guess they got evicted," Joe said. "Nobody home."

He went to check in the bedroom. She waited, remembering seeing the man standing there. The man who had the same blurred face that she'd seen in Michael Diamond's mirror.

Julie's imagination began to run wild. *You're a fool. You can't have seen anything in the mirror. You can't have seen a man with a blurred face anywhere. It's the dreams you've been having. It's Hut's death. It has gotten to you and instead of dealing with it, you've been dancing around it. You*

saw the video with Mel. You saw that all you filmed was
yourself, maybe dreaming of sex with Hut. Maybe dreaming
of things because the raw deal you got with his murder was
too much for you to handle. Hut was part of some psychic
study as a kid. No wonder he never talked about it. But he
did talk to Livy about her brain radio. He did try to tell
her—she was sure of it—that something bad had happened
in his childhood. Maybe when he talked about the Hutchin-
sons being horrible to him, he was confusing it. Maybe his
memories had been like crossed wires. Or maybe Michael
Diamond had been telling the truth: that the fire in the
building took the memories. Blocked them. That's nuts, to
think any of this is real. You don't genuinely believe it . . .
but the Streaming session with Diamond had seemed too
real. She had never felt someone else's consciousness inside
her like that. *Am I going insane? Is this what it is?* But she
could answer her own question: it was as if someone was
fucking with her. As if someone had already crawled inside
her mind and was screwing with the way she saw things.
The way she perceived. The video. The Streaming. It was all
about her brain itself hitting short-circuits. It was not insanity. At best, it was shock and paranoia. Posttraumatic stress.
Seeing her husband's body on a metal table. Seeing how
he'd been carved. Seeing Matt's arm, with its carvings.
That's all it was. Seeing things. It wasn't that she herself was
losing her mind. It was a problem of vision. It was a problem of how things are seen, and what happens when a shock
occurs.

She waited for Joe, and her mind spun until she just
wanted to feel as if something made sense.

Joe came out of the bedroom and said, "Nothing there, either."

She could see in his face the doubt. Even Joe, who believed in psychic phenomena wholeheartedly, thought she
had gone off the deep end.

"Look," he said, anticipating her mood. "You've had some shocks. I'm not saying that none of this adds up to anything. But I think if we're going to call the police, we need more. I'll look up some stuff and call some friends who are more experts on this. I'll find out more about Project Daylight. Don't worry about this. Let me drive you home, okay?"

7

Joe drove her back in her Camry, and when they got near Rellingford, he offered to spend the night, but she could tell he wanted to get home. She insisted that she was all right. So they drove to the train station and she saw him off. She enjoyed the ride back with all the windows down and the slight wind blowing through the car, giving her a nice chill. She felt better. She wasn't sure what to make of Michael Diamond or what she'd seen—or hadn't seen—at his place. But she'd handle it later.

When Julie walked in the front door of her house, her sister was on the couch in the living room, covered with a blanket, with Livy, in her jammies, curled up around her.

Mel opened her eyes. "How'd it go?"

"I'll tell you tomorrow. Thanks for coming over," Julie whispered, lifting Livy up in her arms. Livy was so sound asleep that she barely stirred as her mother carried her to her bedroom.

Julie was too tired to clear out the guest room for Mel, so she and her sister slept together up in the big king-sized bed in Julie's room. When Julie got up in the morning, Mel already had coffee made. The kids had gone off to school. It was after eleven.

Mel hugged her. "I love you, Julie. You're the best little sister in the whole world. But I don't want you going into the city anymore. I don't even think your friend Joe was much help to you. And I certainly think that Michael Diamond was bad news from the start. I wish I'd told Mom to go by herself to that stupid show."

Julie said very little, and certainly didn't want to add to her sister's sense that she was losing it by telling her about Project Daylight and Michael Diamond and seeing blurred faces and burned bodies. As the thoughts spun through her head, Julie giggled a little and then noticed Mel's unforgiving look. She knew what Mel was thinking. *You're thinking that I am a terrible mommy and I need to somehow be strong and pull through and just focus on mommydom and forget that I had a husband, forget that you saw me masturbating on videotape while claiming that I saw a dead man molesting me in my sleep, and you think that I need meds and a good long rest and you're probably even thinking of taking Matt and Livy away for a while until I get a good doctor and end up like the Numbah One Wife, Amanda Hutchinson, who thought I had big hairy balls.*

Absurdities encircled her thoughts, and nothing made sense, and she knew that the longer Mel watched her, the worse she would feel, the more she would go whirling into an oblivion of fear and belief and shadow. Julie thanked her for the coffee and for cleaning the house. She thanked her for taking care of Matt and Livy. She told her that she knew she'd been experiencing crazy thoughts. "Eleanor called it posttraumatic stress disorder," Julie said. "But I'm getting good care. Honest. I am."

8

"You went to see this con man again?" Eleanor asked on the phone. "Julie, you have been through a trauma. Your husband was murdered. Do you think your mind is going to work right at this point in time? Do you think you're not going to wish you could see him? Wish you could hear him?

When soldiers come back from war, they often suffer from posttraumatic stress disorder. Why? They've witnessed atrocities. You have experienced a personal atrocity. Your husband, the father of your child, was murdered in a terrible way. Psychics like this man are preying on people like you. They may be worse for you than anything else. He may be giving your subconscious mind permission to break down."

"Can I see you?"

"Immediately," Eleanor said. "I'll be at my office in twenty minutes. I consider this an emergency."

9

A bald man in a gray, expensive suit sat in the overstuffed chair that Julie normally occupied during her sessions with Eleanor.

He rose up as Julie entered the room. She had the sense that he had too high an opinion of himself. *He must be a doctor.*

"This is Dr. Glennon, from Hillside," Eleanor said.

Julie shook his hand and went to sit on the couch next to Eleanor.

"I've brought Dr. Glennon in, Julie, because I thought you two might talk more openly. I feel I'm a little too close to the situation to be of much help."

"But . . ." Julie began. Then, "The situation?"

Eleanor smiled. "What you're going through. Your sister called last night. She was worried about you."

"She called you?"

"Now, don't be angry with her," Eleanor said. "She's thinking of your well-being. You've been through a lot, Julie, and my fear is that I haven't been as much help as I should've been."

Julie picked at the hem of her skirt. "All right." Then, to the other doctor: "You're a psychiatrist?"

Dr. Glennon nodded.

Eleanor patted Julie on the knee and then got up and walked over to the doorway. She stepped out of her office, shutting the door behind her.

Julie glanced back toward the door, feeling like a little girl being left behind by her mother on the first day of school.

10

An hour later, she stopped by the pharmacy to fill her prescription for some drug she'd never heard of, a mild sedative. She wanted whatever would be necessary to somehow help her mind clear up. Glennon had told her, "You can take them together, and they'll act fairly quickly. Take them when you're feeling rundown, or when your mind seems to be doing that thing you called letting off sparks." He seemed like a good man, and he told her that the drugs had few side effects and would just be for the short term.

She took the pills with some Snapple when she got home, and then she went to lie down in the bedroom and let the supposed relaxing benefits of the new miracle drug take her over.

At first, she watched the ceiling with its swirls of patterns, and then she felt as if she were moving into the patterns. She felt quite wonderful and rested and only vaguely sleepy. The sex dream came, of course, and in the dream she had no fear at all. Hut parted her legs, his mouth pressing into her, his hands reaching up and around to grasp her breast and stroke her. It wasn't like the nightmares of sex and lust—this was lovemaking. *Thank God,* she thought, *for drugs and psychiatrists.* This wasn't posttraumatic stress, this was love, this was love that never died, this was no ghost making love to her, but a man of flesh and blood, and the world was fuzzy—she remembered Amanda's phrase, "the warm fuzzies"—that's what this was, the warm fuzzies had her in their thrall. She felt taken care of again, secure in his arms, his ministrations, and she realized he had never done this before, when they were married, he had never taken her like this in real life, this pounding and battering and swirling and lifting, but with the warm fuzzies, he transformed into this sexual dynamo who wanted her and her alone, wanted to be within her, want to find her pleasure and press into it, delight her, awaken her, but the warm fuzzies pulled her back, ah, she could not be awakened. She could not. The warm fuzzies drew her down into a rich comforter of Hut, his body, wrapping around her as he moved upward, kissing her navel and flicking his tongue within it. She didn't care that several cameras were filming them—it was a porno movie, she saw people filming them as he took her again and again and she gave herself to him. Then moving to her breasts and taking each nipple in his mouth, like he was a baby, like he drew strength and comfort from her, like she was his mother and his lover and his wife and his whore and his savior.

And when he came up to her face, when she looked in his eyes, his eyes were normal, his face was normal. Not milky white. Not a nightmare at all.

His body was covered with strange markings, whirligig drawings and little sunbursts etched into his skin, but it was him. It was Hut.

She was sure.

He pressed himself into her, inside her, and she opened, she blossomed—ah, the warm fuzzies made it easy. *That new drug sure could get a girl in trouble,* she giggled softly. Had she said it aloud? She didn't even have to move or struggle or embrace him. Her arms and legs felt as if they couldn't move, but it didn't bother her. She liked that he had taken control. She liked that Hut was there, taking her. Taking her the way men took women in fantasies. She loved this fantasy.

She awoke several hours later. In the dark. *God, another insane dream,* she thought.

Someone had screamed.

As the seconds passed, she was sure of it. But the house was silent. No, not a scream. It was as if the silence itself had made her wake up.

The scream, or cry, must have been what had snapped her out of sleep. Or was it in a dream? She couldn't quite remember—like a spiderweb of a dream that she'd somehow broken through.

11

A headache from hell battered at her, but she managed to dress. Had she undressed herself? She couldn't remember. She went into the hall and flicked the light switch but it didn't come on. *Have to change the bulb. Damn it.* She went down to Livy's room. It was dark, but everything was in place. She looked in at shadow upon shadow—the toys, the doll collection, and then the small, perfect bed, piled high with pillows, which was how Livy liked to sleep. Hokey Pokey Elmo sat square on the bed as if watching her. She saw a bit of Livy's hair over the pillow. Livy liked to scrunch down under the blanket at night, "like an oyster in a shell," Hut used to joke. She stood in the doorway, feeling a bit of relief. But when she passed Matt's room, she stopped. Then she turned the knob. It was locked. She had allowed him his privacy like that, ever since she'd walked in on him masturbating the year before. She had felt more embarrassed than he had, and she didn't blame him for locking up now and then. She could easily unlock it with a credit card or even the front door key, so she wasn't worried. Matt was fine. In fact, she thought she heard him snoring a little through the door.

She felt a chill from the hallway and went down the stairs

to the living room to check to see if a window had been left open.

Instead, the front door was open wide. She glanced at the small plastic box that housed the burglar alarm system. It no longer had its little green lights flickering. *Damn* it. She'd forgotten to turn it on. Had she even left the front door open? Had the damn sleeping pills made her too groggy even to be sensible?

She looked out into the night, and the stars seemed to have dimmed above the trees, against moonlit sky.

Julie shut the door, locking it. She flicked up the living room light switch. It was dead. Then she went to the kitchen and got a flashlight from under the sink. She went out the back door and checked the switches. She toggled them back and forth, unsure as to what she was really trying to accomplish. No light came on in the house.

She went back inside with the flashlight, and as she walked down the main hall from the kitchen, the flashlight's beam hit the back of a mirror, and it illuminated the room.

She was sure that someone stood behind her. She turned around quickly, shining the light.

The beam of light hit Michael Diamond's face.

chapter twenty-one

1

"Julie," he said, his hands going up. She kept the flashlight on his face. She thought about the gun upstairs in the bedroom. She thought about how fast she could run there. Could she get there fast enough? Could she lock the bedroom door behind her? Could she get the key out—in the dark—and open the metal box and get the revolver and get back out to make sure her children were safe from the man who she was now sure had murdered her husband?

"Julie," he said. "I'm not trying to scare you."

"Shut up," she said. "You broke into my house."

"No," he said. "The door was open. The lights were off. Please. Let me explain."

"What in hell are you doing here?" she asked, and then wondered how long it would take for her to find the cell phone and call the police.

"Please. I can understand every single thought you're having now. I was the boy who was burned."

"You said he died."

Michael didn't respond to this. "But my memories are like flashes of lightning, Julie. I can't see everything. You know what I did with you. You know where I took you. You showed me what was inside you. You were there. You aren't crazy. This makes sense if you believe, Julie. If you believe. You resisted me. I could feel it when I went into you. You had fear, and fear is the thing that has power over you now. But you've got to let it go, somehow. You know how I Streamed into you. How you went to doors in your mind. You saw things. You relived things. But there's something important now. Something more important than that. There's a door in you that needs opening, but they've blocked it."

"They?"

"If I told you who, you would not believe me," he said.

"Try me."

"Your husband," he said.

"My husband is dead."

"There is no death, Julie," Michael Diamond said. "Let me show you."

He moved toward her, and she stepped backward and felt fear clutch at her. She was sure he was going to kill her. She stepped back and felt for the doorknob to the front door. She turned it, but it was still locked. The chain was on, as well. She pressed her back against the door. Her mind flashed on things—on what she could grab to protect herself. Where she could run. Her heart beat a mile a minute as she began to hyperventilate.

He came nearer, and she kept the flashlight beam on him. He unbuttoned his shirt.

The light shone on his skin. It was scarred and layered. "They set fire to me. They wanted me to burn, Julie. They stood by and watched me die. But I can show you. Just as you showed me what was inside you. I want you inside me. I want you to see this," he said, and reached out and took her trembling hand while she kept the flashlight on his chest. He drew her hand to the middle of his chest and she felt a surge of energy, and she knew it was the Stream because she felt herself—not her body, but her true self, something in her mind—flow into him, sucked along as if she were liquid and were being poured into a dark lake.

2

The first thing she felt was that gradual warmth and a sense of safety, and then a pleasing sensation ran through her. She heard his voice, with her, inside her, guiding her. "Julie, this is the Stream. I've brought you into it." And she tried to resist moving along with his voice, but she didn't feel the same fear as she had seconds before. She saw memory screens inside the darkness: his father holding his hand as he led the little boy toward the doctor who took him through several doors, into a room with a series of beds. Two boys and three girls of varying ages lay on the beds, their eyes closed, small wires attached to what looked like polka dots on their foreheads and just beneath their left nipples. They were in their underwear, sheets drawn up just to their stomachs. He cried when he was told to take his clothes off and get onto one of the beds, and watched in terror as the polka dots and wires were attached to the top of his head, making a slurping sound as they suctioned onto his forehead.

"This one is for your heart," the doctor said as he placed his cold hand near his chest. "It's so we can make sure you're okay."

The lights were kept on, and his arms were tethered to the bed so that he had a range of movement but he couldn't get up. "I have to pee," he said repeatedly, but no one came to take him to the bathroom. He was in a white room with long mirrors on all the walls. He wasn't even sure where the door was.

Eventually, he peed in his underwear and fell asleep, exhausted and a little scared.

Another memory screen: a classroom of twenty children, with three stern-looking women at the front of the class, near the big teacher's desk. He sat in the third row back and they were all being told to close their eyes and try to think of nothing but darkness. But he couldn't. Every time he shut his eyes, he saw something awful, although as soon as he opened them, he couldn't remember what it was.

"You don't go home?" Julie asked in the Stream, shocked that she was able to speak at all.

The little boy answered her. "For some of us, our Mommy and Daddy never pick us up. We stay in that room with the lights and all the mirrors. They put the polka dots on us every night."

It was night, she assumed, but the lights above never gave an indication of morning or midnight. One of the boys plucked the polka dots off his forehead, and laid them on the bed. "Mikey," he said. "They're stealing your dreams."

"Are they?" he asked. "My dad wouldn't do it."

"Don't lie to him," a sad little long-haired boy said. He must've been about fourteen, but he looked younger than Michael, who was almost thirteen. "They're checking for brain activity. That's all. They want to see patterns while we dream. Don't worry, Mike, nobody can steal your dreams."

"They are too," the older boy said. He was at least fifteen, but seemed older. "They're trying to steal from us."

The girl of eleven or so, who Julie thought might be the long-haired boy's sister, piped up. "I just want to go home."

"There is no home," the older boy said. "None of us have parents."

"I do," Michael said.

The little girl nodded. "Me, too."

The older boy smirked. "If you call those people parents. They'd sell you if they thought they could get away with it. Don't you think that, Mikey? Don't you? Since as far back as you can remember, don't you remember how they hated you? How they think you're a freak because of what goes on in your head? They think you're going to go nutso because you keep predicting things—bad things—like you're a bad luck charm. Like you're a jinx. I wouldn't want a kid like that around the house," he said. "Who would?"

The long-haired boy said, "What about you?"

"My parents died," the older boy said. "In a car crash. I knew it was coming, only I didn't tell them."

"That's mean," one of the girls said.

"Is it? I was only four. What did I know? I didn't know people died like that," the older boy said.

"Don't you feel bad?" Michael asked.

"Why should I? I didn't make them die. It was an accident."

"But you saw it coming."

"There's a lot of things I see coming," the older boy said, looking hard at the boy with the long hair.

A voice outside of the memory—Julie's—*"Who are they? What are their names?"* It jolted her off one memory screen and onto another.

There was an isolation booth. A glassed-in cage, but with a doorway that led into a larger room that was the testing room.

"Why is this important?" Julie asked.

"Something bad happened here," Michael said.

Then another memory: the older boy and three girls stood on the stairs, blocking the way for Michael to pass.

"You can't come up," the boy said.

"Why not?"

"We're testing someone."

"You're testing someone? You're not supposed to run the tests. Where's Dr. Stone?"

"Getting a taste," said one of the girls—a tall, wiry one with braces, "of his own medicine." She and one of the other girls giggled.

"If you know what's good for you," the boy said, "you'll just go back downstairs."

Michael noticed the way the five of them had carved spirals and things on their bodies. "Why'd you do that?" He pointed to the girl's arm.

"We're a special secret club now," she said.

"You can't join," the older boy said quickly.

"Why not?"

"You're not good enough," he said. "You're fake. You're one of the twenty-six percenters. We don't want you. We want the ninety-nine percenters."

Another memory screen:

Michael was weeping, wiping his eyes as he walked down the corridor, and when he came to the Sleep Room, he looked through the door window and saw something that scared him.

"What is it? What did you see?"

The doctors and teachers and the parapsychologist, all lying down in the narrow beds as if sleeping, polka dots on their foreheads. Michael tried to make his mind roam into the room, but something blocked him. Why were they just lying there? What had done this?

His mind sped through possibilities, thinking of his classmates, and he knew it was the older boy. Something terrible. Something they had done: the ones who gathered at the top of the stairs. They had scrambled the minds of their teachers, of their doctors, and of Mr. Boatwright, and maybe even his own father.

They weren't dead, he was sure. Their eyes were open, and their lips opened and closed as if they were fish pulled from water, gasping on dry land.

And then Julie heard what sounded like an explosion and saw a little girl screaming as she tried to open the door to a glass booth—inside it was an inferno. The door finally opened, and a boy, on fire, came running out.

Then Julie felt other things. She felt a sense of benevolence like she'd never experienced. She felt kindness. She
felt something sacred. Michael's voice in her mind: "I died,
Julie. I died then. You're with me, feeling that. Don't forget
it. Don't ever forget what you're feeling. It's not a terror.
Death is not a terror. It is the doorway to something sacred.
See, how I felt it? Stay with me. Stay with it."

Wave after wave of elation seemed to sweep through her.
"It's the human soul," he said. "It's the human soul, inviolate. Don't ever forget that, Julie. Don't. Death is just a stop
along the way."

Then she felt herself heave as if about to vomit, and she
sucked air—but it was not her, was it? She experienced his
memory—his fragments. He was alive. They stood around
him, pointing. The other children.

The older boy stepped forward and whispered in the ear
of the boy who had been burned. "You passed the test," he
said.

It was Hut. She knew it was Hut. Hut was the older boy.
Hut helped set the boy on fire. Hut was doing something
evil. Something terrible as a child.

The fear rose up in her, growing quickly, like a raging fire
in her mind, and she felt Michael's consciousness grasp at
her, trying to tug her back. But the fear shot her out of the
Stream and she was once again in her front hall, her back
pressed against the front door, the flashlight fallen to the
floor.

Michael Diamond had released her hand.

"Julie," he said, his breathing heavy. "I did kill him. But
not because of revenge. But because he was bringing things
into existence. He was doing something terrible."

She stood there, breathing heavily also. She crumpled to
her knees and sat down on the cold floor.

"You murdered my husband," she said. "And now you
come here with this. This . . . magic trick."

"You believe," Michael Diamond said. "You can't go back from that. Once you believe, you can't."

3

Inside her own consciousness, without the sense that Diamond was inside her, Julie felt a growing belief, more than she had ever felt anything before. His words: the human soul inviolate. Inviolate. There was something more than just this existence. She'd sensed it, she'd been exposed to it in the past, but she had never believed it because she had no direct experience. But now, it was all laid out. As if it were meant to come to her. As if it were falling into place for her.

He murdered Hut.

"I want more," she said, feeling hungry. "I want to be inside you. I want to see more. I can't live like this. I can't be like this. I can't have all these things in my head. What I've seen. What I've experienced."

"It's unexplainable in words," he said. "Here, take my hand. Just take my hand. I can bring you back inside me, but there's something inside you that's still blocked, Julie. Something they blocked."

"They?"

"There are at least five of them still. They've done terrible things. Worse than you can imagine. If I were to tell you . . ."

"Show me."

4

In the dark, he took his shirt off and crouched down beside her. Then he guided her hands to his chest. "Accept the Stream," he said. "I'll bring you in. I'll show you what you want."

Soon, she felt as if she were flying into shadows. She

knew from her reading that this was the astral projection that was often written about—the remote viewing, where one consciousness invaded another. And she saw the memory screens again—it was like blinking, and each time a new image or moment of his life came up.

She saw his early life and his first experiences with Ability X (even his language invaded her mind, and she understood and accepted it) when he was seven and his father, in his military uniform, in a boardroom of some kind, tested him with cards. Then the mind games, where the boy had to tell what he saw in pictures from his father's thoughts. The little boy scribbled houses and horses and cats and women and his father each time nodded, and then the boy was in a room with his little sister Margie, and more tests. And she saw the building that was the Chelsea Parapsychological Institute, and she was there when the sleep study began, but Michael's consciousness guided her through these screens, into other memories, after the fire. Of the hospital where he spent nearly a year. She watched from above as skin graft procedures were done, and painful saltwater treatments. The boy in the bed howled in pain and begged his father to let him see his sister. Then roaming through the open Stream— floating down the halls of the hospital while the pain intensified for the boy in the room. Moving through windows, out into daylight, out into the world and traveling above the trees until finally, coming to a graveyard, drifting down among the oaks like a kite falling to the ground, coming to rest at the grave of a little girl named Cassandra Diamant. His sister. More screens came up, and Julie blinked through them, feeling as if she were swimming underwater with her eyes only half-open.

And then operation after operation while the boy recovered, a teenager, nearly a man, and learning to test himself, test his abilities, but still too weak. Not fully recovered. And then she went further, and felt as if she were going into the whorls of a dark shell. She was inside him, behind his eyes, seeing what he saw. It was as if he were directing her back in time to look out through him. She saw the clippings on the wall—the murders. And there was Hut. Somehow he'd Streamed to Hut, Hut when he was in his late twenties, with Amanda, who looked more beautiful than Julie imagined she had been, more radiant than any woman Julie had ever seen. Then Amanda had Matty, a two-year-old then, and they were in Tompkins Square Park in the city. They were talking, but Julie couldn't hear their words. She saw Hut's face, saw a darkness there—as if there were an aura of ravens fluttering around him—and he was arguing with Michael, he was angry, and some of the words came through: "you idiot," "wasting your life," "you can't see what we're trying to do." Amanda looking as if Hut had frightened her as he picked Matt up and took her hand, tugging her away from Michael Diamond.

And then Michael turned around on the street, and there was Hut again, only it was the Hut that Julie remembered. It was the Hut that she'd seen their last morning together. Again, she couldn't hear the words clearly. But she felt what Michael Diamond felt, and she saw the anger in Hut, and then the two men went to the curb, and Hut told him to get in his car. Hut had a small knife. He was threatening Diamond. But Diamond got into the Audi, and they drove. Consciousness crashed in a wave, and Julie felt herself being pulled into an undertow, deeper into Diamond's mind.

And then, she was at the clearing, and it was Hut with the knife. Diamond argued, and Hut jabbed the air in front of him. Julie understood. Hut had wanted to kill Diamond. In her mind, Michael Diamond said, *"I had been the instrument that allowed him, and the others, to discover about resurrection."*

She shot out of his mind just as violently as if she'd been catapulted.

She opened her eyes, and it was already morning. She was soaked with sweat, as was Diamond. "Oh my God," she said. "Oh my God."

"Try to stay calm," Michael Diamond told her. "Please. It's something that they discovered when they tried to kill me."

"What is it?"

"There is no death, Julie. At least, not how we think of it. Death is like a train station. You leave one train and get on another," he said. "Only some people—with Ability X—can alter the process. I don't completely understand it, nor do I care to. I experienced death briefly. They were testing me, Julie. They've tested others. Most fail. Even with Ability X, the failure rate is high. They've killed some people. Some of their own children."

"Who's 'they'?"

"I've been trying for the past seven years to locate them, but they . . . well, they block me. They can do that." He must have read the shadowy expression on her face. "I know it's hard for you to believe. You've just come to this."

"But if Hut . . . if Hut were really . . ."

"You saw inside me. You experienced it."

"You carved into his body," she said. "And others. I saw them."

"I killed only your husband, Julie. They killed the others. And more that still have not been found. They kill their own children, Julie. Just as they tested me, they've been testing one another for years. They carved the symbols into your husband's back. They were there, watching. That's why he stopped the car at the path into the woods. I couldn't detect them, but I know they were there, and I did my damnedest to make sure that your husband could not come back from the dead. They are a death cult. They have turned their ability into something . . . unspeakable."

She felt a shiver rack her body, and she pushed herself up

from the floor. The ordinariness of the early morning light coming through windows, of the shadows being erased along the living room and down the hall to the kitchen, made her wonder what life was, and where the real and the unreal separated.

"You've been inside me, Julie. I've been inside you. You can't go back. You know—inside you—that what I'm saying is true. I showed you," he said.

She rose up, keeping her back to the door. "I don't know," she said, trembling. "You have this ability. I know you do. I don't know what to think. I just don't. What if you're lying? What if you can show me things that never happened?"

He pressed his hands to his forehead, as if he were stopping a headache. "Don't doubt me. Please, Julie. It's important. I'm here with you because I knew what you were going through. When you came to me, and I went inside you, I knew the pain you'd felt. I knew the desolation. It's because your marriage was a lie. He used you. He is still using you."

"He's dead. My husband is dead," she said angrily. She stepped around him and went toward the kitchen. "I need time. I need time to think."

"There's no time," he said. "They plan to test others."

She half turned, stopping. "What do you mean?"

"Your children," he said. "They have some of their father in them. They have the genetic material for Ability X. You know that your stepson experiences things he can't express. You know that your daughter thinks she has a brain radio. That she communicates with her father. Some of them have already murdered their own children, trying to resurrect them. Do you think your children are safe?"

Julie glanced upstairs to the bedrooms. "Stop it. Please. If that's true . . . My God, if that's true, then why didn't Hut just come here and take them? All these months . . ." She tried to block out the videos she'd seen. *That's insane. It was your mind. It was. Posttraumatic stress. Shock of having your husband murdered. Shock and despair and anger and grief and mourning and cracks in your mind where you fall off a cliff of life and dangle from a thin branch over a chasm. Nervous exhaustion. Night fears. Erotic dreams. Rape dreams. Short-circuiting in the face of an enormous shock. That's what it was.*

"You don't come back all at once," he said. "First, your autonomous nervous system kicks in when Ability X turns on another part of the brain. Then it takes weeks before your memories come back. And they only come back if others with the ability are there to bring them into you. To get inside the Stream with you. To re-open the doors that have been closed. But you've seen him. In your dreams. In the movies in your head. The movies on screen. He is blasphemy, Julie. He violated the sacredness of death. He violates the soul. He does not believe in the soul. He puts himself above the laws of nature, which are here for a reason, Julie. It's what I learned in my death. If I could take away my life now, I would. I've tried. But I can't. Only when my brain itself breaks down will I finally find release and enter the Stream that connects us all. And then my soul will go where it is meant to and not be shackled by this body. I wish I could make it untrue, Julie," he said, getting up from the floor. He came toward her. "I wish I could say I made it all up. That I'm just a murderer. That I murdered your husband and I'm here to hurt you. But it's not true."

"Don't come near me. Please," she said, feeling an immense ache within her.

"You're feeling separation from me. It's all right," he said. "It passes. It's what we feel when we're too much within another. You don't have Ability X strongly enough. Everyone has it to some small degree. Your husband has it to a greater degree than anyone I've ever known. You seem to have a drop of it. But it's enough to make you ache when you separate from going inside someone in the Stream. It's what we all feel," he said, and as he walked toward her, she slowly moved back, through the doorway and into the kitchen.

"I learned something in my death, Julie. I learned about the soul. And death is the sacred doorway. I should not have been pulled back into life. I should not have come back into my burned body. But they were there, and they got inside the Stream, and they drew me back because I was their experiment. I was their guinea pig. But I came back better. They don't always. Sometimes they come back violent. Sometimes they show up with nothing but evil in them. Sometimes they come back as a child who can't learn correctly, who can't remember, who can't express himself, who gets angry and violent and pulls knives."

She stared at him, angry now. "Matt? Matty?"

"Hut killed him. When he was only three. That was too young. But he doesn't care, Julie. It was a test. I know, because his wife came to me. Amanda. She came to me and she was losing her mind with fury for what she'd allowed them to do."

"Matty? He's not dead. He's in his room, sleeping. He'll wake up soon."

"She told me that she fought Hut to make him stop. But what they want, Julie, is fear. Fear makes the adrenaline pump. Fear makes them come back. It wakes up a part of the brain after one part of it turns off. Fear is a switch. It gets the ability going at hyperspeed. They need that. It opens a door that should be permanently sealed in the brain. It turns on something. When one part of the brain diminishes, another part begins to rewire and come alive. Do you know how they did it to that little three-year-old boy? Do you?"

"He doesn't have the carving," Julie said, her eyes watering up with tears. She went to the knife block and pulled out a long sharp knife. She held it up, more afraid than she'd ever been in her life.

"Amanda stopped them from carving into his skin after he was dead. But before he died, they had to frighten that little three-year-old. They had to do something so terrible to him, Julie, that his system would go into shock. They drowned him. They made his own mother do it. Your husband made his wife wrap her hands around the boy's neck and press him into a bathtub. The fear was like electricity, so that even she felt it. But he had some of the ability. He came back, but he came back with problems. But that's what they do, Julie. They think that they're changing the world. They think by doing this, they'll eradicate death. They'll close the door of death. But it doesn't always work. Sometimes the body rots. Three days are crucial. If the mind does not awaken in three days, corruption sets in, and it's too late. If the brain doesn't turn on, then natural death occurs. But they stay inside them for three days. They stayed inside me for three days after the fire. They made sure I turned on and came back from the dead. And they did it with your husband. And his son.

"Julie, there's no time now. I want to ask that you and your children come with me. I'll protect them. They can't really hurt me. They can't do anything to you once you've died and come back."

"No," she said, wiping at her eyes with the back of her left hand. She held the knife up, sobbing. "Matty's a good boy. He's good. There's nothing wrong with him."

"It doesn't make you bad," Diamond said. "But there are no guarantees how we come back. None. Nobody understands how the brain and mind work, Julie. Nobody understands the enormous part of our minds that is untapped. They play with fire. They murder and call it understanding."

"That's insane. You're talking gibberish. This is not real. This is not happening. Please, just leave. Just go. I . . . I'm confused. I don't . . . I don't want this. Please." She tried to reach for the phone on the counter by the sink. He stepped toward her, and she jabbed the knife in the air.

"We've been inside each other. You know this is true. You know it."

"Stop saying that! It's obscene. It's disgusting. He's dead! You killed him. Please. Why don't you leave? Why don't you leave?"

"I know you won't stab me," he said, stepping closer. "I've been inside you. I know you, inside and out. I know."

"Don't, please," she sobbed, slashing at the air less than a foot from him, then crumpling to the floor, wishing the world would disappear, wishing she could feel safe again.

"There's something I need, Julie. You know where they are. But they blocked you. I can unblock it inside you. I need just a little time to find that door. I can stop them for good, Julie. Inside you, you have a memory. You've been to where they're giving their tests."

"66S? Is that what this is about?"

"No," he said. "That was a young woman's apartment. A woman I knew. Her father had been friends with my father, and he gave her the apartment after it was converted into units. A woman named Gina Lambert. Another one of us. But she was the daughter of a girl named Nell who had been in Project Daylight. Her mother was one of them. And they got Gina. They killed her to test her. They killed a boy named Terry West. He was still in college. He had Ability X. They had to create great fear in him before he died. But he still died. He didn't come back. Do you want to know how monstrous they are?"

"I don't know anything, I don't."

"Let me inside you one last time. Just one last time," he said, "Please let me get inside you."

She jabbed the knife at him, almost touching his skin. "No, please, no."

"There's a place inside you. I know it's there. We were

almost there. Almost. I almost found it. If you can let me in, I can stop them. I know I can. There's always hope. It's a blessing and a curse. But sometimes it's all we have. Help me find them. Help me open that one door in your mind."

"Please," she wept, slashing blindly, "go away. I don't want this. It's not happening!"

He reached out and touched the edge of the knife, and then the tips of her fingers. "Let me inside you, Julie."

She felt a spark between them, and a lubricating familiarity as he slid into her. She shut her eyes for just a moment and felt him moving, and now she tried to resist but he was pushing her hard, slamming up against her on the inside, his consciousness roaming and tearing at walls and doors and tunnels into her memory.

And then she saw it at the moment he did.

It was simply a house.

It was a house with glass walls on one side.

She had seen it before but she wasn't sure where. She could not name whose it was. She vaguely remembered a video of Matt's that was just a house on a lake. On the lake, she thought. Their lake. Somewhere right here. Somewhere in Rellingford. She remembered the rich people's houses across the lake, and felt as he searched her memory for who owned this house and why she was there, and she saw a woman coming to the door as she stood out in the side yard looking at the brown lake, and she turned to see the woman more clearly, but the image was out of focus and she almost had a name . . .

And then something exploded. She felt a sudden rush of wind inside the Stream. Diamond was no longer there with her. She opened her eyes.

At first she thought the noise was from outside the windows, a cherry bomb blast.

She looked at Michael Diamond's face. He wore an expression of shock.

He tried to reach around to his back.

He fell hard on the floor.

Behind him, Hut.

chapter twenty-two

She felt the world spinning around her. She saw Michael Diamond wriggling and then trying to crawl. She stared at him. Looked up at Hut, trying to comprehend. Trying to make it all make sense to her. Reason was gone. She knew Michael Diamond. She didn't know Hut. She had never known Hut. He had hidden from her. He had . . . used her. *For what? For making a child? Another child? Another test to pass? Livy? With her brain radio? Was that it? Were they all making children? Stealing children with Ability X? It couldn't be. Why? What purpose? Why kill them? Why do it? The human soul, inviolate. Not to be violated. Not to be played with. The soul's journey along the Stream after death. After life. Beyond life.*

Hut stood there in a white shirt and khakis, the revolver from the metal box in his hand.

"Don't scream," he said softly. "The kids are probably waking up now. They heard the shot. Even the neighbors, although it'll take a little while to identify where it came from. Shhh." Then he bent down and took the knife from Julie's fingers and put his foot against Michael Diamond's throat. "Look at him. He can't die. But he can suffer. He can go toward death. But in three days, he'll come back. Once you pass the test, Julie, you can't die ever again." Then he leaned closer to Julie. She could feel his breath, which was sweet. "If you let me inside you now, I can take all the pain away," he said.

She stared at him, feeling as if she were surrounded by ice.

"This is shock," he whispered, stroking the side of her face gently. "Do you want me inside you?" Hut asked. "If you let me inside you, Julie, I can take away hurt."

Then she felt his consciousness come into her and suddenly she felt sleepy, as if she'd been given a sedative. He was stroking her on the inside, altering the pain, softening her confusion, making her black out.

As she sank down into a dark oblivion, she thought of Livy and Matt, and she wanted to claw her way up from the darkness for their sakes. *Please, Livy. Please, Matt. Don't let him touch you. Don't let your daddy near you. I don't know what to believe. I don't know if I'm really here or if my mind is gone. Please God, help my children. Please, Michael. Please, someone. Hut, please don't hurt them. Don't let this be happening.*

PART FOUR

PART FOUR

chapter twenty-three

1

The headache blasted into the back of her scalp. *Jesus. I have to tell Dr. Glennon that Dalmane is like an ax. Christ, I'll never take it again.*

Her eyes opened. She looked at the clock. It was after three.

She began to get fragments of memory back. They were dreamlike and vague, but then she felt terror clutch at her. She got out of bed and ran down the hall to Livy's room.

Her bed was empty.

So was Matt's.

First, she called the police and talked to the sheriff, but midway through speaking, she could tell that he was patronizing her. "Julie, I'm sorry. Have you checked with the schools? With anyone? Could they possibly be somewhere together?" Then he said, "All right. I'll send someone by."

She demanded Detective McGuane's number, and when she got it, she called and had to leave a message on his voice mail. She spoke slowly and as coherently as possible. She tried not to bring up everything that Michael Diamond had told her or shown her. She was beginning to doubt herself by the end of the message.

She finally went to the kitchen. The knife was on the floor. She picked it up and put it in the sink. She thought she saw something under the cabinetry on the tile. She reached down and felt around to see what it was. It was the revolver.

A police cruiser came by, and she met the two cops outside. She worked hard to retain her composure. She didn't tell them everything. She watched for their reactions to her story. She didn't say "my dead husband," and she didn't say "psychic." She just told them that some crazies broke in. That she passed out. That there was a gunshot, and she had the gun. That her children were missing. They wrote some things down and told her to wait at home, keep the doors locked, keep the phone line clear.

But as soon as they'd left and she returned to her house, she got the revolver and got into her Camry and drove down to the perimeter road of the lake.

2

She drove slowly on the opposite side of the lake. The house in her mind had been a large one. It had a seventies-style architecture—rectangles and squares and too much glass. She stopped in front of several of them, but each time, it just didn't seem right.

And then she saw the house, with a circular driveway in front.

She had been there. She remembered being there before but she could not remember who lived there. Why had she visited it? Had it been another dream? She remembered Matt's video of the house clearly now—he must have been in the canoe. Maybe with his father. A Boys' Day Out. Matt must've held the camcorder up and just videoed the back of the house on the lakeside.

She parked on the road and walked up the driveway. She

did nothing to conceal the gun in her hand. She stepped off the driveway onto the slate walk that went around the side of the house. It was enormous, and although it had huge glass windows, the shades were drawn. She went back to look at the lake, and then to look at the house.

She felt her heart beat too rapidly and a clutching at her throat. She raised the revolver slightly as she walked back around to the front of the house.

She stood at the bottom of three steps that led to the front porch. A slender patch of garden bordered the porch— peonies and pansies and irises.

She took each step slowly, feeling a thudding on the inside. A gentle shivery wind down her back.

When she got to the door, she rang the bell and waited.

No one came. She rapped at it. Waited. The revolver felt heavy in her hand, and she lowered it. She began to doubt her vision. Her memory. Was this the house? Whose was it? Who was the out-of-focus woman from her memory that Diamond's consciousness had brought her back to see?

Who would she know who would know Hut? Would know Amanda? Might have known them years before Julie had ever met Hut? He didn't have many friends outside of people at work. But none of them lived here. Who lived on the lake? Who was it?

When the door finally opened, she already knew. The name just came to her. A name that Michael Diamond had mentioned.

Nell. That had been what she was called as a girl in Project Daylight.

Eleanor, on the other side of the door, looked startled. "Julie?" she asked as if she had expected someone else.

Julie brought the revolver up, pointing it at her. "Where are my children?"

3

She stepped over the threshold of the house as if she were in a dream. How could this be real? How could Eleanor, a therapist, for God's sake, be part of some insane psychic conspiracy? What was she thinking? How was it possible? But possible didn't matter anymore.

"Now, don't get excited," Eleanor said. "You're experiencing—"

Julie cut her off. "I know. Posttraumatic stress. Blah blah blah." She kept the revolver pointed at her.

"Julie, put that thing down," Eleanor said. "Right now. You are not in any danger, believe me."

"Where are they?" Julie asked, her voice hardened.

"Matt's asleep. He needed rest."

"Did you hurt him?"

"Of course not. He was getting violent. You know how he is. We had to . . . give him something," Eleanor said as if she were in her office again, dispensing advice.

"You are good, Eleanor. Or Nell. Or whoever you are. You are good," Julie said.

The man she knew as Dr. Glennon came out of a room down the hall. He spoke to Eleanor. "Well, I can't say we didn't expect this."

"I know," Eleanor said. "Hut's been careless."

Dr. Glennon nodded to Julie. "Mrs. Hutchinson, please, just think for a minute. I know you've gotten some mumbo jumbo from that Diamant character. But he's taken care of."

"Did you give him some Xanax? Or Dalmane? Something to make him sleep? Is that what you gave Matty, too?"

Dr. Glennon held up his hands slightly defensively. "I know what that man told you, Mrs. Hutchinson. But there's more to it. Believe me."

Eleanor said, "Julie, we had to do it this way. We had to

wait until Hut was fully himself again. He's better than he was. He really is."

"You people brought him back from the dead."

"I would've thought you loved him enough," Eleanor said, "to want him back. He has Ability X stronger than anyone we've known. You loved him. He loves you, Julie. Surely, you'd want to be with him."

"Not like this," Julie said. "You're a pack of fucking psychic monsters."

Eleanor shot a look at Dr. Glennon, who sat down on the stairs to the second floor. He looked exhausted. Julie noticed sweat on his forehead. She was scaring them. Just a little. She didn't know how they'd be scared. "You're nothing but zombies."

"Oh, Julie." Eleanor tsked as if she were a child. "This is the human brain. It's not mystical crap like Diamant believed. Project Daylight was a scam. They were trying to find out things to justify war. To justify invasion. To milk little children of their abilities. But we all learned, together. We learned. And we've put it into action."

"You kill. You kill one another. You kill your own children. I didn't even know you had children, Eleanor."

Eleanor began to look at the revolver as if she wanted to grab it. Julie grinned. She was happy to feel that she had power in this situation.

"You've been in the Stream, Julie," Eleanor said. "You know how life and death define the imperfect human brain. There is no death, Julie. There doesn't need to be. Those of us with this ability can change how human beings exist. We can alter the course of the future."

"Not all of you come back. Are you dead yet, Eleanor?"

"I guess there's no reasoning with you," Eleanor said.

And then Hut came around the corner, with others behind him. People she didn't know—three or four of them. The redheaded woman from the video was there. Gina? Was that

her name? She stood with a middle-aged man who had tor-
toiseshell glasses and thinning hair.

"Zombies," Julie said.

"Baby," Hut said, moving toward her too rapidly. He
looked well rested. He looked healthy. He wore one of his
favorite T-shirts and blue jeans, and didn't look like he was
in his forties at all. He looked better than she remembered
him looking. Life was in him.

"No, Hut," she said. She raised the revolver. "I saw you
shoot Michael Diamond."

"He's not dead, though," Hut said. "He's somewhere safe
now. He won't harm you again. And he won't harm us."

"You shot him. And he fell. If I shoot you, maybe I'll feel
good. Maybe it's enough."

"If you shoot me, will you shoot all of them?" Hut asked.
"Will that get you what you want, Julie?"

"Where's Livy?"

Eleanor cleared her throat.

"Matt's resting, upstairs," Hut said. "You can go see him
if you want."

"You drugged him. You . . . you killed him . . . when he
was practically a baby. You *tested* him," Julie said.

"What is it you want, baby?" Hut asked. His eyes seemed
kind. He didn't look like the undead. He didn't look like a
vampire. He didn't look as if he meant to hurt her. She hated
him most for that. She tried to remember Michael Diamond's words. Things he'd said. She tried to remember the
feeling of Michael Diamond inside her and being inside
him. The safety of it. The warmth. The complete connection
between the two of them. "What is it you want?"

"I want my children."

"Yes," Hut said. Dr. Glennon looked up at him as if this
were the wrong answer.

"Julie, you've been through an enormous shock," Eleanor
said, taking a step toward her.

Julie turned the gun on her. "Back, Eleanor."

"Nell, please," Hut said. He stood still, his arms out-stretched. "Julie. You're the love of my life. I hated being separated from you."

"You came to me at night," she said. "You Streamed or you broke in or you did something. And you raped me while I was sleeping."

"In your dreams, you told me you wanted me inside you," he said. "I asked, and you said yes."

"Because I thought it was a dream," she said. "Where's Livy? I want to see her."

"You can't right now," the red-haired young woman said from the back of the hall. "She can't," she added, turning to the middle-aged man. "Can she?"

"Oh my God," Julie gasped, nearly losing her balance. "You killed her. You already killed her."

Everyone remained still in the room. No one spoke.

"She's only sleeping," Hut finally said gently. "You have to believe that."

He motioned to Dr. Glennon on the stairs to move out of the way. "It's all right," he said. "Julie, let's go upstairs. She's upstairs now. You can be with her."

4

At the open door to what she had assumed would be a bedroom, Julie glanced back at Hut, who was close behind her. She kept the revolver ready, because she was deter-mined that somehow, some way, she would see Livy and Matt through this. Her life didn't really matter anymore. Her children were all that mattered. She could shoot at least two of these psychos, and it might buy enough time to get Livy out to the car, and get her cell phone in the glove compart-ment and call the police as she drove away. If she believed in what they were doing, they wouldn't really hurt Matt.

They couldn't, if it was true. If it was true, Matt was already resurrected from the dead. Once the police came back, she'd tell them that they had kidnapped her children. She wouldn't tell the police about psychics and resurrections and Ability X. She would be sane. She would stop this, somehow.

She glanced back at Hut, but he wasn't threatening her at all. She had a pang in her gut—as if the bond of their marriage still existed and was causing her pain. *Fuck that. Fuck it. He's a murderer. He's insane. He's a zombie. He's a psychic vampire. He's not even real. He can't be. But even if he is, he believes everything he says.*

Hut said, "Let me tell you about life after death. The only way to overcome it is to have the talent and knowledge, and 99.999 percent of human beings don't have it and never will. And many of those who have it never use it. I suppose a few have, and have been elevated to the level of gods. But there's no God, Julie. And no matter what Diamant told you about the human soul, there's no soul except for life in the flesh. The brain is the seat of power."

"I don't believe you. You're a liar. You and your doctors from hell." She glanced into the room, but could not yet bring herself to go in.

"Every obstacle, baby, contains the seed of its own destruction. Within my being is something more powerful than the horizon we call death. It's not any goony theory of magic or miracles. It's simply a process that can most likely be described scientifically. My only understanding of it is that I have it. That my brain did not die when my body did, and that there is something that comes from my mind and manages to overcome what you and others call death. I was not really dead. Perhaps no one is, but the poor bastards don't have the ability to summon themselves back to the world of the living. And so they rot and putrefy. But my mind communicates life back into me. Back into my bones. Into my flesh. Not from magic, not from the spirit world. But from an ability that others have, and don't always even know they have it. It's like a vacuum. Sucking at you. Drawing you away. Drawing you out. It's passing from one state of consciousness into another. It's the body that rots. Consciousness can move molecules. Consciousness can raise the dead. I've done it. But I'm still not sure how it happens. I resist death. Three days is all I need. Three days to remain dead, for my consciousness to grow strong again after the point of weakness of the physical death."

"You're talking but I hear nothing but bullshit," she said.

She stepped into the bedroom.

5

Julie stepped into the room, feeling as if she were entering a dark cave. It was just a small bedroom, with the narrow bed pressed up against the far wall. Candles were lit around the child's bed, and Julie noticed others in the gloom—a man of about thirty with thick blond hair sat on a Barcalounger near the shuttered window, and a teenaged girl who had a Sony Walkman in her hand and earphones in a halo over her head. She drew them off, looked at Julie, then at the blond man, and then at Hut.

"Christ," Julie said. She had lost the nervous feeling, knowing she had a purpose here that was not about herself. That was not about weakness. But she saw her daughter's hair peeking out from under the covers and the lump of her body.

The blond man's face betrayed nothing but caution. He had half risen from the chair, and then, seeing Hut, sat back down.

Eleanor's voice behind her. "Now, Julie, you must be exhausted. Why don't you just—"

"I'm not your patient anymore," Julie said. "Talk to your great god Hut."

"He's not a—" the blond man began, and then silenced himself.

Julie said to herself: *Don't be afraid. You don't matter anymore. They don't matter. All that matters is Livy. All that matters is my little girl.*

"You're ghouls, aren't you?" Julie whispered. "I'm not even sure if you're human."

"Good grief," Eleanor said. "Julie, this isn't mysticism. It's pure science. It's just a science we didn't know about."

"I don't need to hear about this death cult anymore," Julie said. She had that one thing left in her. She had hope. Maybe Livy was alive. They'd only had her one day, after all. Not even a full day.

"It's reality. Objective reality," Eleanor said. "It's not a cult."

"It's not the therapy, either," Julie spat back. She pointed the gun at the teenaged girl. "Get away from my daughter."

If you just ignore them, they'll feel your will. Will is everything. They're weak people who believe in nonsense. They think Hut is a god, after all.

Julie turned to face Hut.

If you're psychic, guess what I'm thinking. Guess what my plan is. Guess.

"God speaks but nobody listens," Julie said aloud, her voice flat, tinged with bitterness. She fought to keep her eyes from welling with tears.

She moved to the bed and sat at the edge of it. "Livy," she whispered softly. "Livy."

"She can't hear you," Eleanor said, nearly as softly. "The auditory nerve is—"

"Shut up, Eleanor," Julie said. "Just shut up."

Julie felt a hand on her shoulder. It was Eleanor. *Old friend. Comforter. Therapist. Monster.*

Julie shrugged her away.

"My God." Julie was barely able to get the words out.

Minutes seemed to pass as she turned the words over in her mind.

She's dead. They did it. They killed her.

They tested her.

The way they killed Matty. They used her for their test.

Her own father . . .

She hadn't really believed it would happen. She hadn't believed in her heart that it wasn't all fantasy. That it wasn't all mumbo jumbo. *PSI. Ability X. Resurrection. Death cult. Project Daylight.* Then her voice returned. "My God. She's dead. She's dead! You already killed her. You really did it . . ." Julie murmured, covering her face, the tears breaking from within her, a dam burst, and she could not see when she had brought her hands away from her eyes, for the tears had nearly blinded her. "Monsters! *Monsters!*"

Hut's voice: "She's not dead. I know she's not. Death is a state of consciousness. It's not what you think."

"You sick perverted bastard," Julie thought she said, but wasn't sure, because she felt knocked out, wiped clean, somehow destroyed by the knowledge of her daughter's death.

"Three days," her husband said. "You can't believe the lies Diamant told. You can't, Julie. Matty wasn't right. Mandy and I were too much to produce a child that worked. Two Ability Xs don't work right in bringing children into the world. Livy will work, because in you, like most people, the gene's recessive. I know it will work."

"I don't listen to dead people," Julie said. "I don't listen to mumbo jumbo."

She reached out to touch the edge of Livy's hand.

"It's not some religion," Eleanor said. But it was as if she were off in some fog at the edge of the room. "It's not something as silly as faith."

"It's science," the blond man said. "Pure and simple. It's a truth that's been locked away."

"Locked away by crap mysticism and Christian hogwash," Eleanor added. "And just plain ignorance. There is no God. There's no devil. No heaven. No hell. There is nothing but animal life. We are animals. But we have developed the ability to take this beyond our lifetimes, Julie. Our single lifetimes. To wipe away thousands of years of ignorant mysticism, of this ridiculous Christian magical thinking about life and death."

"Can't blame Christianity alone," the blond man said. "You just can't. Other religions, too. They just . . ."

But their voices receded into the dark background of her mind. They babbled on as Julie leaned forward toward her daughter, her beautiful Livy, and remembered the first moment she had known Livy was in her body, and the first moment Livy had cried out at birth, and how Hut had helped change diapers, and how Julie had somehow believed that her family was wonderful, that she and Hut were a team, and that Livy was going to grow up to be a doctor like her daddy or a nurse like Mommy or to be an actress like Livy wanted to, or grow into a teenager who would go to her prom, fall in love, go to college, experience the world, travel. That she, her mother, would have all those years with her, would watch her as she grew and changed and became the wonder that Julie knew she would become.

Julie lay down on the bed, cradling her daughter's lifeless body.

Around her, she saw others draw together in the shadows. She ignored them. All that mattered was Livy.

She is all that remains.

Let them burn away. Let the world burn away, for all I care, she thought.

She kissed the edge of her daughter's fragrant hair: chrysanthemums and lilacs, musky and sweet mixed together. She didn't want to think about how they'd killed her. About how they needed to create fear before death to make their ritual work right. She didn't want to think about her baby crying out for her mommy while they did something awful and monstrous to her in her last minutes of life.

Julie closed her eyes, blocked out the others in the room, and held her child tightly.

Perhaps minutes had passed, or hours. Perhaps she drank the chai they brought her, and perhaps she nibbled on some cheddar crackers that Eleanor set down on a plate with some cream cheese. Perhaps it was a day that passed. She slept, she woke, she clutched the gun, but no one bothered her. No one tried to move her or take her weapon away. She got up once or twice to use the bathroom in the hall, and when she did, she felt them watching her but she refused to look them in the eyes. She had blocked the others out and only knew her child's body, pressed against her own. She lay on the bed, slept, woke, tried to feel that inside feeling with her daughter that she'd felt with Michael Diamond.

Then she felt life stirring in Livy's body.

Eleanor's voice, beyond the darkness of Julie's mind, "Look. Look!"

It's not real. It's not real.

Julie felt the warmth and the pulsing heartbeat along her daughter's side, and even the smell of life emanated from her.

Had she imagined the slight heat of her daughter's breath against her cheek? The warmth? The trickle of air?

Eleanor whispered something that almost sounded like a prayer.

Julie opened her eyes and gazed at her daughter's face.

Remembering what Michael Diamond had told her.

"There's always hope," he had said. *"That's the last thing to go in life. It's a blessing and a curse. But sometimes it's all we have. Yet, when faced with this, there is no hope. There can be no hope. Do not let hope cloud your resolve."*

"But what hope?" she wanted to ask him now. "What hope?"

And then his voice was in her head again. Not imagined. Real. Inside her. His connection to her remained, somehow, even among these monsters.

"The human soul is inviolate, Julie. There is always hope because of that. The human soul is inviolate."

She tried not to think of Matt. Of how Diamond had said he'd died. Maybe it wasn't completely true. Maybe there was truth on both sides. *I must put those things out of my mind. Only Livy matters. Only Livy.*

The human soul is inviolate.

Her soul was somewhere in her body. It could not die. There was no death except for the flesh. But the soul had its journey. Michael Diamond had moved elsewhere when he was burned at Project Daylight. Opened another door. Passed into a passageway that had remained unseen. And then came back. And he wasn't dead, was he? Not even now? Maybe they'd done something to him. Maybe they'd buried him alive. Or subdued him in some way. But if I can somehow get him to help again . . . But even as she thought this, she felt that she was doing the kind of magical thinking that had never gotten her anywhere.

But Livy did not have to go through that passage. Not yet.

She may not even come back bad. She may not be spoiled, the way Diamond had said others were. She might be the same. She might even be better. Michael Diamond had been better, after all. Maybe Hut wasn't. Maybe Matt had come back with slight problems. But it didn't mean they all did. She believed it. She believed it with a ferocity of emotion. There was no more reason in her life. She had to cling to belief. She had to remember that the world was not all murky darkness. It had benevolence. It had love. It had stronger elements than this death cult imagined.

It had hope.

Even in this murderous circle, there could be good rising from it. A hand could be uplifted. It could be raised in prayer. A hand could be held. Livy would not be alone. I'll be there for her. I will not abandon you, Livy.

I'll help you find your soul.

I promise.

The human soul, inviolate.

She clung to this idea, as she felt her daughter's small fingers clutch at her arm and heard the faint growl of a child's voice.

Douglas Clegg is the award-winning author of many books, including *The Hour Before Dark*, *Neverland*, and *Naomi*. Having lived in Washington, D.C., Los Angeles, Paris, Oahu, and the coast of New England, he decided that New Jersey would be his next place of residence. He currently resides just outside Manhattan with his partner and a small menagerie (dog, cat, rabbit) of rescues. Clegg is a major proponent of animal rescue and suggests that his readers, when in need of pets, first go to an animal rescue organization. His novel *The Hour Before Dark* was recently optioned for the movies.

Clegg invites readers to email him at DClegg@Douglas Clegg.com and subscribe to his free Internet newsletter at www.DouglasClegg.com.

⊘ SIGNET BOOKS   (0451)

"*A master of the macabre!*" —Stephen King

Bentley Little

"*If there's a better horror novelist than Little...I don't know who it is.*" —Los Angeles Times

The Return   206878

There's only one thing that can follow the success of Bentley Little's acclaimed *The Walking* and *The Revelation*. And that's Bentley Little's return...

The Walking   201744

The dead are getting restless...The walking has begun...

The Town   200152

A small town in Arizona—some call it home, but to others it's their worst nightmare...

The Bram Stoker Award-winning novel:

The Revelation   192257

Strange things are happening in the small town of Randall, Arizona. As darkness falls, an itinerant preacher has arrived to spread a gospel of cataclysmic fury...And stranger things are yet to come.

The House   192249

Five strangers are about to discover that they share a dark bond. A haunted childhood. A shocking secret. A memory of the houses they lived in—each one eerily identical to the next.

Also Available:

THE COLLECTION	206096
THE STORE	192192
THE MAILMAN	402375
THE UNIVERSITY	183908
THE DOMINION	187482
THE ASSOCIATION	204123

Available wherever books are sold or at
www.penguin.com

S413/Little